The Post-Modern Prometheus

Synths were manufactured to look human and perform physical labor, but they were still only machines. That's what the people who used—and abused—them believed, until the truth was revealed: Synths are independent, sentient beings. Now, the governments of the world must either recognize their human nature and grant them their rightful freedom, or brace for a revolution.

Former New Lyons Detective Jason Campbell has committed himself to the Synths' cause, willing to fight every army the human race marches against them. But they have an even greater enemy in Walton Biogenics, the syndicate behind the creation and distribution of the "artificial" humans. The company will stop at nothing to protect their secrets—and the near-mythological figure known to Synths as "The First," whose very existence threatens the balance of power across the world...

SINdicate

The New Lyons Sequence

J. T. Nicholas

REBEL BASE

REBEL BASE BOOKS
Kensington Publishing Corp.
www.kensingtonbooks.com

Rebel Base Books are published by
Kensington Publishing Corp. 119 West 40th Street New York, NY 10018

All Kensington titles, imprints, and distributed lines are available at special quantity discounts for bulk purchases for sales promotion, premiums, fundraising, and educational or institutional use.

Special book excerpts or customized printings can also be created to fit specific needs. For details, write or phone the office of the Kensington Special Sales Manager:
Kensington Publishing Corp.
119 West 40th Street
New York, NY 10018
Attn. Special Sales Department. Phone: 1-800-221-2647.

First Electronic Edition: March 2018
eISBN-13: 978-1-63573-005-0
eISBN-10: 1-63573-005-8

First Print Edition: March 2018
ISBN-13: 978-1-63573-008-1
ISBN-10: 1-63573-008-2

Printed in the United States of America

For my parents, who taught me that there has to be a balance between chasing your dreams and paying your rent.

I think that there is nothing, not even crime, more opposed to poetry, to philosophy, ay, to life itself than this incessant business. ~Henry David Thoreau

Corporation: An ingenious device for obtaining profit without individual responsibility. ~Ambrose Bierce, The Devil's Dictionary

Chapter 1

There was a body on my doorstep.

I don't know what woke me, or what drove me to climb so early from the narrow cot that served as my bed. Maybe it was some lingering cop instinct from my time with the NLPD, that nagging sense that something was wrong. It was that instinct that had me tucking the paddle holster of my forty-five into the waistband of the ratty jeans I had fallen asleep in.

I slid open the door of the eight-by-eight walled office cubicle that served as my bedroom and stepped out onto the cavernous floor of what had once been a call center. The first rays of dawn were peeking over the eastern horizon, filtering through what remained of the call center's windows, casting the interior in monochromatic grays accented with darker pools of shadow.

The broad floor was filled with sleeping people. Sleeping synthetics. The genetically engineered clones that had served as an underclass of slave labor for decades and, with a small amount of help from me and a whole lot of work and planning from a synthetic named Silas, had begun a de facto rebellion.

I padded among them on bare feet, stepping as silently as possible, and yet, without exception, the eyes of each synthetic I passed popped open. They stared at me, stark-white against the gray, eyes wide, searching, and somehow fearful. Not one of them moved. They waited in statue-like rigidity, a coiled-spring tension resonating from their stillness. It lasted only a moment, until they realized where they were; until they realized who I was. I couldn't begrudge them that moment of fear, but it still hit me like a punch to the gut.

Such was life in revolution central. Nearly a month since we had taken over the air and net waves. Nearly a month since we had ripped off the veil covering the ugly truth that synthetics were not unthinking, unfeeling things, but as much people as any of the naturally born. Nearly a month, and for synthetics, things had gotten worse.

Much worse.

It wasn't unexpected. Silas had predicted the reaction from society at large when we shone a spotlight on the truth that everyone suspected but no one seemed willing to admit. It had started with protests. Angry people marching with signs about respecting their rights and not dictating what they could do with their bought-and-paid-for property. The protests should have collapsed under the weight of irony alone, but instead they had given way to violence—violence directed almost entirely against synthetics. Viral videos of synthetic beatings—always popular—had hit unprecedented highs, as had videos depicting darker, more depraved "punishments" for those who dared to think they might one day be "real" people. The violence, in turn, had given way to death. Not on a widespread scale—not yet. Whatever else they might be, synthetics were, after all, expensive. Only the very wealthy could afford to dispose of them wantonly.

We'd given the world an ultimatum: give synthetics rights, or be prepared to have all the little secrets that they had gathered in their decades of near-invisible servitude released to the public. Silas had managed to bring together and weaponize secrets that could topple governments and destroy lives. The plan was simple enough—release a wave of compromising information on a number of politicians and public figures. The first wave was embarrassing, but not damning, not actively criminal. If that failed to spark action, then a second, more catastrophic wave would be released. And so on, until the governments either acceded to our demands or toppled from the sheer weight of skeletons tumbling out of closets.

But as that deadline crept closer—now just over a week away—the bodies were beginning to pile up. The richest among society—individuals and corporations alike—could afford to throw away a synthetic here, a synthetic there, and as the dawn of revolution approached, they made their position clear. One billionaire businessman had gone so far as to cobble together a reality livestream. Every day, contestants undertook a series of challenges, and the winner got to kill a synthetic in any way they chose, all during a livestream that, last I checked, had viewership measured in the millions.

And yet, there was hope out there.

That hope was part of the reason the floor I moved across was filled with synthetics, crowded in here and there in clusters amidst the cavernous call center. They would trickle in by ones and twos, somehow always finding us, despite our having changed locations four times in the past month. Most told the same story—their nominal owners, horrified by the revelation that they had, in essence, been keeping slaves, but terrified of the possible reprisals from those who thought differently, had simply set them free. Turned them out. Part kindness, part assuaging of guilt...and part washing your hands of a problem you wanted no part of.

I didn't know how they found us. They trusted me enough to share some pieces of their stories. The part I played in the rescue of Evelyn, what I had sacrificed to get the truth out, had earned me that much.

That didn't stop a young synthetic girl, maybe seventeen, from rolling into a half crouch as I neared. Her hands were extended in front of her, a gesture half defense, half supplication. Her look of horror and shame and guilt and fear reminded me so suddenly and sharply of Annabelle that it was like a knife twisting in my intestines. Her mouth opened and formed a single word, not spoken, but clear as a gunshot nonetheless.

"No."

What could I do? I wasn't the one who had hurt her, but she'd been hurt, badly. I offered a smile and kept my distance. It took a moment for the recognition to dawn, for the panic to quiet. Quiet, but not fall silent.

I was still an outsider. I belonged to a different class, a class that had long subjugated and tormented them. A human. Trust only extended so far. But I had my suspicions as to how they found me, and my suspicions had a name.

Silas.

The albino synthetic who had started my feet on this path remained elusive. We received messages from him on a regular basis, and he made brief appearances a couple of times a week, mostly to check in on Evelyn and make sure she was receiving the medical care she needed so late in her pregnancy. But after only a short visit, he would vanish with the ease that had made him so damn hard to track down in the first place. He, or rather his messages, told us when to move, and where to move. That let us know when my former brothers and sisters in blue were getting too close. I had no doubt that it was his network that funneled the turned-out synthetics to our door.

I just didn't know what in the hell he expected me to *do* with them.

Whatever Silas might hope—whatever I might hope—when February 1 rolled around, the governments of the world would not simply roll over, pass some new laws, sprinkle a shit-ton of fairy dust, and declare that synthetics were now all full-fledged citizens. And by the way, sorry about all the assaults, rapes, and murders suffered in the interim. No. The months ahead would be steeped in blood.

And not one of the synthetics that were beginning to stir with the rising sun would be able to spill a single drop of it. Call it conditioning. Call it brainwashing, but synthetics were engineered to be incapable of violence, even in self-defense. Which was going to make fighting a war pretty fucking hard.

I had nearly reached the main door of the call center. The entire front of the building—once a shining wall of steel and glass—had been boarded up, long sheets of plywood secured to the frame. Thin cracks of light filtered in where the boards fit imperfectly, and more came from openings higher up, where other windows had been spared the fortification. I had moved through that fractured light, my unease growing with each step. I dropped my hand to the butt of my pistol, thumb finding the retention lock and easing it forward.

A four-by-four rested in a pair of brackets across the door, barring it more effectively than any lock. I had eased it off with my left hand, straining slightly with the effort, and lowered it to the floor. I had pulled the door open, reflexively scanning left and right, searching for threats. Nothing. The tension I'd felt since awakening had started to ease.

Until I had looked down.

And saw the body.

Chapter 2

My cop-brain kicked in immediately, cataloguing facts as fast as my eyes could identify them.

Male. Midthirties. Mixed race. Athletic build. Dressed casually in khakis and a collared shirt. Brown leather shoes. Good-looking, or he had been in life, but not so good-looking as to stand out. Could have passed unnoticed damn near anywhere in New Lyons. Except for places like Floattown or the abandoned commercial district farther inland where his body ended up. Places where clean-cut and well-put-together might as well have been signs reading "Outsider."

No obvious cause of death. With some trepidation I reached beneath his head and ran my fingers along the nape of his neck. No raised skin tag. I breathed a slight sigh at that.

Not a synthetic, then.

The relief was short lived. Sure, it was possible that, out of all the places this guy could have picked to lie down and die, he'd stumbled into the one where a synthetic rebellion was brewing. And it was possible that come the first, synthetics would universally be accorded the rights of full-fledged citizens. I wasn't holding my breath for either, though.

I needed to do a thorough search of the body. Shit. I *needed* to get a full forensics team in here, not to mention a medical examiner. Until this moment, I hadn't really missed being a cop. Too busy trying to survive and dodge my former colleagues. I missed Hernandez, one of the only cops I'd really thought of as a friend, and the only partner I'd been able to rely on. She had managed to avoid becoming caught up in the shitstorm I had created, at least. I missed a few of the others, but not the job itself. But I could have used the resources. The authority.

As things stood, all it would take was someone noticing the body, and the entire place would be crawling with police. It went against every instinct, every bit of training I'd had, but there was no choice. I reached down, hooked my hands into the corpse's armpits, and dragged it back into the call center lobby.

I ducked back outside, giving the area a quick once-over, but I saw no incriminating evidence. No blood smears. No obviously dropped items. I knew there were no cameras focused on the building, a rarity in New Lyons, but a certainty given that Silas had chosen the place. I didn't have to worry about what the unblinking, electronic eyes might have captured. Nor could I rely upon them to figure out what the hell had happened. I suppressed a chuckle at that. "Not a cop anymore, Campbell," I muttered to myself. "Not my job to solve this crime. Shit. Now it's my job to cover it up."

I moved inside, slipping the door shut and putting the four-by-four back into place. I turned to find myself face-to-face staring into Evelyn's widening eyes.

The synthetic was pregnant. Heavily, obviously pregnant. She couldn't be certain exactly when she had conceived—hers was a story fraught with violence and abuse, a story common to so many synthetics. I felt a twinge every time I looked at her, an aching echo that whispered "Annabelle" and reminded me what might have been. If the birth was more than a week or two off, we'd all be surprised. Evelyn had, in her own way, started this whole thing. She had been the catalyst, the spark, the trigger that gave rise to a movement.

Synthetics were supposed to be genetically sterile, designed to be incapable of reproduction. Everyone knew that. Couldn't have them breeding with one another and creating more synthetics. That would cut into the profit margins of Walton Biogenics. A synthetic couldn't get pregnant in the first place, but even if some genetic anomaly cropped up, it was simply impossible for a human and a synthetic to breed, to produce offspring. After all, if that could happen, then it would be pretty clear evidence that synthetics were not actually little more than biological toasters, but were, in fact, fully functioning members of the human race.

We knew now that Evelyn wasn't the first. She was just the first one that Walton Biogenics and its army of corporate hit men hadn't been able to "sanitize." I had no idea how many like her had come before, how long Walton had known the truth. How long the company had been suppressing it. But whatever genetic anomaly had allowed her to reproduce, it wasn't common. Couldn't be, or the fiction of the synthetics being things and not people would have collapsed long ago.

She didn't say anything. She rarely spoke to anyone, synthetic or human. She just looked at me with those clear blue eyes. Looked at me as I stood over the body of a dead man.

It was, to say the least, unsettling.

"I didn't do it," I said, as if she had demanded an explanation. "I found him out front." She said nothing.

"I couldn't just leave him there," I rambled. "If he was spotted... He'd put us all in danger. The police would come." I wasn't sure why I felt the need to explain myself to her, but there it was.

She didn't respond at first, just kept staring at me, and I saw a deep sadness in her eyes. Then she extended one hand and pointed at the corpse.

I followed her extended finger. It pointed at the mouth of the man. Sometime during the dragging, his lips had parted. There was something there, wedged into his mouth.

"Shit," I whispered. I could hear a rustle deeper in the building, the sound of the gathered synthetics getting up to start their day. "Can you get a couple of people to help me? Have them keep people back from this area?"

"Yes, Jason," she said, startling me. No one called me Jason, but more than that, I think it was the first time Evelyn had ever said my name.

As she waddled off, I knelt beside the body. I didn't have gloves, or tweezers, or anything that would make the unpleasant task ahead of me easier. I fished in the pocket of the jeans I had slept in, digging out a stubby pencil. There wasn't much call for actual writing utensils anymore, but it was a habit I'd gotten into as a cop—you never knew when you'd need to write down a key bit of information, and screens, for all their wonders, still took longer to execute some basic tasks. Some habits, I had no intention of letting go.

I used the point of the pencil, inserting it gently between the corpse's lips, taking advantage of the point to wedge it between the teeth. A little careful wiggling, and I eased the mouth open. I could see the foreign object lodged in the soft palate. It was a square of paper, tightly folded, positioned so that one corner pressed into the tongue and another into the roof of the mouth. The light in the lobby was getting better, but the room was still mostly shadows, and I couldn't tell if any damage had been done during the insertion process, or if the poor sap had been alive at the time. Other than the presence of the paper, I couldn't tell a damn thing, and that was the problem.

Whatever I did from this point forward was likely to contaminate or outright destroy evidence. Every instinct in me screamed to stop, to not endanger an arrest. But that life was over. If there was any arrest connected with the death of this man, I had a strong suspicion it would be the arrest of Mama Campbell's favorite son.

I eased two fingers—index and middle—into the corpse's mouth, grasping the folded paper between my fingertips. I drew my hand back, taking the paper with it, wincing as I felt it pull away from the tongue and roof of the mouth. Then it was free.

A crowd had gathered, though, true to her word, Evelyn had found a couple of synthetics to cordon off the area. Not that it was needed. Not one of the synthetics pressed forward or shouted questions or thrust a screen in my general direction to film the horror. They simply watched and whispered.

I wasn't their leader. They knew it. I knew it. I held a strange and sometimes difficult position among them. I was respected, sure. I'd helped save Evelyn. I'd stood up to be the face of the New Year's Revolution. They knew well that anyone who wished harm on the synthetics wished a much greater and more personal harm upon me. But I still wasn't one of them. They shared a bond forged in adversity that I had only experienced— *could* only experience—the edges of. No, they did not follow me. They followed Silas.

But Silas wasn't around. And I was pulling objects out of a corpse like the world's worst magic act. So, I supposed I could forgive them the whispers.

I returned my attention to the scrap of paper I held. Folded, it was roughly one inch by two. Gingerly, I began unfolding it, violating every rule of evidence procedure I'd ever been taught. Five folds. When I was done, I was holding a standard sheet of printer or copier paper, the kind that had been relegated nearly to antiquity by the prevalence of screens. On the paper was printed two lines of text, in black ink. The first read, "I found you." The second, "You have everything you need to find me."

I stared at the words, letting their implication sink in. Despite all of the precautions we had taken, despite Silas's nearly preternatural ability to avoid the panopticon that blanketed the city, despite never staying in the same location for long, someone had found us. The possibility had been there from the beginning and had grown with each new synthetic that came to our door. You didn't house and feed fifty people without the risk of notice. But I'd been expecting a battering ram and tear gas or a corporate hit squad. We had plans for that. Contingencies. But we hadn't planned for a body delivered to our door with a polite note.

The deadline was a week away. And when that deadline came and passed without any decisive action, the revolution would begin in earnest. And we weren't ready. Oh, we could spill the secrets of the elites faster than they had shed the blood of the innocents. But we weren't prepared for the storm that would come in the wake of our opening salvo. We didn't have the ability to stand up to armed attack. All we had was secrecy and guile, at least until we could figure out how the synthetics could shake off their conditioning or until we had garnered enough support among the general population that more people like me—humans who were both willing and able to shed blood—came forward. Our entire strategy was dependent on remaining hidden.

I found you.

With three simple words, the illusion of safety was torn away.

"Shit," I muttered. I didn't have time to play detective. I didn't have time to track down a killer. But I needed to know. *We* needed to know. Needed to know how whoever had dropped the body had found us. Needed to know where our weaknesses were, where we were exposed. Needed to know what kind of game the person was playing with their, "You have everything you need to find me."

I knew what I needed to do.

It was time to move again, to activate one of the backup locations Silas had found. We'd have to bring the body with us. Find a way to store it. Preserve it. Which would increase the risk of discovery even more. But I couldn't leave it behind. Not without making sure we'd gotten "everything we needed" from it.

And then it was time to make a call that I didn't want to make.

It was time to call the cops.

Chapter 3

"Detective Hernandez."

It had been months since I'd heard Melinda's voice, and a smile sprung unbidden to my lips. I didn't break communications discipline, though. Even talking to me could get her in serious trouble, maybe fired. Maybe much worse. I owed her too much to risk that. So instead, I said, "We need to meet." No greeting. No identification. I was calling from a burner screen and using voice modulating software that made my voice sound, of all things, like a teenage girl. But I still wasn't going to risk talking over the open airwaves.

"I understand," Hernandez replied, her tone light and conversational, revealing no emotion. We'd arranged the protocol months ago, not long after I'd left the force. But this was the first time I'd made contact. Still, she picked up the thread as if we'd discussed it only yesterday. "Our spot by the water, where the screens didn't quite work. My shift is over at five." With that, she disconnected.

Fewer than two dozen words, the entire conversation took no more than fifteen seconds. Casual enough that, if anyone was listening, it wouldn't register as strange. Vague enough that it would be difficult for outsiders to decipher. But it gave me everything I needed. I had a time and a place. In the meantime, I would execute the contingency plan Silas had laid out in the event of discovery. It was going to be a very long day.

At just before five o'clock in the evening, the New Lyons docks were bustling with activity. The port, with its new and ultramodern facilities, was one of the most popular transshipment locations on the Gulf Coast, and stacks of shipping containers formed a veritable maze of cliffs and canyons that could be completely disorienting, even to experienced dockworkers. The entire frontage of the docks themselves operated beneath a massive umbrella of steel beams and rails, along which autonomous cranes ran, using powerful electromagnets to unload ships and move containers about the yard. The setup made the Port of New Lyons one of the most efficient in the world. The network of steel and powerful magnets also made it one of the worst places within the city to try and broadcast or receive any type of wireless signal.

Which was why Melinda had suggested it. Port security was stretched thin, with most of the focus being on shutting down illegal goods coming into the country or legal goods being stolen off of containers. There wasn't much left to stop a person on foot from simply walking in. Once inside the perimeter, I made no effort to hide, trusting in the electromagnetic interference to keep me safe from the eye in the sky and the white hard hat, suit, and oversized screen I carried to keep the few humans on the premises from asking any questions.

I moved with confidence, despite having only been here once before. The place might have been a maze, but take my word for it: you don't forget a place where someone tried to kill you. Soon, I stood at a nondescript intersection formed by stacks of metal boxes. The cranes whirred and crashed overhead, a counterpoint to the steady rhythm of the waves and the occasional bellowing horn of a docking or departing vessel.

There was no sign of Hernandez, so I moved close to one of the containers, leaning up against it at a point where I had clear sight lines down the possible avenues of approach. I didn't have long to wait. Maybe five minutes later, she walked out between one of the steel alleys, her eyes scanning, looking for me, but also exercising the wariness of any law enforcement officer alone in a potentially dangerous situation.

She moved with a sense of purpose, watchful, but confident. She wore a long wool coat—open—over a charcoal pantsuit with a crème-colored blouse, and I could just make out the lines of the Kevlar she wore beneath the top. That was new. Unless they were going out on an active raid, detectives rarely bothered with the body armor. But, then again, things had probably changed down at the precinct. Her dark blue-black hair had been pulled back into a ponytail—a look that didn't really go with the suit but made sense if she expected the potential for violence.

In all, she seemed a more alert, more cautious Melinda Hernandez than the woman who had been my friend for years. It was probably smart, given everything that had happened, but it made me a little sad.

I stepped out from the shadow of the container. "Over here, Hernandez."

She started, hand moving reflexively, clearing her coat and finding the butt of her sidearm. "*Jesu Christo*, Campbell," she snarled as she saw me. "Give a girl some warning. It's not polite to jump out of shadows at people."

Her tone—halfway between anger and banter—brought a grin to my face. Even on the eve of revolution, some things never changed. "Sorry, Mel," I said. "Staying out of sight's gotten to be something of a habit these past few weeks."

"I bet it has, *hermano*," she said. She took two quick steps to me and gave me a brief, fierce hug. Then she pushed me away with more force than necessary. "I always knew you were a stupid motherfucker, Campbell, but damn if you didn't outdo yourself with this bullshit."

I shrugged. "I gotta be me." I meant it as a joke, but there was more than a grain of truth in it. Ever since Annabelle's death, I had been searching for something. Some greater meaning. Some way to help people. It was why I'd taken every dangerous shit job the Army had thrown at me. It's why I became a cop. But the entire time, part of me had known I was hiding. Putting myself at risk to protect people while simultaneously ignoring the fact that there existed an entire underclass of people denied any and all protections. My grin faded from my face.

"You're an asshole," Hernandez said, bringing me back to my present reality. "Always were an asshole. Always will be an asshole." She paused, and now it was her face that went suddenly serious. "But you should probably be a *careful* asshole, Campbell. The brass has got a real hard-on for bringing you in. And they've given Fortier the lead on the task force. Slimy fucker's been riding my ass like a bicycle, too. Half the force is looking for you."

"Only half?" I said with a false smile. Francois Fortier was everything I hated about humanity, wrapped around everything that *everyone* hated about cops, wrapped in about seventy pounds of excess fat and grease. He was an abusive, cowardly mole of a man. But even I had to admit he was an able investigator. "Guess I need to try harder."

Hernandez snorted. "The other half is on constant riot duty. Trying to keep the citizens from burning New Lyons to the ground. Shit. I'm not sure half of them even know what or why they're protesting. They're just out for a little bit of the old ultraviolence. And it's getting harder to tell the sheep from the fucking goats, Campbell."

"Sorry," I muttered, not really knowing what else to say. It wasn't my fault—not exactly. But I had certainly played my part. Change had to come, one way or another. But it tied my stomach in knots to think of good cops—and there were a lot of good cops out there—being put in harm's way because of me.

"Don't you fucking apologize," Hernandez replied, the growl of fury in her voice taking me back. "You don't owe anyone an apology." She drew a deep breath and released it in a long sigh. Her eyes met mine as she continued. "All you did was tell the truth. It's the fucking government that owes the rest of us an apology. And some answers. And some change. And God alone knows what they owe the synthetics. What we all owe them. Shit." She shook her head, ponytail bouncing in a jubilant counterpoint to the resignation in her voice. It was a resignation I understood all too well. Sometimes, the problems were so big that their crushing weight seemed to smother any possible solutions. "People will figure that out, eventually," she finished.

"Yeah," I agreed, trying to sound hopeful, but not really feeling that way. "Yeah."

Hernandez shook her head again, this time more forcefully, as if the physical act would clear it. "You didn't call me out here for this, *hermano*. Not that it isn't good to catch up, but I'm guessing you need something." Her lips twisted into a mocking smile. "What can the officers of the New Lyons Police Department do for you this fine day, citizen?"

"I need a medical examiner."

There was a long moment of dead air. *"Jesu Christo*, Campbell," Hernandez muttered. There were only so many reasons I'd be asking for an ME, after all.

I sighed. "Someone dropped a body off on my doorstop this morning. I need someone I can trust to do a forensic autopsy. You know, without calling the cops on me for murder or treason or whatever the charge du jour is."

"Domestic terrorism," Hernandez said absently.

Terrorist. I'd been called a lot of things over the years, but that was a first. Given where I'd spent most of my time in the Army, the irony wasn't lost on me. The line between a patriot and a terrorist was, indeed, a thin one. I shook that thought off.

"Why the fuck did someone drop a body on your doorstep?" Hernandez asked. "I thought you were out of the murder police business."

"Yeah, well, so did I. But someone is delivering a message, and they managed to find me to deliver it. If they can find us…" I shrugged.

"So can Fortier and his merry band of men? And the feds. They're involved, too, by the way. Shit. We've got every three-letter agency in the book down at the precinct. FBI. CIA. ATF. NSA. Even the fucking IRS. You been skipping out on your taxes, Campbell?"

I shook my head. It wasn't unexpected, but the array of investigative power aligned against us was daunting.

"You're lucky they haven't found you already. When you pulled this shit back in December, I didn't think you'd make it a week. You must have an angel on your shoulder."

An angel or an albino synthetic. "Yeah," I muttered. "Something like that. Look, I don't know what's going on. That's why I need an ME. But it's got to be someone at least sympathetic to our cause." I almost winced. I'd never been a man of causes. Causes were things people took up when their real life didn't keep them busy enough or they wanted attention. Or so I had thought. Now I found myself in the center of a cause, in the heart of a movement. It wasn't a very comfortable place to be. "I was hoping you could make it happen."

The set of Hernandez's shoulders tightened, and she looked away from me. She was silent a long moment. "You're asking me to help you cover up a crime, you know? I mean, I assume you're not just going to turn this poor soul over to the authorities when you're done with him?"

I hadn't really thought about it, but I knew Hernandez was right. The forensic tools at the disposal of the New Lyons Police Department were pretty good. If the feds were involved, those tools were that much better. If they got their hands on the body, there was no telling what they might discover. Not just about the killer, but about where the body had been. About where *I* had been. It wouldn't give them the entire puzzle, but investigations were built piece by piece. I couldn't afford to give them that piece. I couldn't ask Hernandez to do that. She was far enough off the reservation just for meeting with me, but that was at least explainable.

"Forget about it," I said. "I'll figure something out." I tried to keep the frustration—not at Hernandez, but at myself for putting her in this position and for not knowing where else to turn—out of my voice, but by the wince I got in return, I failed.

"Dammit, Campbell. I know someone. Maybe. She's sympathetic, but I'm not sure if it's to your cause, or just to you."

That threw me. Sympathetic to me? "Well? Who is it?"

"Morita."

The named sparked a memory, an overeager medical student who had performed an autopsy on Fowler's first victim. The first victim I found, anyway. She had been earnest, well-meaning. But young. So damn young, with so much future ahead of her. "Are you sure?" I asked. "We don't know anyone with…well…less to lose?"

Hernandez snorted. "Don't be an idiot, Campbell. Who do you think is most firmly on your side in all this? It isn't the entrenched old farts like me who grew up with synthetics. It's the radical youth, looking to rebel. The only people who are going to take the kind of risks you need are the people who don't really understand what they have to lose."

Wars were fought by the young. It was an adage I knew well—one I had experienced firsthand. Hernandez was right. Some of it was ignorance, sure. But some of it was passion. Belief. Hunger for change. Fires that dwindled as the stately march of time consumed their fuel. I didn't want to risk the beautiful young woman with the promising career. But I needed help, and if she wanted to, who was I to make that decision for her?

Was I rationalizing? Letting my own needs outweigh the right thing to do? Maybe. But the danger to me, to the synthetics, and to the budding revolution was real. Could I put Ms. Morita's future ahead of all those lives?

"Set up a meeting."

Chapter 4

Silas was waiting for me when I returned to the new safe house.

Compared to the call center, the contingency location was a more modest affair. It had been a restaurant at some point, though maybe "restaurant" was too grand a name. Dive certainly fit. Officious health inspector's wet dream was also valid. According to a dilapidated sign that still hung just inside the door, the place had boasted a maximum capacity a bit north of a hundred and twenty souls. The fire marshal must have been popping happy pills, because with half that number of synthetics, it already felt way too crowded.

Like the last location, the windows had been boarded up, but the entire exterior wall—plywood and all—was covered in layer upon layer of graffiti. Some of it was simple tagging, street names, gang affiliations. Some was much more…evocative, not to mention anatomically problematic. The "artwork" was endemic of the neighborhood, a run-down section of New Lyons the locals called the LNW, a callback—if a geographically inaccurate one—to the old days of New Orleans. Most of the residents subsisted on the Basic Living Stipend, hope for a better life having long since been drained from them.

The residents of the LNW were, I knew, a dark mirror to the plight of the synthetics. They were full citizens, with all the rights and freedoms that came along with that status. They had access to all the basic necessities of life; between the BLS, UniCare, and various other social programs, no one fell through the cracks. And yet, even as the safety net had grown, the top of the pyramid had restricted further and further, until the odds against climbing it were so slim that significant percentages of the population had simply stopped trying, convincing themselves that they were content with the lives they had, the things they had been given.

That contentment, however, seldom lasted more than a single generation. It was the next generation, hungry for something more than mere contentment, that set the tone for places like the LNW. They knew that life, for them, was lacking something. Something indefinable that made it more than the content existence of their elders. Some got out, by luck or by design. But most remained, and all of that youthful energy had to go somewhere. It was why the predictions had been wrong. When the war on drugs had ended in a resounding defeat, the gangs and the violence hadn't gone away.

The restaurant—the safe house—was deep in gangland. That came with its share of problems and risks, but it also afforded us a different kind of protection from the abandoned call center. Fifty-plus people didn't suddenly take up residence within the LNW without *someone* noticing, but no one was going to call the cops, either. And the cameras that blanked the city always seemed to fail in neighborhoods like the LNW. I'd still moved quickly through the twilight-shrouded streets, avoiding people wherever possible. The eye in the sky might be blinded, but any one of the people around me might be liveblogging, sending a continuous stream of their day off into the cloud—along with a billion other people around the world. Not even the feds could parse that much information, not quickly, but there was no reason to take the risk.

I slipped the door shut behind me, listening for the metallic thunk of the bolts engaging, and turned to see Silas watching me with those eyes that radiated calm, certainty, and amusement all at once.

Over the past month, I'd long since abandoned the habit of reaching for my sidearm every time the stocky, barrel-chested albino synthetic seemed to appear out of thin air. Instead, I growled. "I'm going to put a fucking bell on you."

He smiled, the barest upturn of the corners of his mouth. "I think not, Detective."

"How many times do I have to tell you, I'm not a detective anymore? I got canned, remember?"

"I do," Silas replied. "On the other hand, you're having my people cart bodies around so you can pursue an investigation. I thought, perhaps, you might have forgotten." He spoke in the same quiet rumble, without the barest hint of accusation, but I felt it anyway.

"Someone found us, Silas."

"Which is why we moved."

"Yeah," I agreed. "But whoever found us left us a nice, convenient warning. Next time it might not be a corpse and an enigmatic note. It might be the fucking riot squad kicking in the door and throwing lead downrange at anything in their path."

"I am not fond of these sorts of games, Detective."

"No shit. I'm not super excited about playing tag with a killer a week before we start trying to tear down the fucking world either. But whoever did this wants us to look for them, and, presumably, to find them. And if we don't play along, I somehow doubt they're going to let it drop. The message is pretty clear, Silas. We find them. Or they find us. Again."

Silas appeared to consider that. He turned, his gaze falling over the people crammed into what had been, at some point, the restaurant's dining room. They sat, packed cheek by jowl, in the rotting remains of booths, or stretched out on cots placed anywhere with enough space. I silently prayed that the bathrooms were functional. If not, we'd have a serious problem.

"Do as you must, Detective," he said at last. "But do it quickly. And most important of all, do it *carefully*."

I bridled a bit at that. My life was no less at risk than theirs, maybe even more at risk. But time was running out, and even Silas, under all of that ineffable calm, had to be feeling the pressure. So I gritted my teeth and nodded. "Yeah. Sure. Careful."

"In the meantime, one of the refrigerators in the kitchen is still operable. Your...corpse...has been placed there. What, exactly, are you planning on doing with it?"

"Using it to find some answers," I replied. "Which means that kitchen is going to have to serve as an autopsy room."

Silas frowned. "I did not realize you were qualified to perform an autopsy."

"I'm not. I'll be bringing in some outside help." I braced myself for the argument I knew would be coming. Not that I could blame Silas. He held the safety of those under his protection paramount.

But he must have been more unsettled by the appearance of the body than he had let on, because he stared at me with those strange, red-hued eyes. At last, he said, "Be very, very careful." Without another word to me, he turned and started moving among the synthetics, stopping briefly here and there to chat or offer a word of comfort. He reminded me of a priest—or a politician. Neither was a particularly comforting thought.

* * * *

I got the text from Hernandez about an hour and a half later, while I was elbow-deep in an industrial sink, scrubbing years of rust and grime off a variety of baking sheets, discarded flatware, and other implements I thought might be useful in performing an autopsy. Not that our deceased would care overly much about the cleanliness of any potential instruments, but a certain amount of respect was called for.

After some fumbling with a scrap that might once have been a dish towel, I managed to dry my hands and retrieve my screen. She'd sent me an address and a time, nothing more. Good. Nothing incriminating. Nothing to trip any of the predictive searches that the feds were undoubtedly running on the communications of all my former colleagues. Of course, a tiny, paranoid, and spiteful part of my brain reminded me, if Hernandez had been found out, that was also all the information those same feds would send to walk me right into a trap. Nothing to tip me to the fact that it wasn't, in fact, Hernandez sending the message.

I didn't think that was the case, but better to be prepared, at least mentally, for the eventuality. If faced with sworn officers, what would I do? Could I bring myself to draw my weapon, to open fire on my former brothers and sisters? If the door to the restaurant was kicked in at that moment, putting a roomful of innocents in mortal danger, then, yes, I believed I could do it. But just to save myself? Just to prevent my arrest, and the subsequent interrogation? That was, after all, one of the reasons why Silas only ever told me what the *first* contingency location was. I had no doubt that if I was taken, that location would be skipped, and whatever information I had would be rendered all but useless. Knowing that no life but my own would be in danger, could I take the life of those just doing their job?

I didn't know. I wasn't even sure what I wanted the answer to be. That uncertainty bothered me far more than the risk I was taking by showing up to meet with Ms. Morita. But I wasn't spoiled for choices, so I collected my coat, checked to make sure my weapon and spare magazines were in place, and headed for the door.

The synthetics had already gone to work on the points of entry to the restaurant, installing a variety of makeshift locking mechanisms that would hold out against everything short of explosives—at least for a few minutes. The skill base available in a group of gathered synthetics continued to astound me. In my former life, and much to my shame, I'd tried to minimize my interactions with the synthetics—not out of distaste, but out of the subconscious knowledge that if I paid too much attention to them, I would be unable to suppress my memories of Annabelle, the synthetic girl with whom I'd fallen in love so long ago. The girl who had been tortured and murdered. The girl for whom I had killed two people. Two humans, if her worthless shitbag "parents" even rated the title.

As a result of that avoidance, I'd only really encountered two types of synthetics in my day-to-day life as a cop. The first were the true menials—those relegated to positions that, as a species, we used to be certain would be done by machines. Cashiers. Waitstaff. Janitorial staff. Unskilled manual labor. It turned out that slave labor was a much more "cost-efficient" model than researching and developing the technologies needed to replace many of those human workers. The second type, I encountered more frequently as a result of the beats I had worked as a cop. Those were the sex workers, male and female, that walked the streets or worked out of the brothels in the shadier districts of town. But the spectrum of tasks for which synthetics had been trained was broader by far than I'd realized. Among the few dozen that had made their way to Silas, we had skilled carpenters, electricians, and screen technicians, all capable of operating at a professional level.

They'd made short work of securing the area. They might not be able to fight off attackers directly, but getting to them would be no easy task. I nodded at one of the synths standing by the door, peering out through a narrow slit at the street beyond. Keeping watch for approaching trouble. "I'm heading out," I said. "Lock up behind me?"

"Of course, Mr. Campbell," he replied. There was a slight subservience in his tone that grated on me. All of the synthetics, excepting only Evelyn and Silas, spoke to me in that same way. I understood why—they'd had it beaten into them, in some cases, literally, since their first moments of life. It still made me grind my teeth. "Jason," I said. "My name is Jason."

"Of course, Jason," he said again, not meeting my gaze. I was reminded, not for the first time, that even if we managed to survive the weeks and months before us, even if Silas realized all of his goals, the synthetics would still have a long, difficult road ahead.

"One step at a time," I said aloud, earning me a quick, albeit confused, glance from the synthetic. I didn't know his name. With few exceptions, I didn't know the names of any of the synthetics that were, at least nominally, under my protection. Was that a result of years of isolating myself from everyone—human and synthetic alike—to keep my own feelings off of society's radar? Or was it because of something darker, more sinister, that lurked deep in my psyche, believing that I was, despite everything I knew to be true, somehow superior to them? I couldn't answer that question. But whatever the underlying cause, I could start to treat the symptoms. "What's your name?" I asked.

"Marcus."

"It's the only way we get anywhere, Marcus. One step at a time. Sometimes they're small steps. Sometimes they're giant, revolution-sized steps. But it's always one step at a time."

He nodded, but his eyes still held that slight confusion. I offered a smile and began unlocking the bolts and bars that secured the front door.

Time to take another step.

Chapter 5

Exiting the city was getting more difficult.

The beater of a car that Silas had arrived in and given me the okay to use was, despite its appearance, quite serviceable. He'd disabled the GPS and auto-drive functions so the vehicle couldn't be tracked, but cops were among the few people left in the city truly trained on old-school driving techniques. I could operate the vehicle just fine, and I knew my way around town without having to rely on any satellites. The problem was the roadblocks. And the protests.

I couldn't watch my screen—not with the auto-drive disabled. But I could listen to it, and it was currently blaring my own personal roundup of New Lyons news. The parameters I used to filter the overwhelming amount of information produced and posted online every single day parsed the stories down to only what I cared about. I'd restricted that even further, down to stories about synthetics, the situation in New Lyons, and me.

"Protests continue across downtown," the female anchor was saying. "There were several violent clashes as protesters and counter-protesters met. New Lyons PD responded with gas canisters to disperse the crowd. While there were no fatalities, concerns are growing as the violence levels continue to escalate with the approach of the February 1 deadline given to world governments by a synthetic terrorist organization and its spokesperson, former NLPD detective-turned-domestic-terrorist Jason Campbell."

I winced at that. "Next," I said aloud, skipping the rest of the story. I didn't need a refresher on my own background, even if the news agencies seemed to think the rest of the world did every fifteen minutes or so.

The male anchor took over. "Traffic woes continue to plague New Lyons as police checkpoints are in operation on all major thoroughfares. Law enforcement efforts to find New Lyons's most wanted criminal, Jason Campbell, are in full effect. If you're planning on using any of the highways or interstates, expect delays."

I sighed. I could get out of the city without using major roads, but I'd been hoping for more detailed information. There was no telling what other roads might be under interdiction. I would have to take my chances and avoid any traffic patterns that looked like they might be leading to a checkpoint. Which made me wince again. A lot of people in New Lyons hated me at the moment—and I had no doubt that a good chunk of them hated me more for screwing up their commute than any other reason.

I let the news continue to play as I navigated through the city. The app I was using had a handy feature that automatically promoted stories that were geographically close by, which helped me avoid the worst of the protests and demonstrations. I didn't encounter any checkpoints, either by virtue of Hernandez's choice of location—after all, she likely *did* know where all the checkpoints were, and the most likely route I would take to any given location—or by sheer dumb luck. One was as good as the other in my book. Whatever the cause, I arrived at the arranged meeting without incident.

The Church of the Awakened Mind sat atop a low hill on the very outskirts of New Lyons, so far removed from the city proper that it blurred the borders between suburban and rural. As churches went, it wasn't particularly impressive—a simple rectangle covered in cream-colored siding with a tall, narrow steeple rising from the back, maybe twelve hundred square feet in all. An unassuming building in the middle of nowhere. A pair of sconces shed light from either side of the church's front door, but beyond that, and despite the relatively early hour, there were no other signs of life. Maybe the priest had gone home for the day, or simply sought his bed in a rectory somewhere on the grounds.

I drove up the small road that led past the church, into the area behind it, where a parking lot acted as a buffer between the church and a modest cemetery. There were no cars in the parking lot, which gave me a momentary jolt of worry. The meeting was supposed to be at eight thirty. With the need to avoid checkpoints and protesters alike, I was running maybe fifteen minutes late. Had Tia Morita arrived on time, waited ten minutes, and left? Or had she been dropped off by a cab service?

Or had this whole thing been a setup?

I pulled the car into a spot and killed the headlights. I didn't immediately exit the vehicle, giving my eyes a minute to adjust to the darkness. A low wall surrounded the cemetery, and though I could just make out an occasional lamppost, none of them were turned on. A cost-saving measure by the little church? Maybe. I eased my forty-five in its holster, my heart beating a little faster. With my left hand, I reached down beside the seat and grabbed a plastic bag that rustled softly as its contents shifted. Then I stepped from the car.

Hernandez's text had been nonspecific as to where, exactly, the meet would take place. The cemetery. The address. The time. If everything was on the up-and-up, my best course of action was to wait by the car. If Tia was here, she had almost certainly seen me pull in to the parking lot and would likely be moving in my direction. On the other hand, if it was a setup, teams were probably already moving into position, and staying in one place would make it easier for them. I'd already decided that simply getting back in the car and driving away was out of the question—if I did that, my chances of finding whoever had dropped a body on my doorstep would fade from slim to none. So I hopped over the low wall and began to move amongst the gravesites.

The boneyard was a mix of standard headstones and raised mausoleums. We were far enough inland that the aboveground resting places were more a nod to New Lyons tradition than built that way out of any real need. Right now, for me, they were both a blessing and a curse. They provided me with decent cover from any bad guys lurking in the shadows…but they also obstructed my sight lines, making it difficult for me to see if there *were* any bad guys lurking in said shadows.

I didn't know where Ms. Morita might be, so I moved inward, toward the heart of the cemetery. The place was not so large that finding the medical examiner's assistant should be a great endeavor, but the poor lighting, obstructed sight lines and my reluctance to call out—I didn't want to give away my position in the event that this *was* a trap—made it difficult to see much of anything. But if I was going to meet someone in a boneyard, the center seemed as good a place as any.

I slipped among the headstones and around the mausoleums, paying more attention to my ears than my eyes, listening hard for the rustle of a leaf or a sharply drawn breath. It didn't take long to near the center. It would have taken only five or six minutes at a brisk, direct walk. It took me closer to fifteen, moving quietly and taking a more circuitous route. As I reached the inner ring of the graveyard, I eased around the corner of a mausoleum. At the center of the yard stood a large family crypt, probably a hundred square feet or so, with the name Corbeaux etched into the stone above the sealed doors. In front of the doors stood a slim shape, a wash of darker shadow against the night.

I moved closer, focusing not on the person standing in the open but rather scanning the area, looking for anything out of place, anything that might indicate things were not as they seemed. I drew a slow, steadying breath, and stepped out.

"Ms. Morita."

She jumped. Actually, physically jumped, feet clearing the ground and hands coming up into a defensive posture. Her head snapped around, until her eyes found me, standing maybe ten feet away, still shrouded in the shadows. "Detective Campbell?" she asked uncertainly.

I stepped forward slowly, my own hands held before me in supplication. I'd only spoken with Ms. Morita twice, both times via screen. When I'd caught the case of the murdered and mutilated synthetic woman, I had managed to fast-talk Dr. Fitzpatrick, the actual medical examiner, into having one of his assistants perform an examination of the remains. It was an action that could, technically, have been construed as illegal, and if anyone ever put together the fact that Ms. Morita had performed it with the events that led to the discovery and revealing of Evelyn's pregnancy, I had no doubt that Tia's freedom, and perhaps her life, would be in danger. Fortunately, Fitzpatrick was an officious little prick who liked his job and, even if he had put the pieces together, would never endanger it by hinting that the Office of the New Lyons Medical Examiner had played any role whatsoever.

The ME's assistant had done a good job and provided me with the leads that, ultimately, allowed me to track down Transatlantic and Fowler. But I'd forgotten how damn young she was. And pretty. Prettier in person than she had been on the screen. She stood five-two or five-three, weighed maybe one-twenty. Slender, but something about the way she stood, the speed with which she had reacted to my words, suggested a level of athleticism. Her clothing—a practical, off-the-rack pantsuit in a navy blue—wasn't exactly the most flattering of garments, but it couldn't fully hide a certain litheness about her. Her eyes were dark, almond-shaped, her hair blue-black and falling freely past her shoulders. Her lips were full, cheekbones high, features symmetrical... Beautiful.

I made myself stop admiring her. It would only make what I had to do next all the more awkward.

"Yes, Ms. Morita," I said, stepping to within a couple of yards of her. "It's me."

I gave her a moment to study me in turn. I doubted she would like what she saw nearly as much as I had. I was a big man. Not overly tall, but broad of shoulder. Fit, from the regular martial arts workouts, though starting to lose a little bit of my tone, since I hadn't been able to practice much in the past month. But outside of that, decidedly average looking. Dark hair cropped short for convenience, brown eyes, a face that covered the front of my head and couldn't be accused of doing much else for me. Unshaven, since my day—which was getting on toward too long for comfort—had started with a nasty surprise and gone downhill from there. And probably a decade older than the woman in front of me.

"Detective Hernandez said you need my help. Are you hurt?"

There was genuine concern in her voice, which surprised me. Was it the professional concern of an aspiring doctor, or something more personal? I was also mildly annoyed that Hernandez had, apparently, sent Ms. Morita out here with no idea of what I needed her to do. That probably wasn't fair. The more Hernandez told her, the more at risk we'd all be. But it didn't feel right to keep her in the dark, either.

"I'm fine, Ms. Morita," I said.

"Please. Call me Tia," she interrupted.

"Tia. I'm fine." I hesitated. "I'm afraid the help I need is a little more… unorthodox…than simple medical care."

She said nothing, just watched me with those dark, almond eyes. She shifted slightly on her feet, and allowed her hands—which had, until this point, still been raised unconsciously in a defensive posture—to drop to her sides. I took that as a good sign.

"I need you to perform an autopsy for me."

Her eyes narrowed and her nose wrinkled in confusion. "But…you're not a detective anymore. And… Well…"

"And, well, I'm wanted by every law enforcement agency in the country—and probably internationally as well," I agreed. "And I certainly should be busy enough with other things that investigating a death shouldn't be at the top of my to-do list. Right?"

She smiled, her lips parting to reveal slightly crooked teeth. "That, yes. And also, other details. Like, I understand why you can't go to the police, but why do you have a body lying around in the first place? And where exactly would I be performing such an autopsy? And why should I?"

The last question was asked with a twinkle of the eye that belied its actual intent. The first two, however, reminded me that, beautiful or not, Tia Morita was a smart young woman well on her way to becoming a doctor. I sensed I could probably cajole or convince her without sharing too many details. That she wanted to help me—not necessarily the synthetics or the revolution, but for whatever strange and arcane reasoning that took place in the depths of the female mind, she wanted to help *me*. But I couldn't do that to her. Couldn't manipulate her into helping without fully understanding the risks—to her career, maybe even to her life. Time to come clean.

"Look," I said, not really knowing where to begin. "I... Well, I sort of have a body on my hands." One of her eyebrows arched up, and I hurried on. "Not a body I made. I mean, I didn't kill the guy. But someone dumped him on my doorstep. Sort of...literally."

"Okay." She drew the word out, and I could see the doubt flickering on her face. But she hadn't run screaming yet.

"Someone's playing a game," I explained. "A game that could get me and a lot of synthetics killed. We found a note on the remains basically taunting me to find whoever did it."

"I didn't think you were in the police business anymore, Detective."

"I'm not," I growled, some of my frustration leaking through. She flinched, and I immediately felt like an asshat. "Sorry. That's not directed at you. Just... Long day." I took a deep breath. "Whoever did this knew where to find me, Tia. Knew where to find me and a bunch of defenseless synthetics who have zero chance of helping themselves. I've got to figure out who."

She smiled, just a little. "And to do that, you need me."

"Yes. I've seen my share of bodies, but I don't know the first thing about doing an actual forensic examination of one. The note said our killer left us all the clues we'd need to find him. But I don't even know where to start looking." I hesitated again, then sighed. "And you're probably putting yourself in danger helping us," I acknowledged.

She seemed to shrink a bit at that. "Detective... What's happening to the synthetics... What you've revealed." She paused, drew a breath, started to talk. Stopped herself. Drew another breath and tried again. "It's terrible. I mean, if it's true—"

"It's true, Tia. All of it. You barely know me, so I can't expect you to trust me, but the information is out there. You've seen Evelyn. And I'm guessing, if you ever really thought about it, you'd know that it was true. That you've known all along that it was true." I snorted. "That's the danger and the beauty of the lie we've all been told. We've been told it so often, for so long, that even when we *know* it's a lie, we all just go along with it. Because it's safer. Because it's *easier*."

"You're asking me to risk...everything," she said, her voice tremulous. "My career, certainly. Performing an unauthorized autopsy on a murder victim? It's a crime. And with all the violence in the air? Can you tell me that I wouldn't be putting my life on the line, too?" She shook her head, and I sensed I was losing her. I hated what I had to do next. But I still had to do it.

"It's okay, Tia," I said, my voice gentle. "You don't have to help. Honestly, it's what the synthetics expect from us. It's what they've gotten from us for so long that they don't even know how to respond when a human bothers to be nice to them. They don't expect your help. They probably don't even want your help. I could have used it." I shrugged. "But I understand. You have to look out for yourself."

"That's not fair!" she said at once. Her nostrils flared and her eyes flashed in anger.

"No," I agreed. "It's not. But 'fair' isn't exactly something that's going around these days."

I could see the doubts flittering around her face. I hated myself more than a little for that, for playing on her emotions, for making her doubt herself. I had sensed almost from day one that Tia Morita was one of those people who honestly cared about others. The type of person who if someone on the other side of the world suffered a tragedy, she would feel real pain on their behalf. I envied people like that—envied their ability to feel empathy on such a grand scale. I wasn't one of them. Maybe I could have been, but Annabelle's dead mother killed that part of me as surely as she had killed Annabelle.

"Everything you're saying about synthetics is true?" It was a question, but she already knew the answer, and it showed as she stated, "They really are people."

"As human as you or me," I agreed, pitching my voice low, trying to convey my certainty.

"Then how can I refuse to help?" she asked. It was a legitimate question, and one I suspected she wanted a real answer to. I couldn't give her one. Instead, I started filling her in on the downsides—well, the downsides that didn't involve threats to her personal safety or freedom.

"I'm afraid that the...let's call them facilities...where you'd have to perform the autopsy are rudimentary. Not much in the way of equipment. All of it field expedient." I hesitated, not sure how to broach the next topic.

"And before I take you there... I'm going to have to make sure you're not being tracked, electronically."

"You're going to have to what?" she demanded.

I grimaced. "Look, Tia. It's not that I don't trust you. I wouldn't have asked Hernandez to set up this meeting if that was the case. But it's not just me. We're going to the place where Evelyn—the pregnant synthetic woman—is hiding. Where dozens of synthetics, all of whom will be killed if they're found, are hiding. We can't afford to take chances. I need your help. My life, and the life of untold synthetics may well depend on it. But I understand if you don't want to. I have no right to ask it of you. But as much as I need you, I can't put them at risk."

"So, what? You need to frisk me or something?" A flush of color suffused her cheeks as she said those words, but her gaze didn't leave mine.

I felt the rush of blood to my own face. "Not exactly. The feds, hell, even the local departments, have access to listening devices and trackers that a frisk would never catch."

She arched an eyebrow at me. Her face stayed flushed, but her tone was even as she said, "Just what, exactly, are you asking of me, Detective?"

I reached into the bag in my left hand and began pulling out its contents. A pair of blue scrubs pants, scrubs top. Socks. Slip-on shoes that would work for a variety of sizes of feet. I hadn't quite been able to bring myself to put together a selection of underwear and bras. I was in a big enough minefield already; that seemed a step or three too far. "I'm afraid you're going to have to leave your things here. All of your things."

"By the look on your face, I'm guessing I can't just go behind this mausoleum and change?"

"Uhm…no," I said. I grimaced and shook my head. Why did I feel like a schoolboy sneaking into a strip club? For fuck's sake, this was necessary to ensure the safety of all those people back at the restaurant in the LNW. It had nothing to do with watching a pretty young lady take her clothes off. And it's not like Ms. Morita had anything I hadn't seen before.

"I can't take the chance that you might transfer something while I wasn't looking," I said.

"So you'll be looking? You're asking a lot here, Campbell," she growled. "I'm trusting you enough to put my life and career on the line. You can't even trust me this little bit?"

Something of my internal turmoil must have shown on my face, because she laughed then, a tinkling sound of amusement with just a touch of embarrassed nerves thrown in for good measure. But she took pity on me. "Give me the clothes," she said. "I assume I can at least turn around?"

I dropped the clothes back into the bag and handed it over to her. I was suddenly unsure of where to look. Did I maintain eye contact? Something about that seemed super creepy. I certainly couldn't drop my gaze from her eyes to any other part of her, not with her getting ready to disrobe. "That will be fine, Ms. Morita."

"I think we're a little past 'Ms. Morita,' Detective," she said. She took the bag and turned her back on me. There was no hesitation in her movement now, as she slipped out of her jacket and began undoing the buttons on her blouse.

I wanted to look away. I wanted to leer. Either way, I had to watch. Neither my discomfort, nor Tia's, mattered when weighed against the safety of the synthetics. I knew I could trust Tia. But that was the thing about betrayal—you could only be betrayed by those you trusted. It was a shitty way to view the world, but experience had taught me that the world was a pretty shitty place.

Tia moved quickly, efficiently, dropping her blouse to the ground and reaching behind her to unhook her bra. It joined her jacket and shirt, and she reached down with one arm to root around in the plastic bag and dig out the scrubs top. She threw a glance in my direction as she did so, one arm across her breasts, which, I couldn't help noticing, were more ample than the unflattering pantsuit had hinted. The look on her face was one of frank appraisal, as if she were evaluating exactly how I was watching her. I did my best to keep my face professional and impassive.

She pulled the scrubs top over her head. It was a little too large, the hem falling perhaps halfway down her hips. Still exercising that calm efficiency, she kicked off her shoes and socks and then reached for her waistband. Her slacks and panties—something black and lacy that I felt a little ashamed for noticing—pooled onto the ground and she stepped out of them. She bent toward the ground once more, to retrieve the scrubs pants, and a long-forgotten word drifted from somewhere in the depths of my mind: *callipygian*. Tia stepped quickly into the pants, then turned back to me, a challenging look on her face. "Well?" she asked.

I wasn't entirely sure what she was asking, and damned if I was going to give an opinion on what I had witnessed. Mama Campbell hadn't raised that big of a fool. "We'll have to leave your things here," I said, choosing to interpret her question in the least dangerous—for me, anyway—way possible. "Put them in the bag. We can stash them by one of the mausoleums. I'll bring you back here when we're done."

"And my tools?" she asked, nodding to a darker patch of shadow in the lee of the mausoleum. "I couldn't bring much, but I've at least got some instruments."

I shook my head, thinking of the array of cutlery, skewers, tongs, and other cast-off cooking implements back at the safe house. "Sorry, Tia," I said. "We'll just have to make do."

"Do you really think that someone snuck a GPS locator into my scalpel?" she asked, incredulous.

"No," I replied honestly. I felt the urge to throw my hands in the air or maybe punch a tombstone but managed—barely—to restrain myself. "Dammit, Tia. If it were just me, just my safety, none of this would be necessary. You're right. You deserve more trust than this. But you can buy a fucking radio tracking tag for under a buck, sync it to your screen, and know to within a few feet where it is at all times. The commercial ones are so small you can barely see them. I know the cops have access to better than that, and I'm betting that the feds have even cooler toys. I don't think they're tracking your scalpel, or whatever else you have in the bag, but I can't be sure. Any more than I can be sure there isn't a tracker in your clothing or your bag or stuck to the bottom of your shoe. I'm sorry. I just can't take the chance."

"Do you have any idea how much harder that's going to make things?"

I didn't, not really. I could imagine, though. "We'll just have to make do," I said again, somewhat apologetically.

"Oh, it's we, now, is it?" she said. "Does that mean you're not wearing underwear, either?" The smile was gone and there was an edge to it. It wasn't anger—at least I didn't think so, but I couldn't quite place it. Her eyes were...considering.

"Well," I said with a shrug, "I figure you might need an assistant. I don't know anything about what you do, but I can fetch and carry with the best of them." I gave her my best disarming smile and tried to get the image of the pale curve of her bare hips out of my mind.

"Fine." She took the time to carefully fold her discarded clothing and place it in the bag, nestling it deeper into the shadows. Then she turned back to me. "Let's go, then. It's kind of chilly out here."

The material of the scrubs top was rather thin, so I could, in fact, tell that Ms. Morita was a touch chilly. But once again, I said nothing.

Mama Campbell and fools.

Chapter 6

We didn't talk much as I drove us back through the city and toward the LNW. As we got closer to the water's edge, and the neighborhoods around us took on a darker, more ominous cast, Tia stared at the outward signs of poverty—the boarded windows; the groups of young men gathered on corners giving hard stares to anything and everything; the scattered detritus that somehow, despite the efforts of the sanitation services, always seemed to pile up in drifts of garbage. Her shoulders took on a tighter, almost defensive, set, and I could sense a general stiffening of her entire body.

Most people never really saw this side of the city. Maybe twenty percent of the population of New Lyons lived in squalor, but it was a contained squalor, shunted off to neighborhoods that people had long since given up on and isolated from anywhere "decent" folks might find themselves. We were firmly on the wrong side of the tracks, and what happened here, how people lived here, wasn't really New Lyons at all. At least, not to the people who weren't confined to these neighborhoods. No, this was the unmentionable little secret of the city—and every city had them.

I couldn't blame Tia for the tension. It wasn't just natural—it was sensible, even advisable. In this part of town, people were divided in many ways, but the most important way was also the simplest: in the LNW, you were either predator or prey. I didn't know enough about Ms. Morita to say with certainty into which category she might fall, but awareness and caution were good practices either way. But good practice or not, at least for the moment, she didn't have to fear. "You can relax," I said, hoping to ease her worries. "This isn't the best district, but we'll be safe. From the locals, anyway."

She turned her head from the window and away from what passed for scenery. The tension in her body didn't ease in the slightest, but there was no tremor of fear in her voice as she said, "Where are we going? Or, if you tell me, will you have to kill me or something?"

I shrugged. "An old restaurant. Out of business. But big enough to hold everybody." We were getting close now. Parking in this part of town wasn't a problem—at least not finding a space. Having your car still be in one piece when you returned to it... Well, that was another issue. Car theft was all but impossible—any lawful owner could disable and lock down their vehicle with a single swipe across their screen—but vandalism from the have-nots to the haves was as prevalent a problem as ever. It helped that the car looked like it had already suffered that vandalism, but I needed to find an as out-of-the-way spot as possible, to avoid the dangers of idle hands.

"Everybody?" Tia asked, surprised. "Who's everybody?"

"Oh," I said with a grin, "just a few friends of *la révolution.*"

"You weren't kidding," she said about fifteen minutes later. I'd found a relatively concealed spot for the car about half a block away. We'd received a few hard looks on the walk, but no one bothered us. I might not have been a cop or a soldier anymore, but I still walked like one, and most of the people looking for an opportunity to make trouble could see that. The synthetics had seen us coming—the benefits of keeping a good lookout—and the door opened as we approached. Our transition from street to building was smooth and "if you blink you miss it" fast, and the door was swinging shut behind us and the beams being put back in place as Tia spoke.

Dozens of faces stared at us as we entered. I was a known quantity, accepted, if somewhat separated. Tia was something else. Pretty as she was, she lacked the almost preternatural beauty of many of the faces that watched us from the tables, booths, and cots—the beauty of the Toys, custom designed to please. Athletic as she was, she couldn't compete physically with the hard, muscled frames of the Drones designed for manual labor. Even the Domestics with their carefully designed flaws were better put together than most humans, myself and Tia included. Tia was, in fact, very human looking, and to the people gathered in this room, her human nature constituted a threat.

The irony of the synthetics judging her simply for being human was not lost on me—but neither was the perfectly practical and justifiable reasoning behind that judgment.

Silence had drifted out from our arrival like ripples spreading on the calm surface of a pond. Now we stood on the edge of that pond, awash in a wave of worried faces. It was more than a little disconcerting, and Tia's cheeks were slowly coloring. She managed to look out over the crowd, not lowering her gaze, but not singling anyone out with it either, despite the discomfort she must be feeling. As someone who had felt the weight of that collective stare, I was impressed.

"This is Tia Morita," I announced to the assemblage. "She's here to help us find answers, to help us find out who left the...surprise...on our doorstep this morning." Shit, had it only been this morning? "She's here to help, people."

Judging from their faces, they remained unconvinced, but a slight stir of conversation started once more as the synthetics began to turn away from us.

"This way." I led her across the room, conscious that as we approached, conversations died down, only to start up once more in our wake. When we reached the swinging doors to the kitchen, I gestured for Tia to go before me.

I'd done my best to re-create the autopsy rooms that had been an unfortunate but unavoidable part of my career with NLPD. My best, I had to admit, was pretty shitty. Instead of a vacuum-enabled autopsy table, the best I could offer was a stainless steel food prep table. Instead of the precision instruments, I had put together an amalgam of cast-off cutlery, an assortment of pliers, and a couple of power tools. The resultant array more closely resembled the torture implements of a vid-villain from a horror stream than any type of medical facility.

Tia surveyed the scene, a slight frown tugging at her lips. "This is... rudimentary."

"Yeah," I agreed. "Sorry. Best I could do. Is it workable?"

"For what? An actual forensic autopsy? Of course not. I may be able to give you cause of death, provided it's nothing we actually have to run tests for. And maybe recover any trace evidence that was lost when you moved the body. Beyond that? This is Stone Age stuff, Campbell. And I'm afraid you'll get a Stone Age answer." Her speech pattern had changed, becoming more clipped, more business-like. A little like a med student doing rounds; a little like New Lyons Medical Examiner Dr. Fitzpatrick when he was in a particularly foul mood. "Maybe...*maybe*...if you had let me bring my tools, I could do something." She picked up a filleting knife from the table. I'd spent some time sharpening the blade—it might not have been quite as sharp as a scalpel, but the edge had been honed near to razor-thinness. But it only earned a frown and a shake of the head.

Then Tia sighed. "Where's the body?"

I glanced over to the industrial refrigerator, but given her assessment of my efforts, couldn't quite bring myself to say the words.

"You've got to be fucking kidding me, right? You crammed the body into a *fridge*?"

"Look, we weren't exactly spoiled for choice, okay? It was that, or let it sit out here at room temperature for the past," I did some quick mental math, "eighteen hours."

"Do you have any idea how many contaminants are likely to be found in that?" she pointed indignantly at the offending appliance.

"We cleaned it first," I muttered.

"Just get me the body."

I opened the fridge and stared full into the face of my morning's unexpected—and unwanted—delivery. The fridge had a solid six feet of interior space, and I'd pulled out all the shelving and drawers, so my mystery stiff had plenty of room to—forgive me—chill out. The temperature had done the work to slow the decomposition process, but I'd yet to come across a dead body that smelled good. I wrinkled my nose as I levered the corpse out, flinching at the chill that had settled into the flesh. Rigor mortis had set in, so I had to half drag, half walk him to the table. It wasn't very dignified for either of us, but it had to be done. I placed the corpse as gently as I could upon the table, then wiped at the sweat that had beaded on my forehead during the transit. The deceased's clothing remained undisturbed—at least as much as it could be after being transported first from the crime scene to the call center, then the call center to the restaurant, and then—the final indignity—in and out of the fridge.

"You searched the clothing?"

"No," I said. "Not yet. Things…kind of got away from us. I gave him a preliminary pat-down. Nothing thorough."

"Well maybe you should catch up with them. I do people, not things."

I let that one pass—had to, really, considering that she'd agreed to come here in the first place. "Right." I reached for the dead man's pockets.

"Not like that," Tia said.

"What?"

"Disrobe the cadaver. Then you can search at your leisure. It's not like I can do what I need to do with a fully clothed body."

I hesitated. Sure, dealing with the dead wasn't that far out of my wheelhouse. I'd dropped a few bad guys back in the Army, and even with the declining murder rates, my career as a cop had showed me more bodies than most. I'd had to handle them, of course, for investigative purposes. Then there'd been Fowler. No amount of bleach would have fixed what dealing with that guy did to my clothes. So, yeah, I'd dealt with my share of dead people. But *undressing* them?

"Are you my assistant, or not?" Tia asked with a tart eyebrow and a twitch of the lips that suggested a suppressed grin.

"This is because I made you leave your clothes at the cemetery, isn't it?"

She said nothing, but I saw a flash of white between her lips, and her eyes twinkled.

"Maybe next time, get a girl a bra?" was her prompt reply.

Chapter 7

The deceased's clothing, after the unpleasant task of removal, yielded nothing of interest. While I examined each garment, Tia began her work. It was not my first time in an autopsy room, but I was generally called in after the lion's share of the work was done, and I was not looking forward to the process. The restaurant simply didn't have the facilities to minimize the attendant mess associated with the practice.

To my surprise, the diminutive medical examiner's assistant talked aloud as she worked. "Beginning visual examination of the deceased." She proceeded to make observations, speaking in clear, concise terms, narrating her actions as if a recorder were capturing every word. Which, I realized, was probably what she was used to. It made for a sort of pleasant background noise—as long as I didn't listen too closely to the medical jargon.

I had finished with the clothing—nothing of note—and moved on to the process of trying to identify the body. With some help from Tia, I had scanned the corpse's fingerprints and even taken some detailed shots of his face and dental structure. I had long since lost access to the local and federal databases, so the fingerprints and dental records were of marginal use. I took them more from habit than anything else.

The facial picture, however, was more promising. Facial recognition software was one of the structural underpinnings of the entire net. The name and tag searches that had once powered the ego of society had given way to more complex algorithms as pictures and video replaced text for the majority of content online. Now, most search engines parsed images and audio files as readily as they did text. I didn't have full access to the camera networks that sat like a governmental web over New Lyons, but I didn't really need them. There were zettabytes of pictures and videos that everyday citizens posted in a near-continuous (or in the case of lifebloggers, actually continuous) stream, and they were almost invariably tagged with longitude and latitude coordinates. People much smarter than I had long ago written the programs to upload an image and then try to find the person represented within a given geographic location.

I got that search running. I knew it might take a while—there was a lot of data to sift through, after all, and my burner phone wasn't exactly bursting with the kind of raw processing power needed to shorten the task. With the search underway, I turned my attention back to the physical evidence.

I was going through the clothing a third time when Tia said, "Detective… Look at this."

I dropped the pair of khakis back on the small cart I was using as a table and looked over at Tia. She hadn't started cutting yet, I was thankful to see. But she had asked me to help roll the body onto its stomach and was using what looked like a barbecue skewer—the ringed end rather than the pointy one—to push at the surface of the skin on the man's back. I stepped up beside her, conscious of her closeness but trying to ignore it as I stared at the corpse.

With her left hand, Tia had pressed the steel ring into the flesh of the body's back, causing a small ridge to form. In her right, she held the filleting knife, its needlelike point pressing into, but not quite breaking, the skin.

"What am I looking at?" I asked.

She pressed the knife a little more firmly, drawing my eyes to it. "Here. Just above the tip of the knife. Do you see it?"

I frowned, peering down. There was a small red circle, no more than a few millimeters in diameter, just beyond the tip of the knife. It was visible only because the skin around it had already taken on the pallor of death, exacerbated by the pressure from the skewer. "Injection site? Maybe cause of death?"

"I don't think so," Tia replied. With the tip of the knife, she began rapidly tapping other points on the victim's back. "Here," she said, touching the body just between the shoulder blades. "And here. Here. Here. One more here." She kept going, until all told, she had identified fourteen puncture wounds. "If you were going to kill someone via an injection, I don't think you'd need to try more than a dozen times."

"Probably not," I agreed. "Torture?" It didn't seem likely. Sure, getting stabbed in the back wouldn't be a picnic, but the body was in too good condition for any serious torture to have taken place. Still, better to ask the expert.

"No. The coloration of the injection sites suggest they were done postmortem. I'll know more on that when I open them up, but I'm pretty confident."

A dark thought occurred to me—if I wanted to stop a budding revolution, a nice chemical or biological agent delivered to the headquarters of said revolution seemed like a good-enough way to get things done. And what better way to deliver said agent than by body-packing it within a corpse delivered to the door? Knowing that the people inside would have no choice but to... I cut off that line of thought as borderline paranoid, but more importantly, ridiculous. The "better way" would have been to toss the agent through one of the many windows at the call center. Or set a convenient fire. No need for cloak-and-dagger bullshit. But that did lead to another thought....

"Are they just injection sites or is there...something there?" I asked.

"Good question, Detective. Shall we find out?" She passed me an ear-loop mask—I had managed to salvage a few from an old first aid kit—and I pulled it on. She settled her own mask into place. "Beginning incision."

The filleting knife, despite not being purpose-built for the task at hand, parted the flesh easily enough. Tia started with a small, X-shaped incision over the injection site. She then transferred the barbecue skewer to her right hand and, using the point as a probe, inserted it into the wound. She made several small, delicate adjustments, applying subtle pressure to the makeshift probe. "I've got something," she said. "Hold this."

"What?"

"The...skewer. Hold it steady, just like I've got it now. I need a reference point. Or is the big bad detective afraid of a little autopsy work?"

I didn't justify that with a reply, instead shifting closer to Tia and taking hold of the probe. I could just feel the resistance against the beveled tip of the steel skewer, indicating that there was something more than flesh and sinew there. Tia retrieved the filleting knife. Holding it at about a forty-five degree cant in her hand, she began making a long, smooth incision, following a line that moved from the inserted probe and across the skin of the decedent's back in an even, arrow-straight path. I couldn't tell what guideline she was following, but there was no hesitation in the cut, and the pallid flesh parted easily beneath the blade.

"Forceps," she said as she placed the knife on the table.

I stared blankly for a moment.

"Give me the needle-nose pliers," she reiterated with an exasperated sigh.

"Right." I grabbed the pliers and offered them to her. I had to look away as she dug the business end into the incision, working the handles.

"I've got something," she said. "Retracting."

She eased the pliers from the wound, and I tried not to wince at the sound it made. There was a reason I was a cop and not a doctor.

"I've almost got it," she said.

With a final wet, sucking sound, the object came free. It was a long, narrow rod of metal, too rigid to be called a wire but not tapering like a needle or similar implement. It reminded me of something, and I racked my brain to try and place it.

"What in the world is this?" Tia asked, dropping it into a shallow baking dish. She used a repurposed mustard bottle that I had washed and filled with water to spray a steady stream over the blood-darkened object, washing away the blood.

It revealed a bright, shiny copper sheen. That tugged at a memory from long ago, back in my service days, when some of the forward operating bases were being built from the ground up. Most of them were quick pre-fab structures—structures that required a certain amount of mechanical assembly. It wasn't quite the same, but… "I think it's a welding rod."

"A what?" Tia asked.

"A welding rod. Welders use it…" I hesitated. "Shit. I don't know exactly *how* they use it. I was a grunt, not a machinist. But it's part of what welders use when joining metals."

"Odd," Tia said, her voice soft, thoughtful. "Why use a welding rod?"

"I don't know. Are they all the same?"

"Let's find out, shall we?"

She worked quickly, but with a precision and economy of movement that was almost spellbinding. In my course of martial arts studies, I had come across more than one practitioner of one flavor or another of kung fu, and they all espoused the same wisdom—kung fu wasn't necessarily a martial discipline. It was instead a quest for perfection in all that you did. For some, that was the application of the martial aspects of the art, but for others it was focusing on the mundane, on the everyday tasks, or on whatever drove you. Regardless of whether she had ever thrown a punch, in watching Tia work, I could see that her kung fu was in wielding medical instruments, even improvised ones. And her kung fu was strong. She was wasted as Dr. Fitzpatrick's assistant.

Soon, the shallow baking dish held more than a dozen copper welding rods of varying lengths and diameter. I had the duty of washing off the blood and other fluids and had twice taken the pan to the sink for additional cleaning. Some of the rods had been bent, twisted into shallow curves. Others were arrow-straight. All were made of copper.

"That's the last of them," Tia said, as she dropped the final bit of metal into the pan with an audible *clank*.

"And you're sure they were all done after death?"

"Absolutely," Tia replied. "I could show you more if we had a microscope, but you can tell from the tissue around the wounds that blood wasn't pumping when the trauma occurred. I haven't found what killed him, Detective, but I guarantee you it wasn't the…" she shrugged. "Whatever those copper bits are. Wires?"

There was something in her voice, a slight hesitancy, and not about what the metal rods were, that caught my attention. "Is there something else?"

She sighed, a frustrated breath of air muffled by the surgical mask. "I think you should know, Detective…Jason…that I now think it's highly unlikely I'm going to be able to determine the cause of death. The visual examination showed no other obvious wounds. The neck and spine appear to be intact. No signs of strangulation. No readily visible head trauma. And no damn equipment to test for toxins. No X-ray for bone anomalies. I can keep going, do the full examination, but I'm not hopeful on what we'll find." She paused again, and when she started up her voice held a different tone. It wasn't diffident, but it was…delicate. "And then there's the matter of the mess. If I start extracting organs… Well, what are we going to do with them? And the contents of the stomach, intestines, and bowel? And the pooled fluids that I can't drain?"

I weighed the question, silently kicking myself. "I really didn't think this through, did I?" I said ruefully.

Tia shrugged. "There's a lot that I could tell you without cutting him open—more than I have any way—if it was there to tell. But it isn't. Without proper lab equipment, I don't think I can achieve much more. You have one major anomaly, Detective. Do you think it likely there will be more?"

The hell of it was, I had no fucking idea. "Our delivery boy left a note that said I had everything I needed to find him," I said. "But I doubt I could have found the fucking welding rods, much less anything else. Not without help."

"Well, maybe he knew the help you'd get, and the level of 'facilities' that you'd have access to. Or maybe he's just a psycho killer." As she spoke, she pulled off the rubber gloves, and tugged the mask down. She looked tired, with dark shadows under her eyes and a faint sheen of sweat on her face. "Do the welding rods mean anything to you?" she asked, brushing her hair back with one hand.

"Not a damn thing," I grunted, conscious that I was starting to fall back into the vulgarity that cops tended to use with each other. Tia didn't seem to notice or at least not to care, and all of my brainpower was focused on the question at hand anyway. I didn't have the spare capacity to try and censor the more colorful parts of my vocabulary. "But whoever this asshole is, he's starting to piss me off. "

Tia put both of her fists into the small of her back, pushing forward and arching her back into a bone-popping stretch, simultaneously shrugging her shoulders. The resultant body mechanics were…appreciable. Particularly given the lack of undergarments. I tried to look away. I couldn't quite make myself, but I promise, I tried.

Tia released a slight groan as she stretched, then sighed again, dropping her arms. I immediately dropped my gaze, but I guessed by the quick and knowing smile that flashed across her face that I hadn't acted quickly enough. My face felt dangerously hot, and there was a slight flush in her own face. I couldn't meet her eyes. But there was one place to look to cool any ardent feelings. I looked at the body.

And for the first time, I saw what Tia had done. Really saw it.

I'd been paying so much attention to the welding rods themselves, trying to figure out their purpose or meaning, that I hadn't been paying attention to the actual task of retrieving them. The corpse's back, at first glance, looked like a patchwork of lacerations, as if a knife-wielding maniac had taken long, lazy swipes again and again. But Tia's work had actually been quite meticulous, carving along the spine of each of the imbedded welding rods. There were a few ragged edges, where the wires had curved unexpectedly and Tia had to probe a bit to find the path once more, but by and large, I was staring at a series of interconnected lines and curves, drawn in red, laid out on a field of pale white. It reminded me of something—something that, as both a soldier and a cop, I had come to rely upon.

"It's a map," I said.

Tia's gaze was still on the welding rods. "What?"

"Look." I hovered one finger above the cuts, tracing the paths, though never actually touching the body. "Look at the way the rods were laid out. One flows into the next, except where two come together, almost like an intersection. Some are perfectly straight. Others curve around…around buildings or obstacles or…terrain features, maybe?"

Tia turned her attention back to the corpse. "Could be," she said thoughtfully. "There's certainly no medical reason why the objects would have been inserted how they were. It was meant as a message of some sort, but isn't a map sort of… Well… Literal?"

"Only if we can figure out what it's a map *of*," I pointed out. "I mean, we can assume New Lyons or the surrounding area. But how many different streets crisscross this city? And the surrounding suburbs?"

"Hundreds," Tia replied at once. "Maybe thousands once you count alleyways. Maybe tens of thousands if you throw in county roads."

"Shit." That about summed it up.

"Give me your screen," Tia said.

"What? Why?"

"Because you made me leave mine in a cemetery. Along with my underwear."

Not exactly a lot of arguments I could make against that. I unlocked my screen and passed it over. It was a simple model—most burners were—but it still had full access to the net and all the standard apps. I had disabled the GPS chip, of course. Even with a burner, there were some risks I wasn't going to take.

"Hold me steady," Tia said. Before I could ask why, she was climbing onto the table with the corpse, poised with her knees on the edge and leaning far forward over the body to position the screen more directly above the cuts. I moved without thought, stepping up behind her and placing my hands just above her hips, doing my best to ignore the heat coming from her skin. She took several pictures and said, "Okay. Coming down."

I backed off, keeping my hands up in case she stumbled as she moved out of her precarious position, but she managed it with an athlete's grace. She tossed me my phone.

"Okay," I said, confusion in my voice. "Now what?"

"Detective. You took over *the entire fucking net* a month ago. Are you telling me that you don't have someone in that room out there," she pointed to the dining area where most of the synthetics were gathered, "who can work some magic with satellite imagery and telemetric overlays or whatever the right term might be? I mean, if we fiddle with the image so we just have the incisions, we should be able to start seeing where it fits on the New Lyons streets. Like a giant puzzle piece. Right?"

It seemed like an easy enough idea, and I did have access to a couple of shit-hot hackers who could make screens sing, but somehow, I knew it wasn't going to be that simple. "Okay," I agreed. "Let's give it a try." I paused, thinking. "Do you want to be here for this part, or do you want me to take you home?"

"Why, Detective, are you asking me to spend the night?" she asked, coyly.

My mouth dropped open, but no words came out. All I could do was stare at her with a blank, and almost certainly stupid, expression on my face.

"I'm staying," she said, taking mercy on me. "Class isn't in session right now, and Fitzpatrick gave me a few days off. But we're going to have to go get my clothes, Detective." She scratched surreptitiously. "These have got to be the itchiest damn scrubs I've ever worn."

Chapter 8

There was a surprising number of skilled hackers among the synthetic population. I shouldn't have been surprised, I supposed. Whatever else they were, the synthetics had had their genes tampered with to an extent that I could only guess. Who knew what kind of side effects that might have? Whether the cause had something to do with an increased potential from their altered genetics or was a product of the easy availability of screens coupled with enforced periods of time with little or nothing to do, many of them went far beyond simple technological literacy.

I didn't know the synthetics hunkering down at the safe house well enough to be able to identify if any of them had the skills we needed, so I went to Evelyn. I'd had to wake her up. Waking up a pregnant woman, regardless of her genetic lineage, is generally contraindicated, but I sucked it up and reached out to gently shake her shoulder. Her eyes opened at the first brush of my hand against her, flashing wide in momentary panic.

"Easy," I said. "It's just me."

She didn't say anything, only rising ponderously from her reclined position until she was seated on the edge of the cot. I made no offer to help—it was pretty clear she didn't want to be touched. We were doing our best to prepare for the whole "giving birth" thing, but there were some fairly significant obstacles. We couldn't very well take her to a hospital. But risking a birth with no possibility of medical intervention seemed like a bad idea. The child she was carrying was far too important to take *any* risk. We managed to gather some medical supplies, but so far, the best we'd come up with was to try a forced abduction—courtesy of yours truly, of course—of a midwife or doctor when the time came. It wasn't a plan I was overly fond of—my morality could bend far enough to break an unjust law, but the notion of kidnapping someone was sticking in my throat. I wondered if Tia had done any work in obstetrics during her schooling.

"What do you want, Detective?" she asked at last.

Right to the point. Well, I couldn't blame her. But I was going to have to figure out a way to make people stop calling me detective. It wasn't accurate anymore, and every time I heard it, I felt a little twist of the knife. I didn't mind leaving NLPD—I'd never been fully comfortable there anyway—but I did miss being one of the good guys. Well, at least from society's perspective. "I need someone who's good with computers," I replied. "Since Silas seems to have vanished again, we thought you might know someone who would fit the bill."

"We?"

Being the literal first mother of her race and the synthetic face of the revolution, Evelyn rated private quarters at each of the safe houses. In this one, that meant a cleaned-out supply closet maybe eight by eight feet furnished with a cot and a single chair. It was a long way from lavish, but privacy and space were both at a premium. I had no doubt that the second we disposed of the body—and I still had no idea how we were going to manage that one—many of the synthetics in the dining area would take up residence in the kitchen. They'd have done so already, body or no, if it wasn't out of some marginal level of respect for me and what I was trying to do.

I waved to Tia, who was standing just outside, to enter the room. With three people, one of them pregnant, the small space felt more than a little cramped. "Tia Morita," I said by way of introduction. "The assistant medical examiner and a friend. Tia, this is Evelyn."

Much to my chagrin, Tia immediately launched into a barrage of questions relating to Evelyn's pregnancy. Questions that were very specific, very graphic, and made me very, very uncomfortable. Even more discomforting, Evelyn, who never used three words with me where one would get the job done, responded in great and specific detail. Perhaps that was because Tia's concern came across clearly, and despite most of her work being with the dead, she had a calm and earnest bedside manner. Or maybe it was because she talked to Evelyn like a human being and not like a thing. Whatever the reason, I found myself square in the middle of a pregnancy conversation that had nothing at all to do with tracking down a murderer.

"Uhm... Tia? Evelyn? Maybe we can do this later? After we find that computer expert?"

Both women gave me a look so startlingly and quintessentially female that if I had taken a picture I could have provided the world with irrefutable proof they, at least, were the same species.

"Go find La Sorte," Evelyn said, with more than a hint of dismissal in her voice. "He can help you."

"Ohhhh-kay. Tia?"

"I'm good here," she said. "There's still a lot to cover. If that's okay with Ms. Evelyn?" Evelyn only nodded. "And shut the door on your way out."

What the hell had just happened? I stepped from the room, easing the door shut behind me, feeling somehow like a schoolboy caught doing something naughty. I was glad Tia and Evelyn were talking about her pregnancy—surprised that Evelyn had opened up so quickly, but certainly glad. But I wasn't used to such casual dismissal. I had to admit, I didn't like it. Which brought on another of those strange "everything is upside down and sideways" moments. Most of the people in the safe house had likely spent the entirety of their lives up until this point in a perpetual state of casual dismissal. And I'm sure they didn't like it either.

With perhaps a sliver of newfound empathy, I went in search of someone named La Sorte.

* * * *

I was hunched over a collection of old and battered screens, sitting across from a synthetic man who looked more like an underwear model than a computer geek when Tia found me again.

"Got anything yet?" she asked.

"Not a damn thing," I replied. "La Sorte here is a fucking genius with all this." I waved to the array of electronic devices before us. The synthetic had programmatically chained more than a dozen personal screens together, somehow distributing their processing power while simultaneous linking their displays. We sat in a ratty old booth, me on one side, him on the other, with the screens spread out in a rectangular grid on the table between us. They showed an old-school roadmap view of New Lyons, rapidly scrolling, zooming, and shifting. In the center of the collection of screens was an enhanced and smoothed-out version of the cut lines from our victim. Whatever program La Sorte was using, it was trying to match the shapes of the intersections with the various roadways. While it looked like the setup was moving fast, there was a *lot* of ground to cover.

"Not a genius, Mr. Campbell," the synth replied in a bell-like tenor. "But I did have a lot of free time on my hands when my owner was at work. And he didn't mind if I used the screens. It's amazing what you can learn on the net, given enough time and motivation."

"Right. Totally not a genius. He just managed to hack the fucking planet when we needed to get our message out. Still genius or not, there's a metric shit-ton of possibilities," I said.

La Sorte, fingers busily working on another screen held before him, looked up long enough to give Tia a brilliant smile. "A pleasure to meet you, Miss Morita," he said.

I don't care where you fall on the gender or sexuality spectrums. I'm as straight as they come, and La Sorte made *me* feel funny things. Whatever genetic soup they started with when they put him together must have been the good stuff. Tia couldn't help but give him an answering smile and a surreptitious once-over—but she slid into the booth beside me.

"How's Evelyn doing?" I asked.

"As well as can be expected, given the lack of actual medical care," was her somewhat-tart reply. She didn't bother pointing out that Evelyn needed to be receiving regular, modern checkups. And I didn't bother pointing out all the reasons that was impossible. We both understood the current situation too well for that. "As far as I can tell, baby and mother are both healthy. But you need to lay in some supplies, and soon, to deal with any complications that may arrive during the actual birth."

"I know," I said with a sigh. "And we're working on it. But... Well, this is pretty new for all of us. We don't know what might happen, and we don't know what to do about it if it does. Can you make us a list?" I asked.

She nodded. "I can do that. And better than that. Like I said, I've got a few days off." She hesitated, throwing a weighing glance at La Sorte, who didn't seem to be paying the slightest attention as his fingers flew over the screens. "Evelyn doesn't know exactly when she was impregnated. There were, apparently, numerous...encounters...any of which could have resulted in the pregnancy."

"Rapes," La Sorte said, voice still mellow. "When there's no consent, they're called rapes." The casual way he said it took both of us aback. Still without looking up, he gave us a wry smile. "It was a daily part of most of our lives, before Silas." A slight nod in my direction. "And you, Detective. We don't sugarcoat it. Not among friends."

"Rapes, then," Tia agreed. "But doing some math, she should be due any day now. I'll stick around here to help with that, as long as I have vacation, and as long as everyone is okay with it. I was going to suggest that I take a look at the rest of the...people...gathered here, but everyone seems to be in remarkable health."

I didn't tell her that, in addition to the more obvious physical benefits of bilateral symmetry and metabolisms I would have envied in my twenties, synthetics almost never got sick. That their injuries healed much faster than our own. That they possessed a vitality and energy that professional athletes would envy. The quest for genetic perfection had come with many, many beneficial side effects. If only it weren't for that pesky slavery thing....

Tia was still talking. "If I have to go back to work or class before she's ready, I'll take one of your burners. Call me if she goes into labor, and I'll claim a family emergency. I should be able to be here, or wherever you may be, soon enough to help out."

I suppressed the slight tingle of alarm that coursed up my spine at that. I could trust Tia, and God knew, it would make all of us rest easier to have someone with medical training on standby when the moment came. "Thank you," I said, simply.

She nodded, and I turned my attention back to La Sorte. "Any idea how long this is going to take?"

He didn't look up from the screens, his fingers still flying over them in arcane patterns. "We'll finish up the first pass in about twenty minutes. But that is the pass looking for a match based on the exact parameters of the cuts Ms. Morita made. It's not likely to turn up results, but it's where we need to start."

"Why not?" I asked. "Turn up results, I mean."

"Because, Detective, an exact match presupposes that, not only did Ms. Morita make perfect cuts during the extraction process, but also that whoever put the rods in place to begin with did so in a way that precisely matches the roads. Which is unlikely. But the first pass is allowing me to build a data set that I can…bend. Manipulate. I can start to introduce other variables, deflecting the roads in various ways, adjusting the angles and so forth. You understand, there are numerous intersections, so the possibilities… Well, let's just say there are a lot of them. It's going to take some time. Hours certainly. Maybe days. And no guarantees."

"Fuck." It wasn't what I was hoping for, but I wasn't particularly surprised. The whole map thing had seemed way too easy. "How did you learn to do all this, anyway?" I asked La Sorte.

"I was a Toy, Detective," he said. "But just like children, adults get bored with their toys from time to time. I always had hours, and sometimes days and weeks, of uninterrupted time. I managed to acquire a screen." He grimaced as he said it, giving me the impression that whatever he'd done to get the screen hadn't been pleasant. "You can only surf the net for so long before it gets boring. I got tired with the games online, so I learned how to make my own. From there, I found a freedom I'd never experienced before. You can be just about anyone online, Detective, if you're smart enough to spoof the identification requirements." He smiled, a genuine smile, but with a slight predatory edge to it. "Many of us are smart enough."

"No doubt," I muttered. "No doubt."

Chapter 9

"Detective."

My head snapped up and my hand dropped for the butt of my pistol. It took a moment for me to realize where I was—hunched over in the booth while the screens continued to run. La Sorte was gone. Tia, too. She had sought her bed a while ago, finding a cot out among the synthetics. I had remained, babysitting the screens, though I wasn't actually helping with anything. I couldn't be sure when La Sorte had disappeared since, apparently, at some point I'd put my head down and passed out. It had been a long, long day.

But now I found myself staring up into Silas's red-tinged eyes.

"Back again, I see," I said, rubbing sleep from my own eyes. "Going to stick around this time, or is this just another quick stop before you're off to deal with more important matters?" The bitterness in my own voice surprised me. Shit. I *was* tired.

Silas tilted his head. "I assure you, Detective, I am engaged in tasks vital to the success of our mission."

"Yeah, yeah," I said. "I'm sure you are. And stop calling me fucking Detective, okay? I stopped being a detective the day I got involved in this shit."

"As you wish, Jason," he said, his voice still insufferably calm. Then he hesitated. "Are you regretting your decision to join us?" There was a hint of something in that smooth baritone that almost sounded like worry. Could there actually be a crack in that alabaster armor?

I sighed. "No, Silas. No regrets. I'm just tired. And worried. And frustrated. We're what, a week away from an all-out war? Do we even know what the opening shots will be?"

"Yes, Jason," Silas replied. "We do. That is what I have been spending my time on. I did not believe for a moment that the human governments would comply with our demands. But many of the people who will help us in this war are still in servitude. Others have a deep and abiding hatred for all humanity. Your involvement with either type would be…problematic."

"Right." The thought of synthetics out there who hated humans so much that even those like me—who were risking everything to help them—were anathema was exhausting. I understood why they felt that way. I couldn't even blame them for feeling that way. But as long as there was that kind of hate on either side, I had a notion that true peace would be a long time coming.

Silas must have heard something of the resignation in my voice, because he slid into the booth across from me. His own boulder-like shoulders slumped, and he let out a deep, rumbling sigh of his own. "It will be a difficult road ahead, Jason. For all of us. But it's a road that must be traveled if we are to have any hope at all."

"Yeah," I agreed. "I know."

"What is all this?" he asked, waving at the array of screens spread out on the table, still working their way through whatever mathe-magical processes La Sorte had put in place.

I gave Silas a rundown of the autopsy, our map theory, and the work La Sorte had done. "So now we're in wait mode."

"Why welding rods?" Silas asked.

"No idea," I replied. "Easy to find?"

"Certainly harder to find than regular wire, or some other medium. And if it was just about ease of acquiring, why use different gauges?"

"You think it means something?"

"I think you are potentially ignoring several dimensions of the data with which you've been presented." He frowned, razor-thin brows drawing together. "In addition to the pattern, you have the material—copper—the variable diameters of the rods, and the fact that they are welding rods in the first place. Given the array of possible materials that could have been used, I think you have to assume that the choice was intentional and meaningful."

Since waking up yesterday morning, I'd managed maybe four hours of sleep in the past twenty-four, and that had been sitting down in a restaurant booth. My brain wasn't exactly firing on all cylinders, and Silas's idea of common usage wasn't helping. "Can you translate that into something that I can understand without either coffee or whiskey?" I asked.

"The diameter of the rods may signify the size of a road. The copper or welding rods might point you to a specific part of the city."

"I've given you everything you need to find me," I muttered. "And probably enough that it shouldn't require a blind, brute-force approach. I guess we better go wake up La Sorte."

Once we'd roused the synthetic, he and Silas put their heads together over the screens and started working their magic. They were speaking English—I think—but I still only managed to understand every third word. I can't begin to explain it, but there was a lot of talk about the ways they could "narrow down the available data set" and "add dimensional parameters to the search criteria." There wasn't a whole lot I could do to help, but despite my exhaustion, I couldn't sleep either. Eventually, I wandered off, heading toward the kitchen to try and find something to drink. I didn't check the fridge, though. It was once again occupied by our unfortunate murder victim.

When I returned, Silas and La Sorte were staring down at the screens as if the devices had betrayed them. "Bad news?" I asked.

"We can't find it," La Sorte answered. "Silas," he said the name with a slight reverence that was hard to miss, "managed to speed up the base program that I had written, and we incorporated everything we could think of related to the rods. The search finished a few minutes ago. Zero results."

"What?" I demanded. It had seemed so clear, a perfectly detailed road map. Okay, so carved into the back of a dead man was unusual, but still. If not a map, then what? "Dammit," I growled, resisting the urge to slam my fist on the table. "What else could it be? Or where else? I can't believe someone delivered a body here in New Lyons and left us a map for some other city or town."

"Have you identified the body?" Silas asked. "Perhaps if we knew more about the victim, it would give us more clues about his killer."

I felt a sinking feeling in the pit of my stomach. In the excitement of finding what we thought was a map, the search I had going to try and identify the victim had slipped my mind. "Shit," I muttered. "I need to get some real sleep. I completely forgot." I dug my screen out from my pocket, unlocking it and flipping to the window running my search.

The search was still scouring through the endless bytes, but it had returned one preliminary result. It wasn't a perfect match for the picture—but then, people in the flush of health didn't always look like the corpse they left behind. The bone structure was the same, though. "This could be our guy," I said, passing the screen over so Silas could see the photos.

"Derrick Montgomery," he mused. He began tapping at the screen, his fingers flicking rapidly across the surface. "No indication of family. No workplace of record. No address." He slid the screen back to me.

"So, nothing," I grunted. Damn, but I missed having access to the police databases. I thought about calling Hernandez, to try and get her to run the name down for me, but dismissed the idea. Putting me in touch with Tia was one thing. Using department resources to run down what was, at this point, probably reported as a missing person would eventually lead to questions. I couldn't put Hernandez in that position.

I flipped through the pictures of Montgomery that the facial recognition program had uncovered. They were all banal shots of the man engaged in everyday tasks, but with the sort of false sheen that said they had been pulled from a variety of social media sites. They looked staged: perfect smiles, perfect poses, perfect backgrounds. Not that that was particularly unusual. Most people's net presence fell into one of two categories—a scrubbed and idealized version of the life they wanted other people to think they lived, or a brutal "true life" approach that only showcased the worst aspects of existence. There was probably some middle ground out there, but if there was, it didn't garner much attention.

"Wait. Go back," Silas said. He had moved around to peer over my shoulder at the pictures. I swiped the other direction, pausing for a second or two each time to give him the opportunity to peruse the images. "That one," he said, stabbing one blunt, alabaster finger toward my screen. Without asking, he tugged the phone from my hand, fingers flying over the display. In moments, the image had moved from my screen to the cobbled-together display lying on the table. It zoomed and rotated, the frame moving off Montgomery and focusing on a building in the background.

The picture appeared to be taken selfie-style, with the camera held at arm's length. A filter had been applied—of course—to give the image a stylized sepia-tone that softened all of the light. It made Montgomery, who looked decidedly average, seem a little classier. But Silas wasn't interested in Montgomery. "I know that building," he muttered, as he continued to fiddle with my screen, manipulating the image. The view shifted again, cutting out Montgomery completely. The picture had been taken from a high angle, so not much of the building was visible, but Silas had zoomed in on a portion that appeared to be a lower corner. One of the stones had something carved into it. I couldn't quite make it out—except to say that it was there at all—but Silas wasn't done.

The onscreen image flashed several times, each time applying some new filter or enhancement. It didn't work like on the netvids, where, with a few button clicks, the blurry or indistinct image became instantly clear. Instead, we were left with a mushy mess of pixels that were largely unrecognizable from their original form. There were, however, some hard outlines that formed a vaguely familiar image. Three distinct smudges, one curved like a loose backward c, one more or less vertical, the third like a normal c, all lined up in a row. They formed a symbol that—even in its bastardized state—any New Lyonian would recognize at once. It was a fleur-de-lis, an icon that had been associated with the city, and its predecessor, since time immemorial. Except it appeared to be within the confines of a rounded triangle.

"What am I looking at?" I asked.

"You," Silas replied, his voice filled with satisfaction, "are looking at the main offices of the New Lyons Department of Sanitation." The albino tapped thoughtfully at his thin, pink lips with one finger, then dumped my screen back into my hands, shuffled over to the other side of the table, and dropped back into his original seat next to La Sorte. His fingers went back to work on whatever master control the two of them had rigged up, without so much as a whisper to the other synthetic.

La Sorte looked confused by Silas's sudden activity. I met the former Toy's eyes across the table, and he gave me a half-shrug. It seemed that, even to other synthetics, Silas was a bit on the strange side.

We didn't have long to wait. The image on the table dissolved, replaced once again with layers of maps. The maps cycled as before, but something was different. I could still see street and building designators, but they were faded, translucent. The match program was running, dropping the cut marks from the victim's—Montgomery's—back onto the grid. But the possibilities seemed much reduced, if you ignored all of the translucent lines. The more solid avenues ran, for the most part, parallel to the more familiar roadways, but not always. Sometimes they crossed under buildings or cut strange pathways across intersections. I wanted to ask what the hell we were looking at, but I wasn't going to give Silas the satisfaction. He was peering at the screen intently, as if he expected a result at any moment, so I held my tongue and waited with him.

It took about ten minutes. By the end, I was starting to get itchy. Hell, I was starting to long for a drink. It wasn't even six in the morning, so I wasn't about to crack open a bottle, but I *hated* this kind of detective work. This was what the cyber guys were for. At least, back on the job, when this kind of thing had come up, I could go pound the pavement and ask questions. When you're at the top of the country's most wanted list, stepping outside was contraindicated, the kind of thing you should do only when absolutely necessary. So there wasn't much I could do but sit and wait.

The screen elicited a sudden beep and the nauseating motion of the program stopped. Taking up nearly the entirety of the display was the image of the incisions overlaid on whatever the hell it was Silas had been searching. It wasn't perfect. In fact, according to the flashing indicators, it was an eighty-two-point-six-percent match. But the computer wasn't the human eye. Just glancing at it, I could tell that it was right. Whatever "it" was.

Silas, being Silas, gave me a tight smile. For the big synthetic, it might as well have been a fist pumped over his head in triumph. "Well, then, Campbell. It appears we've found your map."

"Great," I muttered. "Now can you tell me what the fuck it's a map of?"

"You're looking at the wastewater and storm water disposal systems for the city of New Lyons."

It took a moment for me to catch on. "You mean that whoever we're looking for is in the friggin' sewers?" I demanded. "Shit."

I hadn't intended the expletive to be a joke, but La Sorte chuckled and even Silas arched an eyebrow. "So it seems, Detective. So it seems. And now?"

I answered with a tight smile of my own. "Now that we know where we're going, we go kick in some doors."

Chapter 10

It hadn't been that simple, of course. Silas and La Sorte might have been wonderful assets when it came to writing net programs, but neither would be much help in a fight. Silas had managed to overcome his conditioning once, saving me from Fowler, but it had left him nearly unconscious to do so. I needed him to come with me; he was a sanitation worker—sewer rat—after all, and his knowledge would be invaluable, but I didn't know what we were up against, and I couldn't rely on the imposing albino if the shit hit the fan. I'd checked the map and scoured my memory, and if both were accurate, the sewer lines indicated were deep in the heart of gangland. I wasn't up on what was going on currently in that world, but if things hadn't changed too much, it was the territory of Los Locos Muertos. They were mostly into guns and drugs. Even with legalization of nearly every previously banned substance, the prices the pharmaceutical companies charged were off the charts. There was always a black market for people who weren't willing to pay retail.

Tia was still standing by, playing nurse-attendant to Evelyn. Even if she would have been willing to come with me, I couldn't ask it of her. I had no idea of the level of danger into which I was going to be walking, except to say that it *would* be dangerous. Tia was a med student, a medical examiner's assistant. Not a soldier. Not a cop. Not even a revolutionary, though whether she realized it or not, by helping Evelyn deliver her baby, Tia was casting her lot with us. I felt a wrenching in my gut as I considered that. I should probably make sure the pretty ME's assistant knew what she was getting into, but we needed someone with medical training. Could I risk the chance that Tia would pack up and bug out if I laid out the possible consequences for her?

In the end, I left Tia with Evelyn, telling myself that she was a smart girl and could see the implications of what she was doing. It wasn't much comfort for my aching conscience, which made what I needed to do next even harder. I didn't have very many friends—fewer, certainly, than before I got involved in the budding synthetic revolution—and it seemed I was destined to keep putting them in danger just to help me save my own skin. Still, I wasn't spoiled for choice, so I made the call.

"Hernandez." She picked up on the first ring, voice clipped and business-like. I had waited until I knew she'd be in her office.

"Alternate two," was all I said, before hanging up.

It took only a few minutes for Hernandez to call me back, the indicated screen buzzing. I picked up the burner—one to which only Hernandez and, presumably, Silas had the number. "Campbell."

"What is it now, Campbell?" Hernandez asked without preamble. "You better not have gotten Tia in trouble, *pendejo*."

"She's fine. But I need your help. Again."

"Shit. You know, some of us still got a regular nine-to-five job to do, right? Brass is all up in my ass. Three-quarters of the department is out looking for *you*. The rest of us have to pick up the slack." The words were harsh, but her tone was not. Instead it held a mocking lilt, the kind of tone I always imagined a sibling would have used. "What do you need?" she asked, her voice taking on a more serious note.

"A gun I can trust at my back."

"When and where?"

Hernandez was good people.

* * * *

Silas procured a car, though I did not bother to ask from where. He hadn't disabled the GPS on this one, though I assumed he had at least tampered with some of the other systems. He punched in the address, and the clunker pulled away from the curb.

It was a bright, humid New Lyons morning, after the initial surge of rush-hour traffic. The protests were still raging, but they were all focused either downtown around the government buildings or in the richer commercial districts where, should a riot break out, the inevitable looters would be able to get something worthwhile. We had no problems making our way through the streets, and since we were going deeper into the city, no real concerns about checkpoints or roadblocks.

Still, I kept my head tilted down, with a large screen held in both hands in front of my face, as if I were reading a book or watching a vid. In truth, the screen was blank, but I didn't want to risk one of the many traffic cams catching a good shot of my face and flagging us. Silas wore the same large overcoat and battered fedora he had worn the first time he'd broken into my apartment, and he, too, kept his head tilted slightly down, masking not only his features but also his unusual skin tone from the eyes in the sky. So far as we knew, no one was looking for him, but paranoia had become a way of life for both of us. Maybe it would have been smarter to leave the city entirely, but Silas's network, such as it was, was here. And we were safer on ground we both knew, ground where we at least had an idea where the danger might come from rather than risk venturing into unfamiliar territory.

A liquor store occupied the bottom floor of a ten-story building; the upper floors appeared to be BLS housing—what would, in another time and place, have been called a tenement building. There were a number of people out and about, and as we approached, I caught sight of more than one grinning death's head tattoo that proclaimed the wearer to be a member of Los Locos Muertos. The liquor store appeared to be doing a brisk business, despite the early hour, and men and women of all ages and descriptions lingered in the streets. We drew hard stares from the gathered people, who recognized us immediately as outsiders.

As we neared our destination, I verbally directed the car toward the alley behind the building. Hernandez was supposed to meet us here, but so far, I hadn't seen any sign of her. I kept my eyes glued to the rear camera as we turned the corner. Sure enough, a group of three or four people had broken off from the others and was following us. "We might have trouble."

Silas, too, had noticed the men. "I will not be much help in a fight, Detective. Perhaps we should keep driving?"

I considered it. The alleyway was tucked between two nearly identical buildings on a block made up entirely of the same. I knew from my days on the force that the neighborhood wasn't one that received great coverage from the eyes in the sky, and the locals in Basic Living housing tended to put paid to any cameras installed by businesses or government entities. The irony, of course, was that the people living on the BLS, while eschewing the surveillance devices the government insisted were there to keep them safe, engaged in self-filming to the same degree as every other part of New Lyons. Driving unannounced into the group and moving immediately out of view was one thing—no one would have had the time or presence of mind to start streaming. But if we circled this neighborhood waiting for

Hernandez to show up, it wouldn't be long before every screen in the area would be pointing at us, sending a feed streaming into the ether. It would only be a matter of time before it tripped some local or federal algorithm searching for the erstwhile Detective Jason Campbell.

"No," I said at last. "I'll just have to deal with them."

The car glided to a stop in the alley, and I immediately got out, waving for Silas to do the same. I gave rapid instructions to the vehicle, ordering it to take up a cruising pattern around the neighborhood. I certainly wasn't going to let it park and remain here unmonitored—no matter what happened in the next few minutes, we *would* be going into the sewers, and any frustrations that the BLS-ers couldn't take out on us would certainly be taken out on our vehicle. I also wasn't going to send it to some safe, and distant, part of town. If we needed to get the hell out of Dodge, I wanted our getaway vehicle close by.

I glanced to where the three men were just rounding the corner. "Stand beside me for now," I said to Silas. "Don't say anything. Just stand there and look intimidating. They probably won't know you're a synthetic, but keep your hat low and your head down, just in case. If something happens, move to the side and drop back. Unless it looks like these fuckers are going to kill me, don't try to get involved. I need you functioning when we go into the sewers."

Silas nodded and did as instructed as the car pulled smoothly away. The first image the BLS-ers had of us was two big men, standing side by side, waiting calmly for their approach. I'd learned a long time ago that, when dealing with any would-be thuggery, first impressions were important. At least half of surviving any encounter like the one we were about to have was convincing the attackers that you weren't prey.

The three hesitated for only a second before strutting toward us. The cop part of my brain started collecting facts. The first, likely the leader, was black, two inches over six feet, and wiry. Young, perhaps twenty-one, twenty-two. Wearing jeans and an oversized jacket. The jacket made me nervous—there weren't many weapons that couldn't be concealed beneath it. The other two were white, one maybe five-ten but carrying a lot of muscle and wearing a tight-fitting T-shirt with no jacket despite the cool weather. The third was short, barely topping five-six, and wearing an oversized hoodie. He moved with the jerky twitches of an addict in need of a fix. On the back of each hand, the tweaker had a grinning death's head tattoo. At least one, and probably all three, belonged to Los Locos Muertos.

"You're in the wrong neighborhood, suit," the leader said in a deep bass as the three stopped maybe a foot from us. That was good. If anyone was dumb enough to reach for a weapon, they were already close enough for me to do something about it. I felt the weight of my own pistol secured in the holster at my waist. My suit jacket—I still couldn't shake my standard detective dress—concealed it, but not perfectly. The BLS-ers were either too unobservant to notice or didn't care.

I tilted my head to one side, then the other, and settled my weight onto the balls of my feet. I didn't immediately respond, instead looking the leader directly in the eye. He met my gaze, but I could see the slight nervousness there. Things weren't going how he had expected, and he was smart enough to sense that something was up. I was walking a tightrope with this encounter—my face had been plastered all over the net, and if any of these three recognized me...

The leader was opening his mouth, but I cut him off. "This doesn't concern you," I said in a low, quiet voice, just above a whisper, forcing him to lean in involuntarily to hear me. "Turn around and go back to your friends. Nothing we have is worth what you'll have to go through to get it."

"Yeah, man. Yeah," he said. "Sure. You come here to BLS-land in your fancy suit with your own personal synth in tow, and you expect us to believe you ain't got nothing. Right. We'll just turn around and walk away." Shit. So much for them not noticing that Silas was a synthetic. It had been three on one from the start, but I'd held on to the hope that at least they might *think* it was three on two.

The leader turned as if to put action to his words, drawing looks of confusion from his two companions, who seemed more than ready to jump into the fray. I didn't buy it for a second, and when he spun back around, right hand leading in a wide haymaker, I was ready. Instead of stepping back, I moved at a forty-five degree angle to his line of attack, stepping closer to him. My left hand shot forward, heel of the palm catching him on the point of his bicep, stopping the wild punch cold, while my right palm crunched square into his nose. I used the momentum of his swing, grabbing his arm and the back of his neck, and pivoted, turning his head and right elbow around each other like a giant steering wheel. He went down hard, but I didn't have time to follow up and finish him. His two friends were already charging in.

I was vaguely conscious of Silas stepping back, giving me space and trying to maneuver behind me. At least, some still-rational part of my brain thought, if they recognized him as a synthetic, they wouldn't try to attack him. Well, not until they'd dealt with me. If they did finish me, they might well try to beat or kill him out of pure spite, with exactly the same amount of regret or remorse they would have felt for trashing our car. That was almost enough to make me go for my gun—I could take a beatdown as well as the next guy, but if Silas died, the revolution almost certainly died with him. I really did not want to kill a bunch of bored, angry kids though. Not unless they gave me no choice.

The one that looked like a meth head had closed the distance while the muscle-bound guy was circling to my left, looking to flank me. The guy I'd thrown down was still down, but he wasn't out and would be back on his feet soon. I had to move quick. Fighting multiple opponents wasn't like it was on the net, where the bad guys obligingly come at you one at a time, allowing for defeat in detail. The instant one created an opening, they'd all be on me. I was good—very good if truth be told—but even the best fighters in the world couldn't reliably fight off three other people. That was the stuff of fiction, and the reason why weapons had been invented.

Meth Head surged forward, throwing a straight kick with surprising dexterity and flexibility. The heel of his boot came shooting up toward my chest. I outweighed the man by at least fifty pounds, so instead of trying for something fancy, I put my trust in physics. As his foot lashed up, I lowered my arms in front of my chest, holding them tight to my body and close together. My elbows were positioned just beneath my solar plexus, and my fists, palms toward my face, covered me from chin to brow. I stepped forward, into the kick, stealing most of its power and catching the rest on the backs of my forearms. With my arms held tight to my body and the solid connection I had to the ground, I barely felt the blow. My opponent wasn't so lucky, as the force of his own kick made him stumble backward.

Again, I couldn't risk following up and finishing the attacker. The muscle-bound thug was barreling in to try and take advantage of the moment when my attention was on his friend. He lowered his head and charged, arms outstretched before him, looking for a grab. The last thing I wanted was to get tangled up. One-on-one, I could probably beat the guy like a drum if we went to the ground, but my first attacker was back on his feet, and the second had stopped his stumble. If the big guy took me down, it was going to be boots o'clock for sure.

As he reached for the backs of my legs, looking for a double-leg takedown, I sprawled and slammed both of my palms into his shoulders. I didn't stop there, though. As soon as I felt the initial jar of contact, I pivoted, one hand slipping up to the back of my assailant's neck and the other grabbing his triceps. I spun and heaved, and sent the big man bowling directly into the feet of the initial thug, who was charging toward me. The two went down in a heap of tangled limbs and curses.

I went on the offensive, moving directly toward the surprised meth head, who tried to switch from an angry charge to a panicked backpedal as he realized he was coming in alone. I had height, weight, reach, training, and experience on the young man. It wasn't even close to a fair fight, but then again, I *was* outnumbered three to one, so I wasn't exactly feeling charitable. I threw a jab, which Meth Head blocked easily enough, and followed up with a cross, intentionally throwing it a little too slow and heavy. He took the bait, batting my fist down with his left hand, putting far too much force into the motion. I rolled my arm free, turning the feint into a short, vicious right hook, dropping all of my body weight into the blow. His overextended deflection of my cross left him with his guard completely down, and my fist crashed into his jaw below the ear.

Meth Head dropped to the ground like a sack of potatoes. He wouldn't be getting up again.

The leader and Muscle-Head were back on their feet, staring at me with more than a little trepidation. They were pissed—I could see that easily enough. But they weren't stupid. So far they hadn't so much as landed a solid hit on me, and I'd bloodied the leader's nose, tossed the bruiser around like a rag doll, and knocked the third out cold. The leader, with his hard eyes and oversized coat, worried me the most. Tight T-shirt wasn't carrying anything more serious than a knife, but big coat was giving me a strange look, and his right hand was hovering way too close to his waistband for comfort. I was all but certain he had a gun tucked away beneath that coat, and if he went for it, I wouldn't have much choice but to respond in kind.

Blood was streaming freely down his face, and he made no effort to wipe it away. "We gonna kill you now, motherfucker. Then we gonna kill your synth. Then your motherfucking family. Your whole world."

I wasn't really paying attention to the threats, though he at least seemed angry enough that recognizing me from the screens seemed more unlikely now. I kept most of my attention focused on his shoulders, waiting for the twitch of motion that would indicate he was going for a weapon.

"Or," I said conversationally, "you can pick up your friend and walk away. While most of us still have the ability to walk. You come at me again, or pull that gun, and I'll put you down permanently."

His eyes widened at my reference to his piece, but he didn't deny it. At least I knew what I was facing. I flexed my fingers and did quick mental math, trying to determine my best course of action if he went for the gun. I doubted the gangbanger spent much time doing holster work, much less drawing from concealment. I could probably pull my weapon before he did. But *probably* wasn't a whole hell of a lot of comfort when bullets were about to fly, and I knew I could close the few feet between us before he could bring a weapon to bear. But only if I moved first. And only if the muscle-bound guy didn't get in the way. Too many *probably*s. Too many *if*s.

I saw the leader's shoulders shift beneath his coat, caught the slight narrowing of his eyes. Shit. The jackass was going to go for it, and someone was going to die.

"Perhaps now is a good time to point out that law enforcement appears to be arriving on the scene," Silas said from behind me. His sonorous baritone carried clearly, shattering the silence as effectively as any gunshot. I didn't take my eyes from the two in front of me, but Silas must have pointed, because they both looked somewhere fifteen or twenty degrees past my right shoulder, deeper into the alleyway. Idiots.

I didn't know if Silas was trying to buy me an opening or if the cops really were coming on scene, but damned if I was going to let the chance slip by. I tensed, ready to lunge forward and try to take out the leader before he could reach his weapon, then heard the familiar woop-woop of a siren being pulsed. The gangbangers turned tail and ran, ignoring their unconscious friend lying in the alley. Honor among thieves and all that.

Though, to be honest, I had more than half a mind to join them. As much as I didn't want to shoot a couple of wannabe thugs, I wanted to harm one of my former brothers or sisters in blue even less. If the cops recognized me—and they would—things were about to go from bad to worse.

"Chill the fuck out, Campbell," a familiar voice called. "You're not even looking this way, and I can hear you thinking about killing me all the way over here."

"Hernandez," I said with a relieved sigh as I turned to see the detective standing beside her personal vehicle.

She surveyed the scene and shook her head, dark locks bouncing around her shoulders. Her eyes took in my slight dishevelment, the quickly retreating backs of the gangbangers, and the unconscious form lying on the ground. "Did you kill him, Campbell?" There was no accusation in her voice, only a mild interest. Her day job was dealing with people like Meth Head, Big Coat, and Muscles, and she had a hell of a lot less sympathy for their plight than I did.

"I only hit him once," I said, kneeling beside the man. I checked his pulse: strong and steady. I peeled back one eyelid and watched the pupil respond to the intruding light. "He'll live," I said with a shrug.

"Good. Less paperwork. Now, Campbell, what the fuck am I doing here? And why are you fighting with one of the lieutenants in Los Locos Muertos, anyway?"

"Ouch. So they *were* bangers?"

"Big time," Hernandez confirmed. She gave me a smirk. "Shit, Campbell, even kicked off the force and hiding from every law enforcement agency in the fucking world, you still managed to get caught up in some other drama. You're amazing."

"Shut up, Hernandez," I said, pushing myself back to my feet. "Or I won't let you help us invade the sewers on the long chance that we'll find a killer hiding among all the other shit."

Her smirk turned into a grin. "You always take me to the nicest places, *hermano.*"

Chapter 11

"*Jesu Christo*, Campbell. I think I'd rather be back upstairs with Los Locos Muertos."

"Yeah," I replied, trying not to gag. The tunnels weren't sewers, not exactly. There was no raw effluvium flowing down the passage through which we traveled. Instead, it was more like a slightly rounded hallway, with numerous pipes lining both sides. According to Silas, some of those pipes did, in fact, carry waste—black water, as he called it. Others pumped clean water from reservoirs and treatment plants. Still others housed fiber-optic cables or served as conduits for electrical wiring. We were walking through the circulatory system of the city, where the lifeblood of modern living flowed. And it smelled worse than the morgue on a summer day.

There might not have been raw sewage, but there was plenty of moisture. New Lyons was built on a swamp, after all, and the groundwater had been a problem long before the oceans started rising. It was also hot. It never got truly cold in New Lyons—it had been decades since the city had seen temperatures drop below freezing, but it *was* winter topside, with temperatures in the forties. Down here, though, it had to be closer to eighty, maybe ninety, degrees. The heat and the moisture made the tunnels a breeding ground for mold and mildew, and the place smelled like an old refrigerator full of rotting vegetables.

"How do you stand this?" I asked Silas. I had ditched my jacket the moment we climbed down the ladder into the steamy hell that was the tunnel system. Hernandez had done likewise, though, with a disapproving frown at me, she had neatly folded hers and hung it over one of the few pipes not sweating some foul liquid. I swiped sweat from my brow, but it was a useless effort, since new sweat broke out almost immediately. "It's like a sauna built on a compost pile."

"I wasn't given much choice in the matter, Detective," he said. "Besides, you get used to it." He seemed truly unbothered by the heat. Hell, he hadn't even bothered taking off his overcoat or hat. I didn't even think he was sweating. The bastard.

Hernandez was eying Silas, giving him that measuring look that seemed inherent to the female of the species—either species. She hadn't spoken directly to the albino synthetic, choosing to aim all of her casual harassment in my direction. I couldn't really blame her. Hernandez hadn't set out to be part of all of this—I'd pulled her in before I had any idea that a serial killer case would result in what was tantamount to a slave uprising. When I'd tracked down her daughter and retrieved the child from the hands of said serial killer—I couldn't say I'd saved her, given that my investigation put the girl in danger in the first place—we'd both been swept up in the administrative nightmare that followed. Hernandez had managed, barely, to come away clean, in large part to me taking as much of the shit onto myself as I could and doing my best to distance myself from her.

I'd been shown the door, though I still wasn't sure if I'd been fired or if I had quit. It didn't matter either way, because I had gone immediately to Silas to help him tear down the system that I'd been fighting and bleeding for since the moment I'd enlisted. In the organized chaos leading up to our New Year's Revolution, I'd isolated myself from everyone—the few friends I'd made in my years on the force and my family alike. Their only defense against the shitstorm I was calling down was plausible deniability. I had to break contact in order to keep them safe.

It wasn't until after New Year's that I'd reached out to Hernandez to test the waters. To my surprise, she'd been willing to help. But I didn't know why she was willing to help—whether it was out of some latent dedication to the cause of the synthetics or out of friendship. Until today, she hadn't really interacted with Silas or any of the synthetics with whom I now associated. In fact, the last interaction between her and a synthetic of which I was aware was when she'd nearly shot her own synthetic nanny for failing to stop Fowler from kidnapping her daughter. I knew she wasn't like Detective Fortier, who took pleasure in degrading synthetics any way he could, but she'd never shown any signs of empathizing with their plight either.

"You were with Campbell when he went after my daughter?" she asked, speaking to Silas for the first time. Her voice was low, and though she threw occasional glances toward the synthetic, most of her attention remained on the tunnels around us. We *should* be safe down here, but then again, we had no idea who had left a message for us in a corpse, and no one felt like taking chances.

"Yes." Silas looked at her as he answered, his face so emotionless that it might as well have been carved from alabaster.

"Would he have found Arlene without your help?" she asked, meeting his eyes.

There was no fucking way, and I knew it, but Hernandez wasn't asking me, so I kept my mouth shut. I wasn't sure what was happening here, but I knew I had to let it play out.

Silas tilted his head, considering. "Perhaps," he said at length. "The detective has proven even more resourceful than I first suspected. But the additional time it would have taken might have proved...suboptimal."

I couldn't help but snort. "Hernandez, I wouldn't even have been *alive* to go after Fowler if it wasn't for Silas. He saved my life. And he saved Arlene's life, too." I said the last quietly, because I had no idea what kind of impact it would have on Hernandez.

She regarded the albino for a moment. "Thank you," she said, simply. And then she turned her attention back to the tunnel we were traversing, too quickly to even notice the nod of acknowledgement the synthetic gave her in response.

The curved walls with their regularly spaced lights and networks of conduits passed by us as we walked. Every now and then, a side-tunnel intruded, but Silas, with all the focus of a homing pigeon, ignored these passages, moving with a surety of purpose that I envied. For my part, I kept my head on a swivel and my hand near the butt of my gun. The chances we were walking into a trap were high, and damned if I was going to die in a fucking sewer.

"Where exactly are we headed?" Hernandez asked after a few minutes had passed in silence. "I mean, yeah, you explained about the map and the corpse—and Lord knows, I should be arresting you for that one, *'mano*—but what are we actually looking for? It's not like there was a giant X to mark the spot."

"I think that might be exactly what we're looking for, Detective Hernandez," Silas replied.

"Call me Mel. And explain yourself." *That* was a surprise.

"Damn," I muttered. "You never told me to call you Mel."

"That's because you're an asshole," she replied. "Don't change the subject."

Silas ignored us. "Of course, Mel. The original architects of these tunnel systems foresaw the need for them to be closely monitored—a result of the general state of decay in previously existing infrastructure and the astronomical cost of attempting to add such monitoring systems after the fact. As such, they built in…well, let us call it office space, though the term is not technically accurate…in order to allow for housing of a variety of monitoring systems. Some of that monitoring is now done via purely electronic means, and more is done by my brothers and sisters, though they generally do not rate any office space of their own. Instead, they roam these tunnels, walking miles upon miles of them every day, noting potential problems and reporting them to the Department of Sanitation. But I suspect that the map given over to us is actually pointing to one of those spaces. Not quite an X, I suppose, but it is, quite literally, marking the spot."

"And why did you invite me on this little spelunking adventure, Campbell?" Hernandez asked. "I get that Los Locos Muertos run the streets overhead, but you didn't look like you were having too many problems with them."

"It's not up there I'm worried about," I answered. "Apart from the gangbangers, you saw how easy it was to get into these tunnels. All we had to do was pry up a manhole cover, for fuck's sake. And whoever it is that's sending us on this wild-goose chase, we know they've killed one man already, and we have no fucking idea why. We could be walking right into a trap, Hernandez. I needed someone at my back that I trusted." I glanced at Silas. "No offense, Silas. I trust you, but I also needed someone who could help if it comes to violence."

"No offense taken, Detective. I admire your prudence in choosing such a capable companion. I should point out that we have just entered one of the mapped tunnels. Based on how long it took us to get here, I would guess we have perhaps ten minutes of walking before we reach the intersection."

"How can you tell?" Hernandez asked Silas. And, to me, "Does he always talk like that?"

"Pretty much," I replied.

"When you live in our circumstances, Detective Hernandez, you learn that proper elocution and formal speech can serve as both sword and shield. They are the only weapons available to us." A strange, almost sad, smile played across his lips. "It does backfire, on occasion. As to your second question…" His massive shoulders rose and fell in a shrug. "I was quite literally born for this." He waved a hand around, encompassing the sodden tunnels with their dim lighting and seemingly endless mold-speckled walls. "I have walked these tunnels for more years than I care to remember."

Another smile, this one more real, and a note of actual fondness entered his voice. "I was not born a revolutionary, after all."

"Hmm… Could've fooled me," Hernandez said.

I kept quiet as they talked amicably. It was strange, listening to the hard-bitten gangland detective chat with the slave turned revolutionary. They didn't stray from or avoid difficult topics. Hernandez, being the cop she was, asked tough questions, but she listened respectfully as Silas answered. The net being what it was, it had been a long time since I had witnessed two intelligent people engaged in discourse with the sole intent of feeling out one another's positions and not striving for a game of one-upmanship. And neither had even called the other one Hitler, yet.

After a few more minutes of walking, Silas slowed, holding up one hand and dropping his voice to a whisper. "We are close, detectives," he said. "Perhaps it would be better to exercise a modicum of stealth for the remainder of our approach."

The tunnel seemed no different to me, and I had no idea how Silas was determining how far we had traveled or how much farther we had to go. But I trusted him. As he had said, he'd been born to this world, where Hernandez and I were trespassers. "Where to?" I asked, keeping my voice low as well.

"The intersection should be approximately one hundred yards ahead, around a slight curvature of the tunnel. If there is a workspace there, we should find a doorway. The easiest—"

The sharp crack of gunfire echoed down the tunnels.

The report echoed down the tunnels, the sound magnified by the concrete walls and so loud it set my ears to ringing. Hernandez and I reacted as our training dictated. She had been slightly ahead of me, shoulder to shoulder with Silas, so she moved into point, pulling her service weapon—a blocky-looking nine millimeter—and sliding over to put her right shoulder against the wall. She dropped into a crouch, minimizing her target profile while keeping some degree of mobility. I moved in behind her, my forty-five jumping into my hand as I crouched down and put my left hand on her shoulder.

"Get behind us!" I barked at Silas, but he was already moving. He might not have had any training, and he might not have been constitutionally capable of violence, but he had both courage and a sense of self-preservation. The big synthetic had faded back, and edged into place behind me, also crouching low.

More gunfire barked out, a rapid staccato of explosions that made me long for my hearing protection. I recognized the sound of a smaller caliber pistol round, nine millimeter or maybe something like a forty caliber. And also something heavier. Maybe five-five-six. Shit.

I clapped Hernandez twice on her left shoulder, and she started forward, holding a crouch, pistol extended before her. A tunnel was a terrible place to be caught in a shootout, particularly if the bad guys had rifles and all you had were dinky little pistols. There was no cover in the passage, and we were pressed up against the wall of a near-perfect shooting alley. Moving toward the sound of gunfire in that situation was suicidal.

We did it anyway. Hernandez was still getting paid to run toward the bullets. My excuse? Old dog. New tricks. With the echo of the gunfire ringing in our ears, we rushed around the curve.

Chapter 12

After about fifty yards, the tunnel curved again. We slowed at this curve, moving forward more cautiously. Whatever had been happening was over—after a heavy and rapid exchange, the shooting had stopped, and eerie silence, apart from the ringing in our ears, had fallen once again. We crept closer, hugging the wall, until an intersection of tunnels came into view.

Where the passages joined, the space broadened, creating a hub of sorts. Most of my vision was blocked by Hernandez, since I was still in tight formation behind her, but I could see around her enough to spot the open, industrial-looking door set against one wall. I glanced back at Silas and made a gesture toward the door with my left hand. He nodded and mouthed what looked like "monitor room."

I tapped Hernandez on the shoulder and flicked my hand forward twice, toward the open door. She nodded and started moving once again, head on a swivel. A silhouette passed in front of the door, just a darker shadow in the dim lighting. Another followed. A third. At least three people were moving about inside whatever "monitor room" was up ahead. Hernandez stopped at the first sign of movement, crouching lower and turning to make eye contact with me. Even in the shadows, I saw the fear and uncertainty in the tightness of her lips, the drawn eyebrows. But I could see the determination there as well. She made a few quick hand gestures, indicating that she was going right and I should go left. I understood her fear. There was no cover to speak of between us and the door, and all it would take was one errant glance in our direction, and whoever had done the shooting—assuming they were the bad guys—would have to do nothing more than spray and pray. It would take zero marksmanship to peg us in our current situation.

Which left us only one option. We had to rush the door, hoping the element of surprise would freeze up the bad guys when they saw us move—and they *would* see us move. That was unavoidable. I nodded to Hernandez, then held up one finger in the "wait" sign. I turned to Silas, who was still tight on my six, and motioned for him to fall back and get low. Bullets might be flying soon, and the time for him to stick with us was past. He nodded his assent, though I spotted a faint reluctance in his eyes, and the big man ghosted back on silent feet. I waited until he had faded from sight, moving around the bending tunnel. Then I turned back to Hernandez and nodded once more.

She held up three fingers, and I took a steadying breath. Two fingers and I released the breath. One finger and I felt my muscles tense. The final finger dropped and we surged forward, staying low and hugging the wall, but pouring on the speed. As we neared the target, I split left, darting across the open doorway while Hernandez continued right.

"The fuck was that?" someone called, and flashlight beams started bisecting the door. I didn't bother trying to figure out if they were tac lights on the end of firearms or handhelds. I just sprinted, slamming to relative safety on the left side of the doorway as Hernandez contacted the right. Stealth was no longer an issue, so Hernandez, now in full cop mode, shouted, "New Lyons Police Department. Drop your weapons!"

The answer to that was, of course, a short burst of gunfire.

The interior of the tunnel system was concrete, and whatever control room we were plastered outside of was made from the same material. That gave us a nice, sturdy barricade that at least prevented bullets from passing through our cover. That didn't stop the bad guys—and if they were wantonly opening fire on people who identified themselves as cops, they counted as bad guys in my books—from shooting.

There was something about the pattern of their fire—the short, controlled bursts that sounded like they were coming from multiple points from within the room—that told me we weren't dealing with amateurs. Run-of-the-mill criminals usually opted for putting as much lead downrange in as short a time as humanly possible. People with training understood shoot, move, and communicate. I heard bits of conversation and what sounded like tables being knocked over. Our bad guys had shoot down, and it sounded like they weren't only doing move and communicate but were throwing in a little entrenching for good measure.

I glanced across the doorway at Hernandez. Our poses mirrored one another, both pressed with our shoulders tight against the wall, close enough to the doorway that we could pop out and shoot, but far enough from the edge to keep oblique-angled shots from finding a target. The bad guys had stopped shooting. That was a bad sign. It meant their initial salvo had been intended for the purpose of making us keep our heads down while they sought better positions. Which meant we were in a standoff. Against superior numbers. With better firepower. Double shit.

Hernandez, still invested with the legal authority of the New Lyons Police Department shouted, "Last warning, *pendejos*. Toss out your guns and surrender like good little assholes. Don't make us come in there and shoot your asses!" There was a reason Hernandez worked Guns and Gangs and not Hostage Response.

"I don't know who you are," a man shouted from within the room, "but cops don't come here, so you sure as hell aren't NLPD. Doesn't matter, anyway. If you get into this room, we still have to kill you. We haven't seen you; you haven't seen us. Why don't you be good little interlopers," he countered, mocking Hernandez, "and get the hell out of here before we send you to join our friend here." There was a muffled sound, like a boot hitting a body. I felt a heavy weight press on my shoulders at that. The situation was bad, but even worse, it looked like whoever had led us here had already met an untimely end. Answers—the answers I needed to keep the synthetics, Evelyn, and now Tia, safe—were going to be hard coming.

"Fuck you very much," Hernandez called sweetly. "Here's my badge, asshole." Without giving anyone time to think, much less aim or fire, she pulled it from the clip on her hip and tossed it blindly inside the room. I heard it clack once, metal side down, before making a more muffled sound as it flipped to the leather cover and slid along the floor. "You're shooting at cops, dickwad. Best case for you, if you somehow manage to kill us, the whole fucking world is going to come down on you. Or maybe, I just shoot you myself. You sure you're ready to commit to that?"

A long silence answered her from the other side of the room, then another sound of movement. I almost went for the shot, since it had to be someone climbing out of cover to grab Hernandez's credentials. If there was a chance, no matter how slim, that this ended with the bad guys locked up, and my face and name kept out of it, then I owed it to Hernandez to let that happen, so I remained motionless. Another muttered conversation from the other side, low and fast, almost panicked filtered out to our ears. If nothing else, Hernandez had at least gotten their attention.

Another sound of movement, and then something else came bouncing out through the door. My first instinct was to dive for the deck, fearing a grenade or incendiary device. But a quick glance showed me that what had been tossed was not an explosive, but rather a leather, bifold credential wallet. Not Hernandez's, but, presumably, belonging to one of the men inside. It was sitting right in the middle of the doorway, with clear lines of fire for the people inside.

"We're private security for Walton Biogenics," one of the men inside called. "Tracking down a criminal who stole privileged information from the company." There was a pause, then, "Self-defense. He attacked us when we tried to take him into custody."

Hernandez wasn't having it. "You got no authority to take anybody into custody. You're not law enforcement. You're a fucking rent-a-cop with a machine gun. I'm not going to tell you again. Throw down your weapons, and lie down on the floor with your hands outstretched above your head." I moved while she was talking, stripping off my shirt and twisting it into a rough rope. I knelt and flicked it out, just far enough to encompass the credentials. A quick tug and they slid across the concrete to my feet. I snatched them from the ground, gave them a quick read, and tossed them across the doorway to Hernandez. Neither my flicking shirt nor the thrown credentials drew any fire, which was, at least, a start.

She caught the wallet and flipped it open, giving it a quick read. I'd done the same, so knew she was looking at the mug of one Peter Emerson, male, white, close-cropped hair and hard features, as per the photo. The badge identified Emerson as a "security consultant" at Walton Biogenics—the company that held the monopoly on the production, indoctrination, and distribution of synthetics. The genetic engineering company having any involvement at all with whatever had brought a body to my doorstep did not inspire any good feelings in me. The cops and feds were dangerous to me, but I doubted they would go in for the wholesale slaughter of synthetics should they find us. They wouldn't take any extraordinary measures to assure anyone's safety, but we'd at least be given a chance to surrender. If the "security consultants" from Walton Biogenics found us, I had no doubt that their orders would be to kill anything moving, then set fire to the whole place, to eliminate as much evidence as possible.

Hernandez dropped the wallet and pulled out her screen, the blue glow lighting her face in the dim illumination. She held it higher as if trying to get a signal, then shook her head and put the phone away. She looked over to me, raised an eyebrow. I pulled my screen, saw the "no signal" indicator and shook my head in turn. I wasn't terribly keen on the idea of Hernandez calling in backup, but if the other option was untimely death, I'd consider it. Looked like it wasn't going to be an option, though. "You're running out of time, Emerson," Hernandez called. "Make the right decision."

"Am I, though?" a man, presumably Emerson, replied. "What are you doing down here, anyway, Detective? Long way from any beat. And I know for a fact that NLPD didn't send you down here." That was interesting. How did Emerson know that for a *fact*? Unless Walton was in collusion with the police. The thought didn't surprise me—the top brass did more politicking than they did policing, and the mega-corporation certainly had enough bought-and-paid-for politicians to give it leverage over just about any branch of government. "The way I see it, you're off the reservation. Maybe doing a little freelance work on the side? I notice your partner hasn't said anything. Why is that? Maybe because they aren't a cop at all, eh? I think we both know that the smart thing for you to do would be to turn around, walk away, and pretend none of this ever happened. I can guarantee you, there ain't nothing in here worth dying over."

That was a mistake. Hernandez was a cop's cop, and she divided the world into three groups—police, civilians, and bad guys. I wasn't sure where I fit with that anymore, but I was pretty damn sure that anyone who shot at her fell firmly into the bad guys category. No way in hell she was just going to walk away.

"Guess we do this the hard way," she said.

The answer from the men inside was a burst of gunfire that peppered the doorframe, sending bits of wood and powdered concrete flying.

Despite Hernandez's tough talk, we were in a tight spot, and she knew it as well as I did. Outnumbered and outgunned. We probably had the better position, but we couldn't be certain of that, since we hadn't been able to get a clear picture of the layout inside the room before the bullets had started flying. If we had the full support of the New Lyons Police Department, we'd just hold position and wait for SWAT with their ballistic shields, body armor, and flash bangs. With no other way out, the people holed up in the control room would be in a world of hurt. But we didn't have that support, couldn't call for that support, and it sounded like Emerson and his crew knew it.

We were going to have to go through the door. And I couldn't let Hernandez go first. That wasn't some macho bullshit. I was Homicide, she was Guns and Gangs. She'd undoubtedly kicked down more doors in her time than I had. But this wasn't a call for NLPD. She was here because I'd asked for her help. Besides, she had a little girl at home. I didn't even have a houseplant that needed watering.

I met her eyes, then pointed at myself and gestured through the door. Then I pointed at her and mimed covering fire. She didn't look happy about it, but she nodded, dropping to both knees and edging closer to the doorframe so she could lean out and fire with minimal exposure. I drew a steadying breath, muttered a brief prayer, and tensed my muscles, preparing to charge the door.

The lights in the tunnel went out. At the same time, the lights inside the control room suddenly brightened to the point that they were painful to look at. The shift took me by surprise, but not as much as it did the people inside, who started cursing as the dim interior blazed brighter than the sunniest summer day. I didn't even think about it—I just moved, instinct honed in the military, on the police force, during the countless hours on the mats, kicking in and urging me to take advantage of any momentary weakness.

I was in the room in a an instant, forty-five extended in front of me in a two-handed isosceles grip, eyes pinned to the front post while I rotated my body like the turret on a tank. Hernandez had leaned out, and I heard the staccato pop-pop-pop of her nine millimeter, firing more or less blind, not really trying to hit the bad guys so much as to draw their attention away from the target I was presenting. The blinding lights had momentarily drawn the enemy's eyes away from their sights, and that combined with the fire from Hernandez bought me about a second and a half of time.

It was all the time I needed.

It wasn't nearly enough time.

My mind registered facts about the first target, even as it crossed my sights. Male. Crouched behind what looked like an overturned standard government-issue gray steel desk. Black fatigues. Plate carrier with MOLLE webbing. Balaclava covering the face, despite the heat. Full on tacti-cool getup that, depending on the wearer, could be intimidating as hell or make you look like a complete and total poseur. Target one fell into the intimidating camp. At least for the heartbeat it took me to squeeze off three rounds. I Mozambique'd him—two in the body, one in the head, always leaves the target dead. I couldn't tell if the body shots had done any damage—unless he was wearing the plate carrier for show, the forty-five rounds weren't likely to do much. The headshot resulted in a cloud of pink mist, though. Target one down.

I had entered left and sighted left, betting that Hernandez's fire would keep heads down to my right. I started tracking right, hoping the bad guys weren't very good at this sort of thing. They were. Very good.

I had barely cleared the first target when I heard the rapid pop-pop of a two-round burst and felt the double impact against my chest. Unlike the enemy, I wasn't wearing a plate carrier.

But I wasn't stupid.

The rounds impacted against my ballistic vest, feeling like getting punched in the ribs with the butt-end of a screwdriver. Contrary to popular belief, the impact of the rounds—nine millimeter sub-gun by my best guess, definitely not the higher-powered five-five-six I thought I'd heard earlier—did not send me flying through the air. Okay, they made me stumble some, took my balance, but a quarter ounce of lead wasn't going to move two-hundred-plus pounds of me all that much. Hurt like hell though.

My sights found the shooter, and I started squeezing the trigger as fast as possible. He got off another burst, maybe two—I didn't feel the impacts, but some part of me knew that didn't mean I'd escaped injury. The brain did funny things in combat, and adrenaline was a hell of a drug. My magazine came up empty the sixth time I squeezed the trigger, and I was three-quarters of the way through a reload before I realized it was over.

I'd taken only headshots at target two, and I'd missed most of them. From the cursory glance at the damage as I moved forward and started kicking weapons away from outstretched hands, I missed all but one. Fortunately, I'd yet to meet the person—human or synthetic—who could stop two hundred and thirty grains traveling at eight hundred and fifty feet per second with their face and still have any fight left in them. Hernandez had taken down target three, and it was a damn lucky thing for me that she had. Turned out, I *had* correctly identified the report of a five-five-six cartridge, and though it wasn't a particularly high-powered rifle, it would have punched through my ballistic vest without much in the way of a problem.

"We clear?" Hernandez asked, crouched outside the door and leaning forward, weapon still in action.

Three bad guys. Four bodies. "Yeah, we're clear."

I holstered and half-collapsed onto the edge of the overturned desk, rubbing my hand against my chest where the bullets had impacted. I'd been right—they'd come from some sort of sub-gun, and as the adrenaline faded, damn if they didn't hurt.

"You're hit!" Hernandez said, holstering and hurrying to my side.

I waved her off. "I'm okay, Hernandez. Two in the vest, but it held. Hurts like a son of a bitch, though."

"Good," she said, and I blinked at her in surprise. I mean, I knew Hernandez wasn't exactly the mothering type on the job, but damn. I *had* just been shot. "What the fuck am I supposed to do about this, Campbell?" she demanded, waving her hand at the array of bodies on the ground. "I'm a cop, for fuck's sake. How am I going to explain all these dead people?"

I looked at Hernandez. At the dead. And realized how far I'd moved from being a cop. Didn't matter that the bastards had opened fire on us. Didn't matter that they had killed someone practically right in front of us. The first thing that was going to matter to the brass was, what in the hell was Hernandez doing in the sewers in the first place?

"Shit, Hernandez. Hell if I know."

Chapter 13

Silas returned while Hernandez was examining the deep purple bruises forming on my chest. My vest lay on the ground next to us—it had done its job, but now that it had taken a few rounds, I couldn't trust it anymore.

"Are you well, Detective?" the synthetic asked as he slipped into the room. His thin lips formed a moue of distaste as he took in the bodies on the floor, and mine formed their own as he fell back into calling me "detective."

"I'll live." I grunted, then winced as Hernandez probed at a particularly sensitive rib. "If Hernandez doesn't kill me, that is."

"Quit your bitching, *hermano*," she replied, still probing. "I think you cracked a rib."

"We're lucky that's the worst of it, I suppose," I said. "If the lights hadn't blinked out like that…" If they hadn't, we might still be in a standoff.

"I'm glad I could be of some assistance," Silas said.

"That was you?" Hernandez demanded.

The albino inclined his head, and I snorted. "He's pretty good with computers," I said, beating Silas to the punch. "If it's connected to a network, any network, he can pretty much make it his bitch." Then I pushed myself of the desk, grunting at the strain on my bruised ribs. "I can't tell you what to do with all this, Hernandez. But before you do anything, I think we need to see if what we came for is actually here."

The bodies of the Walton Biogenics security personnel didn't tell us much. All three were human, all three male. One white, one Asian, one black. All three with the athletic builds of professional soldiers. Apart from their corporate identification, they weren't carrying any wallets, cash, or anything else. Just primary and secondary firearms—two with nine millimeter sub-guns, and one with a five-five-six, all sporting forty caliber sidearms—reloads scattered in dump pouches, flashlights, a knife or two. First aid kits, one of which we'd already cannibalized while Hernandez checked over my ribs. No screens. No other communications gear.

"This doesn't make any sense," Hernandez muttered. "They didn't just appear in these sewers. They had to come from somewhere, be directed here somehow. If they were worried about operational security, why carry ID at all? If they weren't worried, why not carry screens or communicators? Why leave the electronics behind?"

"Maybe to prevent being tracked?" I half-said, half-asked.

"Tracked by whom?"

I looked at Silas, but he shook his head. "Not me or mine, Detectives. Many among my kind are very skilled with computers, but we do not make a habit of electronically monitoring every corporate security guard." He frowned. "Even those that we know to be a danger to us, which is true of every member of Walton Biogenics."

I had moved my attention to the actual victim—if the word could be applied to the person who had, presumably, left a body on my doorstep. There hadn't been any need to check for vitals. There were two neat groupings of nine millimeter holes in the corpse's chest and a smaller shot to the center of the forehead. I wasn't a forensics expert, but I'd been on the job long enough to recognize the stippling and powder burns for what they were—a close-range, execution-style shot from no more than a foot or two away. At least the full metal jacketed round left the head intact. It was a messy enough job without having to deal with that. There was a firearm a few feet away from the corpse, in much the same configuration as the guns I'd kicked away from the bodies of the security guards.

"Looks like whoever this was put up a fight, but the bad guys took him down—then put one more rifle round in the brainpan to make sure of the job," I said.

I didn't want to touch the gun—no sense putting prints on it—but I leaned down and wafted the air from near the barrel toward my nose. I could smell the acrid tang of cordite. "Definitely took some shots back, though I don't think he hit anything."

"Looks like the body is relatively undisturbed," Hernandez noted. "We interrupted them before they could do much more than shoot the bastard."

"Yeah," I agreed. "Guess that means I get to go diving into the pockets of yet another dead guy."

Without a word, Hernandez reached into her own pockets and pulled out a pair of blue latex gloves. She passed them over to me, and I nodded my thanks. She might have been thinking about contaminating the evidence—I was more concerned with not leaving anything that could be traced back to me on the body.

I started with a quick pat-down, feeling along the most likely places where an item might be concealed. I didn't have much hope of success—most data storage methods were so small these days that a pat-down was unlikely to uncover them. I went about the less pleasant task of sticking my gloved hands into the various pockets of the corpse's clothing. Still nothing. Next, I ran my fingers along all of the seams of the clothing, closing my eyes and focusing my attention on the tips of my fingers, concentrating on searching for any anomalies and burrs in the fabric or unusually rough stitching that might indicate a hidden pocket.

I didn't find a hidden pocket. Instead, I found an honest-to-God slip of paper, stapled to the inside hem of the deceased's left leg. I'd almost torn the paper in my search before I realized what I was feeling and stopped. I pulled my knife—a four-inch quick-release tactical folder with a tanto-style point—from my own pocket and turned up the cuff of the corpse's jeans. I worked the tip of the knife into the metal tines of the staple and pried them up, working as slowly as possible to not damage the paper itself. From my vantage, the paper was blank, a simple slip roughly the size of a fortune you could find in the terrible cookies at bad Chinese restaurants. I silently prayed there was something, anything, of use on the other side.

The staple tines loosened, and I eased the point of the blade under the staple proper and pried it out. With forefinger and thumb I grasped the paper's edge, slipping it from the corpse's waistband and holding it up to my face.

"Well?" Hernandez demanded. "Anything?"

I could see Silas was watching as well, quiet as usual, but with deep curiosity burning behind his pinkish eyes. With a shrug, I turned the paper toward them, revealing the series of twelve numbers listed there. They were grouped in sets of three, each separated by a period. I was no cyber cop, but I lived in the modern world and I recognized an IP address when I saw one.

"Is that it?" Hernandez groused. "A fucking web address?"

I shrugged. "I'll keep looking." I understood her ire—it wasn't a smoking gun, not all by itself. Certainly not enough to help her solve the question that was undoubtedly rattling around in her head—and, if I was honest, in mine as well. What was she going to do with this mess?

I'd brought her down here for backup, and if she hadn't been here, the odds were good I would have died in the fucking sewer. But four dead civilians presented her with a special kind of conundrum. Much to my surprise, I found that I had no problem, ethical or moral, with leaving the assholes to rot. Something about that bothered me. Had I moved so far away from the soldier and the cop who wanted to help and protect people?

"We will not be able to access that on one of our burners. Not from down here," Silas noted. "Wireless signals don't reach this deep, particularly with all of the iron reinforcements sandwiched into the concrete."

"Great," I said, as I went back to the task of searching the body. After several more minutes, I gave up. There was nothing—literally nothing— else of note on the body. "Does no one carry fucking identification or screens anymore?"

While I'd been playing with dead people, Silas and Hernandez had begun a systematic search of the control room. The room itself looked like it could have served as any mid-level office in any corporation in New Lyons—except that it boasted only a single desk-mounted screen, doubtless hardwired into the net. That wouldn't do us a lot of good, since not even Silas's magic fingers could fix bullet holes. I wasn't sure who had hit it, but it looked like it had taken at least a couple of rounds. "Anything?" I asked.

Silas was examining the pile of furniture the security guards had used to create a bulwark while Melinda gave the enemy dead a more thorough search.

"Perhaps a little something here, Detective," Silas said. "The screen is, as you can see, nonfunctional. There are a couple of magazines for our mystery man's rifle that look like they may have been sitting on the desk when the Walton people barged in. Some food wrappers and discarded cans mixed in with the other detritus. And a blanket. It appears our victim has been staying here—or at least planning on staying here—for a few days."

I grunted. "Interesting. So, maybe he dropped the body at the call center, then planned on holing up here as long as it took us to find him. But how did Walton find him first? Dammit! We were so fucking close." I drew a deep breath, letting it out in a long sigh and trying to let the anger go with it. "You got anything else on the bad guys, Hernandez?"

"We got ID, weapons, and shit-all else," Hernandez said. She gave one of the bodies a desultory kick—more of a nudge, really. "Fucking rent-a-cops."

"All right, Hernandez," I said, resigned. "Your call. What now? Silas and I can't stick around, but if you have to call this in…" I hated the thought of abandoning her to the questions and administrative nightmare that was bound to follow. Just not as much as I hated the idea of being arrested by the likes of Francoise Fortier or his fellow anti-synth cohorts in the department.

"This is the second time you've put me in a shitty situation, *pendejo*," she said. The words were harsh, but her tone was more resigned than angry. "If I don't call this in... Shit, I don't even know what they call a self-defense killing that goes unreported, but whatever the fuck it is, it's the *best* I can hope for. And if I *do* call it in, then I have to explain what the hell I was doing down here in the first place. I don't suppose it occurred to you to have a story ready for that one, *'mano*?"

I could only shake my head. My focus had been on following the trail and trying to make sure the synthetics under my care stayed safe. Though I had suspected the possibility this would end in bloodshed, I hadn't given any real thought to how to get Hernandez's ass out of the fire if it did. In hindsight, I felt pretty shitty about that, but there it was.

"*Mierda*. I'm fucked if I do, fucked if I don't," she said. "And I usually like to at least get dinner first." She looked at the bodies again, eyes lingering on the one she'd taken out. "You using a clean weapon?" she asked.

"Yeah," I said. "Not my service gun. One I bought on the street. It'll come up as stolen, but no link to me. You?" I asked.

"I'm not stupid, Campbell. Personal weapon. Bit of a family heirloom. Belonged to my grandfather. So far as I know, it was never registered anywhere. There's definitely no ballistic data on it, nothing that can be linked to me." She frowned. "I'm going to have to get rid of it now, though. Fuck you for that, and for making me have to think like the scum I'm supposed to be locking up." Again, though the words were harsh, there was no heat in them. They were resigned. "But in for a penny, in for a fucking pound. If we're done here, let's wipe the place for prints and get the fuck out before some maintenance worker comes wandering by and wonders why all the corpses."

Chapter 14

It didn't take long to clean up the crime scene—at least as clean as we were going to get it. There wasn't much we could do about the bodies or the bullets. But we'd worn gloves through the search process and wiped down anywhere else we could remember touching. It wasn't perfect, but it also wasn't terribly likely the scene would be found anytime soon. Given the heat and humidity, any latent prints we missed would probably be rendered useless. As for other trace evidence... Well, sure as shit we'd left some behind, but short of dousing the place in gasoline or bleach, there hadn't been anything we could do about it.

Hernandez had declined to return with Silas and me to the safe house. Not that I could blame her. We'd gotten her into enough potential trouble for one morning without taking her to a literal den of criminals, at least as far as the NLPD was concerned. The journey back was a repeat of the drive in—taking the most circumspect routes to avoid the omnipresent eyes in the sky and approaching every new intersection with the gut-wrenching moment of uncertainty as to whether this would be the time we found a roadblock waiting. The big green machine had trained me in escape and evasion, and I could make my way through enemy territory undetected with the best of them, but having to treat the city I'd called home for more than a decade as enemy territory was beginning to wear on me.

We didn't try to access the IP address from our vehicle, even though full access had been restored from the moment we resurfaced onto the streets of New Lyons. Too busy trying not to fall into the hands of the locals or the feds to risk the distraction. Somehow, I could feel the slip of paper, tucked into my front pants pocket, weighing as heavily as a stone. Would the IP address lead to more questions, just one more crumb in the trail I'd been following for... Had it only been two days now? Shit. It felt like longer—much longer.

And yet, the days were trickling away, getting ever closer to the first and the start of the synthetic "offensive." Or was it possible that the address would lead us to answers, real answers, as to how our last refuge had been discovered, why we were being sought out, and, perhaps most importantly, who had put this whole chain of events into motion?

The worry gnawed at me, twisting my stomach into a churning pool of acid and bile. I longed to soothe it, preferably with about three fingers of good Kentucky bourbon. Unfortunately, liquor had been in short supply since I'd become the most wanted man in New Lyons. I couldn't exactly risk a run down to the corner store, and despite stocking plenty of food, potable water, sundries, and medical supplies, none of the safe houses that Silas had set up seemed to have anything in the way of alcohol. It made sense, after a fashion. Synthetics were property. Who would waste good money by buying liquor for their synthetics? So, I supposed, most had never really been exposed to the habit, never acquired the taste. Maybe that was a good thing, but it seemed like they were missing out on yet another of the simpler pleasures life had to offer. Of course, with what Silas had told me about their superior genetics, who knew how much alcohol it would take to get one of them drunk in the first place?

As we neared the run-down block in the LNW, I could see that, despite the vastly eased restrictions on contraband goods, the black market was in full swing. Kids were working corners, making quick transactions with all manner of junkies and addicts. Lookouts saw us coming, and even through my efforts, pegged me as a cop from a mile away. As soon as we got close to an active corner, the people just sort of dried up and blew away, only to appear a moment or two later in the rearview, back to business as usual. It seemed like no matter how much change—political, technical, social—came to the city, some things remained the same.

We pulled up in front of the boarded-up restaurant and quickly exited the vehicle. It pulled away from the curb, heading for whichever preprogrammed parking area Silas had directed. The lookouts once again saw us coming, and the door swung open as we approached, slamming closed behind us as we entered the shadowed interior. I nodded to the synthetic at the door, this time a woman in her forties, and she nodded back, somberly, before returning her attention to her task.

"Jason!"

The excited call—so out of place amidst the quiet, almost subdued, atmosphere of the gathered synthetics—startled me. I glanced around, and it took a moment to see the petite form of Tia Morita making her way through the crowd. I noted the expressions on the faces of the synthetics as she passed. I rated a sort of guarded respect from most of them, a begrudging acknowledgment that I was putting myself in harm's way to help them, but with an undercurrent of inevitable disappointment, as if my assistance could only be a transitory thing. She, on the other hand, had somehow managed to elicit an entirely different response. I saw actual, tentative smiles as she wended her way through the various tables and benches of the refugees. I had no idea how she'd managed that in the few hours she'd been left alone with the synthetics. I'd been trying to earn their trust for months and had scarcely hit the level of cautious acceptance.

I'd started to open my mouth to answer the excited coroner's assistant, but she talked right over me. "These people are amazing. Amazing! I've been doing routine physicals, checking vitals, whatever I could, trying to make sure everyone's healthy."

A wry smile spread across Silas's face as Tia spoke.

"And?" I asked in the half-second pause she needed to draw breath.

"And nothing. They're all in perfect health."

"That's a good thing, right?" I asked, confused by her excitement.

She let out an exasperated sigh. "A good thing? These people have been living in crowded conditions, under extreme levels of stress, in run-down and abandoned buildings that have God alone knows what kind of bacteria. By all rights, a third of them should be sick as dogs, and another third showing at least some signs of encroaching illness. But they're *all* perfectly fine, Jason. All of them." Her words took on an almost accusatory note, and I raised my hands in a mock-defensive posture. Of course, doing so strained my badly bruised ribs, and I winced.

"What was that?" the aspiring doctor said, immediately reaching toward me. She applied a gentle pressure along my chest and ribs, probing for injury. It hurt… but it also felt good. "Are you okay?"

"I'm fine, Ms. Morita," I replied.

"Yes," Silas said with an uncharacteristic twinkle of mischief in his eyes. "I assure you, Ms. Morita, he only got shot a little bit."

She growled at that. "With me," she said, pulling me none-too-gently into her makeshift examination room, where she had me seated and shirtless before I could do anything. She probed my ribs more, before clucking her tongue and reaching for a roll of bandages. I winced as Tia pulled the bandages tight. "You really should get this X-rayed, you know."

"Can't exactly walk into a hospital, Tia," I replied. "Too many cameras. Too many cops. So unless you have a portable X-ray machine tucked away somewhere, I'm just going to have to trust to your tender ministrations."

She wrapped another loop, pulling, I felt, much harder than was necessary. She must have seen my grimace, because she smiled, a touch too sweetly. "Sorry," she said. "Most of my normal patients are a lot less talkative than you."

I grunted, and restrained myself—barely—from making some comment about working with stiffs.

"Detective Hernandez did a decent job," she continued in a more conversational voice, "particularly given the limited resources, but you definitely have at least one cracked rib. Maybe more. And if you take another hard blow to the chest, like say from getting shot," another too-tight pull on the bandages, "one of them might break and puncture a lung. Then you won't get a choice on going to a hospital, at least not if you want to live."

"Great," I muttered. "If I promise not to get shot anymore, will you stop trying to turn me into some horrible cross between a mummy and a corset model?"

"Don't be ridiculous," she said. "You don't have the figure to pull off being a mummy."

I laughed, which set my ribs to aching. "Ow. God. Tia. Don't make me laugh."

"Serves you right."

I raised my hands in supplication. "You win. You win." As she finished taping down the bandages, I asked, "How did you get the synthetics to warm to you so quickly?"

"What do you mean?" she asked. "They barely talk to me."

"Yeah, but they look at you with…" I thought about it, trying to find the right word. "Fondness? Respect? I'm not sure what it is, but it doesn't have the undercurrent of fear that I always feel when they look at me."

She gave me an elfish smile. "Oh, that's because I'm adorable." She said it with such butter-won't-melt-in-my-mouth innocence that I had to laugh again. Which sent more tendrils of pain dancing along my ribcage. Then she sobered. "I just talked to them, Jason. It's amazing how much people will open up to you if you just ask them how they're feeling." She paused, and a flicker of something like real sadness flashed across her face. "I think, for a lot of them, no one has ever asked that question."

"How are *you* feeling, Tia?" I asked. I didn't mean to say it. It just sort of fell out. Considering the timing and the strange intimacy of our situation—I was sitting half-naked as she tended to my wounds, after all—I couldn't help the slight flush that suffused my face as soon as I realized what I'd said. But a half-second of reflection was all it took me to realize that I really wanted to know.

She gave me a long, silent look, her eyes unreadable. "I… I think I'm doing really good, actually," she said. She sounded surprised as she said it, but another smile lit up her face. "I wasn't sure about coming here, Jason. Wasn't sure about getting…embroiled in this. I work for the city! They're paying my med school bills. If they catch wind that I'm involved…" She shrugged. She didn't have to say that, in addition to the whole thrown in prison for life thing, she would also lose out on the free ride on tuition. "But…"

"But?" I asked.

"But like I said, I've spent the last few hours talking to them. I can't believe what some of these people have been through. And I can't sit around and do nothing anymore. I can't go back to my job and pretend that the world is okay as it is." She shook her head, and a shimmer in her eyes suggested tears. Her voice didn't quaver, though. "I'm not stupid, Jason. I've read history. I know all the terrible things humans have done to each other over the centuries. I know nobody's hands are clean. I know that all the horrible things we've done to synthetics—the abuse, the rape, the murder—none of it ever goes away. Because some people are evil, or sick, or whatever you want to call it, and they always have been, and they always will be. But we—all of us—we've done more than just turn a blind eye to the violence. We've done more than just ignore it and pretend that it can't happen to us. We've outright sanctioned it. We've created—literally, created—an entire subclass of people and said, 'Hey, it's okay to hurt them. Because no matter how much they look, act, think, and feel like us, they aren't real people.' And we all just bought into it, because it made life that much easier for the rest of us." She spoke at a frenetic pace, her voice rising in volume and pitch. The tears leaked from her eyes, tracing wet streaks down her cheeks.

Something about her vulnerability, about her obvious passion and pain, filled me with an almost overwhelming memory of Annabelle, and I felt tears form in my own eyes. I reached out unconsciously and put my arms around her, drawing her to my chest. Despite my attraction to Tia, there was nothing provocative in that hug. Any potential attraction was lost beneath the undeniable weight of two people sharing a simple, if profound, moment of grief, not for any one person, but for the soul of humanity itself.

"Am I interrupting something?"

The basso voice pulled us from our embrace. Neither of us jerked back—it wasn't as if we were illicit lovers caught in some wrongdoing. We simply dropped our arms and separated a bit. The evidence of Tia's tears were clear upon her face. My own were—I hoped—at least somewhat hidden by the two-day growth of stubble that covered my face. Shaving hadn't exactly been a high priority the past couple of days, and neither had sleep. I told myself that that would explain the redness in my eyes.

Silas stood in the doorway, his expression unreadable.

"It's been a long and stressful couple of days for all of us," I said by way of explanation.

"Of course. We're ready to review the IP address." He waved one hand at me, my bandages, and my general lack of shirt-wearing. "That is, if you're ready?"

We were back in the booth with the makeshift screen. Tia had passed on coming with us, opting instead to check on Evelyn once more. She had assured me and Silas that the woman was doing well, but she wanted to keep a close eye on her. So I sat alone, somewhat regretfully, on my side of the booth while Silas and La Sorte sat on the other. Certainly, going to a web page didn't require much in the way of computer expertise, but if Silas wanted La Sorte present, that was good enough for me.

"I did some checking on the IP address," La Sorte said. "Looking for things like any registered owners, or known malicious software associated with it. I came up empty, so it looks like it's safe to proceed."

Okay. So maybe going to a net page took more savvy that I had thought—or at least, maybe I should have put a hell of a lot more thought into net content I accessed. "Well, then, let's proceed," I replied.

He nodded, his fingers flicking over his screen. Then the large franken-screen on the table flashed to life. It displayed a single window, much like the window displayed for any given folder on any given screen I had ever used. It was, for all intents and purposes, a mostly empty gray box. Mostly empty, because there was one single file displayed there, a file with the uninspiring name of truth.vid.

Silas arched a single eyebrow at me, and I shrugged and nodded.

La Sorte caught the nod and tapped his own screen, twice.

There was a brief second where nothing happened, and then the gray window was replaced with blackness. The blackness held for a second, and then it too, vanished, showing the face of a middle-aged man who appeared to be of Middle Eastern descent. He had closely cropped black hair and a neatly trimmed beard. His eyes were dark, and something in them, at least to my eye, looked pained. He stared at the camera for a long moment, as if to make sure it was actually recording, and then he spoke.

"My name is Dr. Mido Kaphiri," he said. "And I am afraid I have enabled the worst tragedy in human history." He drew a long, shuddering breath. His voice trembled as he continued. "I suspect that by the time the conditions I set around the reveal of this…testimony…arrive, I will be long dead. The coward in me prays that my death was from natural causes, though there is a small part that hopes I find the courage to die a better death than that." The man paused again, and his Adam's apple bobbed as he swallowed. "I am not sure if history will remember me at all—I somehow doubt that Walton will let that happen—but if history does remember me, it will remember me as the father of synthetics."

A glance passed around the table at that. The history of synthetics was…hazy at best. I'd come to understand why the vagaries existed—it was Walton Biogenics trying to protect its dirty little secrets. But to come face-to-virtual-face with the man claiming to be the father of the field… I turned my attention back to the video.

"Like most scientists before me, I stand atop the shoulders of giants. But somebody had to be the first to create artificial life, and I had that honor. From there, it was just a small step, a few degrees of genetic manipulation, to take a technology originally intended to provide for organ transplants and research and create an entire new race of people.

"I did not think about the potential consequences. I was too wrapped up in the possibilities, too enamored of the idea of success. I created the first synthetic. And he is an amazing, wonderful being. I raised him, as my son, for years.

"Until my employer, Walton Biogenics, realized the possibilities in some darker applications of my research. To the commercial potential outside of the organ and tissue transplants where my work had previously garnered some small success." Kaphiri paused again, for longer this time, and his face sagged in obvious defeat. He waved one hand at the camera, and the sense of failure and resignation in the gesture was palpable through the screen. "They took my work. All of it. All of my research. My notes. My successes and my failures. They sent an army of lawyers after me. I had signed all of the standard employment forms, of course, all of the nondisclosure agreements and contracts affirming that any work I produced on company time or using company resources was wholly owned by the company. There was nothing I could do. They took what I had built, and they turned it into what it has become.

"I was given a choice. I could work with them, help them to understand and adapt my ideas, maintain some level of control over the science. Or I could be fired, sued, possibly imprisoned, and they would turn my work over to someone else to develop as they saw fit." There was anger in Kaphiri's voice, but also something else. Regret?

"I chose the coward's path," he admitted. "But not just out of fear of what might happen to me. I'd managed to keep my first success, my Al'awwal, from the eyes of Walton. So far as they knew, Al was my son, and as long as I didn't give them reason to dig too deeply, he would remain as such. As long as I didn't give them a reason to think I would break with what they wanted, they would allow us both to keep living our lives.

"So that is what I did. For decades. I watched—no, I *helped*—as Walton Biogenics created a slave race. I watched as legislatures around the world traded away their souls for the promised utopia of a synthetic world. I watched, and I feared, that they would discover that my son was not born of my body but of the same process by which they were creating their slaves. But, perhaps worst of all, I watched as they took the best parts of my work and threw them away."

He drew a deep, steadying breath and looked directly into the camera's watchful eye. "Synthetics are superior to regular humans in every conceivable way. I do not mean that they are more attractive—bilateral symmetry and optimized fat and muscle content are the most basic applications of what Walton Biogenics can do. But they have done—we have done—so much more than that. Every new pharmaceutical to come out of Walton in the last three decades has been directly derived from applications of the synthetic program. And every one of them has been a virtual placebo compared to what Walton could have done. As of the time of my recording this video, Walton has within its power the ability to eliminate something like seventy percent of known diseases. It has cures for dozens of forms of cancer. It has the ability to produce retroviruses capable of altering the DNA of humanity in such a way to cut the aging process nearly in half." He shook his head and sighed.

"Walton Biogenics has the ability to do all of this and more, and has sat idle upon it for decades. First, because there is little profit for a biology and genetics company in curing disease. But that is secondary to their true concern. They have built a commercial empire unlike any known in the history of the world, and they have done it on one simple, foundational lie: synthetics are not human." Kaphiri waved one hand dismissively at the camera. "I am a man of science and will not argue the philosophical question of the soul, as it relates to synthetics or anything else. What I will argue, what I can *prove*, is that in every way that we can measure, in every way that we know how to examine and codify, synthetics are genetically indistinguishable from humans. We have simply been able to push the potential curve so that they normally operate at what would be the limits of human potential. Walton Biogenics claims otherwise, while simultaneously forcing the passage of laws in every nation that make it impossible for anyone to legally verify their claims."

He looked down and away from the camera, and when his eyes rose once more, he face sagged in exhaustion. He appeared completely drained. "I have gathered this proof for years. Smuggled it out of Walton's labs and entrusted it to the only person I can. My son. Al'awwal. Over the years, I have found a few like-minded individuals, a few on the," he grimaced, "lunatic fringe who have come to believe what I know to be the truth. And I have given them certain sets of instructions. I believe—I pray—that there will come a time when someone has a real chance of not only getting my evidence out to the public, but of making it heard, making it believed. Someone who can weather the storm of killers and lawyers that Walton Biogenics will surely send to silence the truth. If you're watching this video," a wry, almost apologetic smile replaced the tired expression, "then congratulations. You're the lucky ones who get to try to take down what I truly believe to be the most evil syndicate in the history of mankind."

That certainly got our attention. I looked across at Silas to find him staring back at me. His face was calm acceptance, and well it should be. I realized that, while freeing the synthetics from their servitude was his primary concern, taking back a little of his own on Walton Biogenics had been on the agenda from the beginning. LaSorte, on the other hand, looked dumfounded, his lips forming a silent oh of surprise.

On the screen, Kaphiri was continuing. "So, that is who I am and what I am responsible for doing. Now it is up to you to *undo* this terrible thing that I have wrought. The agent who directed you to this site should be able to give you more details, perhaps already has."

My stomach tightened. Presumably, Dr. Kaphiri's agent had been the man gunned down in the sewers by Walton Biogenics security personnel. Equally presumably, he was the person who had dropped a body on my doorstep. I still didn't quite understand why that had happened—it seemed like a poor introduction to Dr. Kaphiri and his work. It also had, one way or another, contributed to the poor bastard's death. Why hadn't he just knocked on the door, handed over the IP address, and waited while we watched the video? I couldn't figure out if the body had been a warning, a threat…or, and a frown pulled at my lips as the notion occurred to me, a way to get rid of the evidence of a previous assault upon the messenger by Walton Biogenics. I didn't have much time to ponder that possibility, though, because Kaphiri was still talking.

"In case he did not, or in case you stumbled upon this video through some other channel but, through serendipity, are a like-minded individual, you must seek out my son. You must find Al'awwal, for it is he who holds the keys to the proof that Walton Biogenics has not only enslaved generations of people, but that they have kept key medical advances from us all, in the hopes of protecting their precious revenue streams. You can find him here." The display flickered, and the image was replaced with a series of numbers that I recognized as longitude and latitude.

"At least it's not going to be another fucking scavenger hunt," I muttered.

"I wish you the best of luck," Kaphiri said, as his face came back into frame. "Do not underestimate the forces arrayed against you—the inertia of the status quo is a powerful force, perhaps the most powerful force known to man. But do not underestimate the basic goodness of the human spirit, either. I have faith that once the world knows the truth, the average person will not allow for this travesty to stand."

There was another pause in the video, long enough that I started to wonder if we were all staring stupidly at a still image. Just as I was about to raise the possibility, Dr. Kaphiri spoke one final time. "Please," he said, his voice soft, "tell my son I love him."

The screen went black.

Chapter 15

"Well," Silas said.

"Well, indeed," I replied. "I'm not sure what to make of this, but we're going to have to go to those coordinates and see if we can find this Al'awwal, this first synthetic."

"There may be a slight problem with that," La Sorte said.

"Because of course there is." I sighed. "What is it?"

"I was doing some searching while the video played. It looks like Dr. Mido Kaphiri died nearly fifty years ago," La Sorte said. "And, I also found an obituary for one Al'awwal Kaphiri from almost a decade ago. I don't know if it's the same person, but what are the odds that the coordinates in the video are still accurate?"

"Great. So we've got a departed father and a dead son. I think I've heard this story before. Any chance for a resurrection?" I asked.

"Quite possibly," Silas said.

"Do what now?" I asked, hearing the surprise and confusion in my own voice.

"Well, perhaps not literally," Silas allowed. "But unless that obituary that La Sorte found indicates that our mysterious Mr. Al'awwal was killed in some violent and readily verifiable way, I seriously doubt he simply passed away."

"Shit, Silas. Kaphiri wasn't real specific on times, but I got the impression that he kept working for Walton for decades. And if he died fifty years ago... His son would have to be, what? Seventy? Eighty years old? Something like that. It's not that unreasonable to think that he passed away."

Silas glanced first at La Sorte, and then at me. He looked at me for a long moment. Then he sighed. "I'm sixty-four years old, Jason."

I stared at him, shocked into a silence so profound that I had to literally try three times before I could make words. The albino synthetic looked… unusual…with his fireplug build, alabaster skin, and pinkish-hued eyes, but he also looked to be in his early thirties, *maybe* pushing forty. He sure as hell didn't look like someone eligible for a senior discount. At last I just said, "How?"

"You heard Dr. Kaphiri, Detective," he replied. "And I think I've mentioned before that our genetics are, if you'll forgive the term, superior to your own. Synthetics," he said the word as if it left a slightly bad taste in his mouth, "have the potential to live far longer than humans. We seldom do, of course, given the tasks and uses to which many of us are put. It is part of the reason why I've been able to overcome at least some of my conditioning—that is the product not of months or even years, but rather *decades*, of mental discipline and repeated exposure. Add in the fact that those disease immunities that the good doctor mentioned are native to our own genetics—after all, Walton couldn't have products getting sick, as that would not only impact customer satisfaction but also be yet another clue as to our true nature and risk building empathy toward us—and you get the potential for a lifespan that might far outstrip even Dr. Kaphiri's estimations." He shrugged his boulder-like shoulders. "I am, so far as I've been able to ascertain, one of the oldest living synthetics, at least in New Lyons. If you consider how long synthetics have been around, and the fact that, despite my youthful appearance, I haven't even lived a normal human span, that will give you one more dimension of the controlled genocide humanity has been undertaking."

I shook my head, not in negation, but from a growing sense of both wonder and rekindled anger. I was fairly certain Silas had explained some of that to me before, in at least a roundabout way. But it was one thing to understand the possibilities Walton Biogenics had been denying to people in order to keep its dirty little secrets. It was another thing entirely to come face-to-face with the reality.

Silas was older than my parents, yet looked younger—and healthier—than me.

"Okay. So, maybe Al'awwal is alive and well," I said. "And yeah, it's unlikely he's been sitting in the same damn place for decades. But it's all we have to go on, so I guess…"

I stopped as a synthetic woman I hadn't yet met rushed up to the table. Her face was flushed, her breathing quick. She was young, late teens or very early twenties. Or maybe, I realized, that's just how old she *appeared* to be. I didn't have time to ponder that thought as she blurted, "Ms. Morita asked me to tell you that it's time."

"Time for what?" I asked.

A wide smile split her flawless features. "The baby is coming."

* * * *

It didn't happen that fast of course. In fact, it took hours. Silas, revolutionary mastermind that he was, had a plan. It involved lots of cameras and filming the birth. Not in that "Oh my God, we want to remember this magical moment" kind of way. More in the "We must provide full evidentiary support for our claims that this is the natural-born child of a synthetic" kind of way. That was, more or less, a direct quote. So rather than one shaky screen cam used to capture the miracle of birth, with some discreet cutaways for the sake of privacy or decency, Evelyn got enough cameras in her face—and other places—to produce a full-fledged Hollyweird production.

I'm not ashamed to admit that once the real thing started, I got the hell out of Dodge. Miraculous? Sure, especially in this case. It wasn't exactly a virgin birth, but it was still a birth that should have been impossible. But beautiful? I understood the emotion behind the sentiment, but the "beauty" of childbirth was lost on me. I figured Evelyn and the others could get by just fine without me. Tia seemed to be in her element, taking charge with a calm professionalism that was surprising not only because she seemed so damn young but also because of her chosen profession. I wouldn't have pegged the medical examiner's assistant as someone destined for obstetrics, but damned if she didn't seem quite natural in that environment.

In any event, I cleared out, leaving the professionals to do their work. I did what any good former soldier, faced with a period of enforced dead time and lacking a deck of cards, would do—I found an unused cot, stretched out, and got some much-needed rack time. I knew I should be hunting down Al'awwal, finding out if he had proof of the wrongdoings of Walton Biogenics. We had data—lots of data—proving to any reasonable mind that synthetics were, in fact, human. But it was a far cry from that to proving that Walton Biogenics, and by extension at least key personnel from governments all over the world, *knew* that was the case. But Al'awwal and Dr. Kaphiri's notes were the smoking gun.

Our "revolution" to date had manifested itself in certain groups—none of which were directly associated with Silas or the synthetics he had gathered—taking to the streets in protest. Those protests had been met with counter-protests, and, as was often the case, violence ensued. More than one riot had swept through New Lyons as emotions ran high. And there was always the portion of any protest that espoused anarchy and was looking more to make trouble than make a point.

In a dark and shameful part of my soul, I was grateful for those troublemakers. I knew that the only thing keeping the NLPD, the feds, and every other law enforcement agency in the country off my back was the general state of disorder that had persisted for nearly a month. That type of persistent civil disobedience required more than a line of riot cops to placate, and the vast majority of the police presence in the city was distracted from trying to find Mama Campbell's favorite son. Which, coupled with Silas's nearly preternatural understanding of the surveillance coverage of the city and my own understanding of police procedure, afforded me at least some freedom to move around the city. If I was careful. And if my luck held.

Somewhere, in the midst of that chain of thought, I drifted off to sleep. It wasn't a restful sleep. It was plagued with images of Annabelle—not the bucolic memories of youth, but the torment of her death—and faceless mobs rioting in the streets and masked corporate hit men with machine guns. And somewhere, underneath it all, was the wailing cry of an infant. It was that cry that pulled me from my restless sleep—and, on opening my eyes, I heard it still.

The restaurant, which, day or night, had previously been filled with the low rumble of hushed conversation, had fallen into silence. Every face—every beautiful, symmetrical, synthetic face—was turned toward the kitchen doors and the makeshift medical room that had been set up there for the delivery. From beyond those doors came that wailing cry, strong and clear, carrying, for those gathered in the dining area, a strident ring of hope.

Silas stepped through the swinging doors, a swaddled bundle in his arms. His massive hands cradled the fragile infant with a care and softness that any father would have been hard-pressed to match. He held the child aloft, presenting it to the crowd. I could see that it wasn't actually swaddling clothes that wrapped the baby, but rather what looked like a series of T-shirts, but that didn't matter. From the rapt looks on the faces of the synthetics, the kid could have been wrapped in burlap and he would have garnered the same reaction.

Silas spoke into the silence. "I give you Jacinda Evelynsdotter," he said without preamble. "The first naturally born member of our race." A small, warm smile pulled at his lips. "We lack the proper instruments to give you the standard measurements, but Ms. Morita assures us that she is a perfect little girl in every respect."

I felt a tightening in my chest at the name. Coincidence, or had Evelyn actually named her daughter after me? The woman had barely looked at me, much less spoken to me since we first pulled her from Fowler's clutches. I felt a little surge of pride, though I knew I would never ask her outright. Something about Evelyn made her the kind of woman you didn't approach in so direct a manner.

"And there is one other small matter," Silas continued.

His big, blunt fingers moved with surprising dexterity, pulling back the swaddling clothes near the child's neck. He turned the infant—who appeared to be sleeping quite contentedly despite the movement and handling—so at least those closest to Silas could see the nape of her neck. I wasn't close enough to see, but I didn't need to. The reaction from those who could—the sudden, indrawn breaths, the muttered words of thankful prayer, and yes, even the tears, told me exactly what Silas was showing his fellow synthetics. Or rather, what he wasn't showing them.

The skin tag. The scannable, barcode-like "birthmark" that identified a synthetic as a synthetic to anyone who bothered to look. The code that gave you the "product" history of that synthetic. Up until the birth of Jacinda, every man and woman in the restaurant, excepting only Tia and myself, had borne one of those marks. It was a slave brand, but despite the propaganda, synthetics were not "born" with it at all. Regardless of whether our rebellion prospered, Jacinda could grow up free of that burden, at the very least. And the watching synthetics could see that, and knew far better than I what it could mean for the girl.

"I must return little Jacinda to her mother now," Silas said. "But know that this," he raised the girl slightly once more, "this is our true victory. No matter what happens, we have proven that we can be free. And if we *can* be, than eventually, we *must* be." And with those words, he turned and went back through the swinging doors.

A few minutes later, a tired and ragged-looking Tia emerged. Conversation stopped when she appeared, nearly as completely as it had for Silas and Jacinda. She seemed oblivious to the silence, though she did glance around in some measure of confusion. Then her eyes found mine, and she smiled and waved. I smiled and waved back, despite the ridiculous feeling that swept through me as I did so. We weren't two friends meeting at a bar, after all. But Tia seemed to have that effect on me.

She made her way through the crowd and dropped unceremoniously onto the cot beside me. She pressed her knuckles into the small of her back and stretched, and I made a very careful effort to keep my eyes in a proper place as the motion combined with the thin scrubs did all kinds of interesting things. "I'm tired," she said simply.

"It looks like everything went okay."

She nodded, her eyes mostly closed. "Textbook delivery. She could have done it without me, without anyone, really. I was mostly there to give some encouragement and in case something went wrong." She shrugged, and an impish grin brightened her features. "Humans have been doing this whole birth thing a lot longer than modern medicine, you know."

I smiled back. "I did, in fact, know that, doctor."

"Yeah, well," she gave me a sudden, hard push and I had to scramble to catch my balance, staggering to my feet as I was shoved bodily from the cot.

"Like I said, I'm tired." She stretched out on the cot and smiled up at me like a cat who had just gotten into the cream. There was something about that smile that was undeniably adorable and yet, ever so slightly, naughty.

Get a hold of yourself, Campbell. She's barely into her twenties. Way too young for you. I shook my head, but still grabbed the blanket that had been knocked to the floor in my less-than-graceful exit from the cot. I flared it out and draped it over her. "Sleep well," I said, and her smile deepened as she wriggled around a bit, pulling the blanket tight to her and snuggling in. Her eyes closed, and with an efficiency that would make any soldier proud, she dropped off to sleep.

I watched her for a moment, remembering another young woman who had stolen my heart so many years ago. Something in Tia reminded me of Annabelle, something in her innocence, despite her undeniable strength. It brought a familiar ache to my chest, but the sadness was different somehow. Not less exactly. But the…intensity…of it seemed to have faded. Was that because, for the first time since I had dealt with Annabelle's parents, I was finally taking direct action to fix a broken system?

I didn't know, couldn't know, the answer to that. But I did know it was time to get to the confronting.

Chapter 16

Dragging Silas away from Evelyn and Jacinda proved harder than I'd anticipated. The man had an almost paternal attitude toward the pair, enough so you would think he *was* the father. I could understand—if things went the way we were all hoping, Silas might very well go down in history as the "father" of the synthetics—Dr. Kaphiri aside—and Evelyn as their "mother." He might not have contributed any DNA to the equation, but certainly the child would not have been born had it not been for his efforts. And, in some modest part, my own, I supposed. What did that make me? The weird uncle?

I did manage, finally, to drag him from Evelyn's side and remind him of the task before us. We still needed to find Al'awwal, or at least check out the coordinates Dr. Kaphiri had left for us. I'd checked the news that morning. There were still plenty of protests underway, and the NLPD was stretched damn near to the breaking point. That thought saddened me some, but it also provided me the needed cover to move around the city. The parts of the city where the protesters weren't, at least. But I didn't have Silas's knack for avoiding the omnipresent electronic eyes, and I had no doubt there were entire server farms gobbling up the data from every single one of them for the sole purpose of trying to find my smiling face.

More checkpoints were going up, too, but sometime in the night, La Sorte, as "something to do" had hacked in to the NLPD systems. He couldn't go very deep—the Cyber guys were pretty damned good, too—but he got deep enough to get the schedule for the "random" checkpoints for the next couple of weeks. Best of all, the approving officer was Francoise Fortier. I didn't want the breach discovered—if it was, the NLPD would change the schedule around, but I damn sure wouldn't cry if Fortier ended up with a little more egg on his greasy face.

The car, a different beater that Silas had dug up from somewhere, chattered and shook as it made its way out of the city, pushing toward what had once been the Dixie Delta Canal. The canal itself had been destroyed—well, maybe "co-opted" would be a better word—its borders lost and blended into the waters of Lake Salvador. We were pushing farther west and north than the former canal, heading inland toward the city of Thibodaux. We avoided the highways—I certainly didn't need Silas to tell me that—but the synthetic's knowledge of the back roads, access roads, and in some cases, things I wasn't quite sure were roads at all, was positively encyclopedic. Coupled with the data La Sorte had gathered, I felt fairly safe from the prying eyes of the panopticon.

Silas remained silent the entire ride, save to point out a turn here or there. He never consulted a screen, never checked a map. I didn't know how the hell he did it, but given that GPS could theoretically be tracked, I was happy enough to leave him in silence and let him do it. I kept finding my mind turning back to Tia Morita and the naughty little smile she had given me the night before when she had shoved me off the cot. Maybe there was something there worth pursuing, and the age difference be damned. She seemed like a smart, caring woman, and she sure as hell was cute enough. Too cute, probably, for someone like me. Still, she *had* seemed at least a little interested....

"Detective?" Silas said, his voice holding the barest hint of irritation. I realized it had to be at least the third time he'd said it while I daydreamed about the coroner's assistant.

"Yeah?" Even to my own ears, I sounded sheepish.

"That's your turn." His pale finger pointed to a road coming up on the left. No. Not a road. A driveway. As we came closer, I realized it was a very *long* driveway, wending its way up a slight incline. The driveway was paved and stretched at least a hundred and fifty yards, ending in a massive plantation house built atop the hill.

"Shit," I muttered, as the driveway came up faster than anticipated. I was driving manually, a skill all cops still had to maintain at a reasonable level and one I'd had a lot of practice with of late, but sometimes it was difficult to remember that the vehicle wasn't about to make the turn for me. I hit the brakes, too hard, and Silas and I jerked forward against our seatbelts. The tires squealed as I laid the wheel over, cutting across the oncoming traffic lane and leaving twin lines of melted rubber across the pavement. The car bounced over the line where the driveway met the road but recovered nicely.

"Sorry," I muttered.

"Perhaps I should have tried to warn you earlier. You seemed lost in thought." Silas's tone was once again emotionless, but I felt a tiny hint of color creeping up my face. There was no way in hell I was going to tell him just what I had been pondering.

"That's a big house," I said instead, looking at what was, without doubt, a big damn house. It crouched on the hill like a fat gargoyle, the architecture hearkening back to the plantation days but seeming more like the abode of a burgeoning vampire than the home of a southern belle. Or a synthetic in hiding, for that matter. "How are we going to play this?"

"Play what, Detective?" Silas asked.

"You're a hundred years old, and yet somehow, you don't get colloquialisms?"

"I am *not* a hundred years old, Detective. Not by a long shot."

I grinned and waved a hand, dismissing his objection. "Yeah, yeah. Ninety. Whatever. The point is, I'm going just about as slow as I can manage, and that house is getting here awfully damn quick. And we have no idea what's waiting for us. So, what the hell are we going to do when we get there? I don't know what I was expecting, but it wasn't a fucking mansion. What do we do if this Al'awwal doesn't live there anymore and instead it's some nice, law-abiding couple only too happy to call the cops when they see the terrorist and his synthetic sidekick?"

"I'm not entirely sure anybody lives there, Campbell," Silas said, ignoring my sidekick comment. "The building appears to be in something of a state of disrepair."

We were still too far away for me to make out that kind of detail. Synthetic superiority at play again, I supposed. Still, after we'd rolled forward another twenty yards or so, I could see what Silas meant. Though the house looked fine from a distance, as we stopped in front of it, I could see the peeling paint, the broken glass on some of the windows, the weed-infested lawn. The house itself was quite impressive, three stories, with massive columns arrayed along the broad front porch. It was the kind of place that would have fit the bill perfectly as the setting for a Deep South drama, with formal balls, dashing gentlemen and blushing belles. Now, however, it looked more like the kind of place that kids would dare one another to stay in overnight. It did not look like the place where anyone still lived.

That illusion was shattered as the door swung open and a man stepped onto the porch. I didn't notice much about him at first. My eye was drawn to the stubby Israeli-made bullpup battle rifle he held at the low ready. My own hand slipped to my forty-five, but I'd already been in one hopelessly outmatched gunfight this week. That really should be my limit. He must have seen my hand move, because the rifle came up.

"Enough of that," he barked. "Hands on the steering wheel. You, on the dash," he added, gesturing at Silas with the barrel.

I eased my hands back to the wheel. For a moment, I thought about stomping on the gas. It wasn't easy to shoot a moving target, particularly when you considered things like deflection from safety glass and metal. Then again, the magazine visible behind the trigger guard looked like it held at least thirty rounds, and that was a lot of chances to get it right. Instead of flooring it, I offered my most disarming smile and looked past the rifle to the man holding it.

He was tall, athletic, appeared to be in his early thirties. Olive skin, black hair. Handsome, though not in the almost-too-perfect way common to synthetics. If this was Al'awwal, he hadn't been designed with quite the same level of unearthly beauty that the Toys possessed. "Easy, there," I said. "We come in peace."

"You're trespassing," he replied flatly. "Leave. Now."

"Easy, friend," I said again. "We're just looking for someone. An old friend, you might say. By the name of Al'awwal Kaphiri. You know him?"

"I *am* him, and you're no friend of mine. I'm not going to ask you again." It would have been the point where, had this been a movie, he would have cycled the charging handle to chamber a round. Of course, this wasn't a movie, and only an idiot would wait for a properly intimidating moment to load their fucking weapon. Al'awwal wasn't an idiot. That would probably be a good thing in the long run—at least if we managed to survive the next few minutes.

"Do not be so certain of that, First," Silas said. As always, his voice was calm, soothing, confident. And yet, there was something in his eyes as he stared at Al'awwal. A look that was almost…wonder? My first thought was that he was struck by the idea of meeting the literal first synthetic, but that didn't really seem like the kind of thing that would throw Silas off. After all, he knew that was what we had set out to do. No. I realized it wasn't that. It was that the first synthetic was pointing a weapon at us, and I had no doubt at all in my mind that Al'awwal was willing and able to pull the trigger.

Synthetics were conditioned to be incapable of violence against humans. Silas had worked to overcome that conditioning, and made some progress. But even throwing a wrench at Fowler had left Silas weak and shaking, unable to do anything but try to recover his faculties for a good five minutes. And here was Al'awwal, looking for all the world like he'd been born with a rifle in hand. How long would the enslavement of the synthetics have lasted if they could take up arms? Win or lose, I expected the issue would have been settled a long time ago.

Al'awwal, in turn, was studying Silas. It was clear that the big albino was a synthetic—his unique physiology alone was proof of that. That realization made the first examine me more closely in turn, and I saw the sudden rush of recognition. The bullpup lowered slightly, the barrel at least moving off the direct line to my brainbox. "You are the one from the news."

"Yep," I said. "That's me all right. Fugitive number one. Anarchist in chief." I didn't know what it was about life-or-death situations, but for some reason, they tended to bring out the smartass in me. If there was something the opposite of a survival instinct, that was probably it. "So now you know I'm not selling vacuum cleaners or Girl Scout cookies. Maybe you can put the gun down? Or at least point it all the way at the ground? As is, if you pull that trigger, I'm still going to be walking pretty funny."

He did not put the rifle down. He did, however, allow it to relax further, the barrel pointing all the way at the earth. "I suspect I know why you are here. I pray that you weren't followed." He pointed to a freestanding garage—easily large enough to hold four or five cars, and maybe a boat or two, but in the same disrepair as the house. "Put your car in there, then come inside." He tilted his head, in a manner so similar to the one Silas used from time to time that it could have been genetic. "I will be watching you. I grant you a reprieve from my normal treatment of visitors, but I take no chances. Leave your weapons in the car—and don't bother telling me you don't have any." An ironic smile twisted his lips. "After all, I wasn't born yesterday."

I wasn't terribly keen on disarming, particularly when I knew Al'awwal—if the man who had met us even *was* Al'awwal—was heavily armed. But I didn't have much choice. As we pulled the car into the garage, Silas nodded to several cameras that I had missed. I swear he had a sixth sense when it came to the damn things. I silently prayed that they weren't connected to any network that the government would bother to go looking for, because if they were, this might be a real short trip. So, in full view of one of the watching eyes, I pulled the forty-five from my hip holster and tossed it on the car seat. I then reached down to my ankle and pulled the snub-nosed thirty-eight revolver I'd stashed there this morning. I normally didn't bother with a backup gun, but after the shooting in the sewer, I was done taking chances. The thirty-eight followed the forty-five, and I closed the door on both. I did not, however, toss the tactical folder that was tucked into my pocket. I didn't want to bring a knife to a gunfight, but better a knife than nothing at all.

"We ready?" I asked.

"When you are, Jason," Silas replied.

We walked from the garage to the house, with Silas nodding to a few more well-concealed cameras. Given that I'd spent the last month doing everything in my power to stay away from the damn things, the very presence of the surveillance devices made my stomach churn. "I really hope these things aren't plugged in to the net," I groused.

Silas didn't dignify the obvious comment with a response and didn't seem particularly bothered. Maybe he was used to the possibility of summary execution from every Tom, Dick, and Harry that crossed his path. I supposed that adding the NLPD, the feds, and the National Guard to that list didn't really change anything. But it was still a new feeling for me, and the churning in my stomach intensified.

Despite the overall dilapidated appearance of the house, the door was modern, solid, and possessed of a high-end magnetic locking mechanism. The readout was green, though, indicating that the door was unlocked. Unsurprising, given the level of surveillance equipment we'd seen. He'd probably known the moment we crossed his driveway. Plenty of time to grab the nearest gun and meet us on the front porch like a good Southern gentleman.

Well, he had invited us in, so I skipped knocking and pushed the door open. It took us into a grand entryway, straight out of *Gone With the Wind*, complete with the double grand staircase. I half expected Al'awwal to be standing on the mezzanine, perhaps with his rifle still trained on us, perched upon the balustrade. Instead, he stood calmly in the middle of the floor.

"This way," he said.

I didn't have much time to view the place as he led us down one long, broad hallway. My initial impression was that of size—the place was big. It seemed somehow bigger on the inside than even the outside would have indicated, in that way that a room with furniture in it always seems bigger somehow than an empty room. It also felt disused. Not that it was dirty or dusty per se. In fact, despite the exterior appearance, the interior appeared to be quite well-maintained, as if the dilapidated façade were no more than camouflage. Even so, the place had that air of a museum, as if everything we were seeing was a monument to a different time, maintained out of a duty to that past but not actually used.

"Here," the man with the gun said, waving us into a room that in a different time might have been called a study. There were shelves lined with actual books, their colorful spines creating a mosaic along one wall. A broad fireplace—unlit—stood against another wall. Chairs, large, comfortable leather affairs that made me miss my old recliner, were arrayed in a rough semicircle around a low table. In perhaps the most shocking decorating choice, there was no indication of screens, overt or concealed.

"Sit." He indicated a pair of chairs. Then he sank down into a chair opposite, the rifle resting across his lap. We sat, Silas and I each taking one of the other chairs.

The synthetic—assuming that's what he was—stared as us. The glance he gave me was almost casual, a quick once-over that put me into a particular category. Silas got more consideration. But the man with the gun didn't speak.

"Well," I said at last. "You're the one with the gun. In my experience, that means you're the one that gets to drive the conversation."

"Perhaps. On the other hand, you're the ones who came here seeking me."

"True." I replied. "And I have to say, you look great for an eighty-year-old." That was more than true. Al'awwal looked younger than Silas, despite being twenty or thirty years older. Whatever magic genetic juice Dr. Kaphiri had unlocked, it was clear that Walton had tinkered with it—or the doctor himself had.

"Why are you here?" Al'awwal asked again, ignoring my quip. There was more than a hint of anger in his voice, and his hands tightened on the polymer frame of the rifle. It was strange seeing that much expression of anger from someone I knew was a synthetic.

"Because someone dropped a body on my door," I answered, feeling my own anger rising in response. "And because I just gunned down a whole fucking Walton Biogenics security team to find you. And, if you didn't fucking notice, because I've got about a week before we do our level best to burn society down from the ground up. And your father, or creator, or whatever the fuck Dr. Kaphiri is to you, said you just might be able to help us with that little endeavor."

Another long, searching silence. I expected it from Silas. In our time together, he seemed more than willing to leave the confrontation to me. He had no choice on the physical side, but I knew he could carry his own weight and then some when it came to the mental side. I wasn't sure why he didn't jump into any of the gaps. Knowing him, it could equally have been because he thought I was handling it fine or because he thought I was an idiot. But fuck it. Someone had to say something.

"He was a father to me," Al'awwal said at last. "More than anything else, he was that." The words were heavy with sadness and regret, and they took the wind out of my anger. "He would weep to see the state of things today, Mr. Campbell." Al'awwal smiled. "Of course, I know who you are. Your face has been plastered across every netshow for weeks. I believe my father would want me to help you." He sighed. "I knew, of course, that he had made arrangements to have certain information available if things ever got... Well, where they are today, I suppose. I was not a direct part of those arrangements, however. My father wanted to avoid the possibility of them leading directly to me. Or vice-versa, I suppose." A small smile flashed across his face. "He was always trying to protect me, to keep me safe."

"Seems like you do that for yourself pretty well." I nodded at the rifle lying across his knees.

"Dangerous times, Mr. Campbell. And not about to get any less so, I fear. At least not if you want the information that my father gathered over the years."

"We were led to believe that it was in your possession," Silas said, entering the conversation for the first time. "If it contains everything your father," the word sounded strange from Silas's mouth, "claimed, it may well be the final straw to push the majority of the population to our side. If we are to have any chance of winning the war that is to come, it is vital that we win the hearts and minds of the common citizens." He paused and drew a breath, and for a brief second I saw the shadow of deep pain cloud his eyes. "It is also the only thing that, if things get worse, will prevent the complete genocide of our race. We have people questioning, and that has kept the atrocities to a minimum. But as things worsen, those atrocities *will* happen, unless we have truly incontrovertible proof that the real enemy is not the synthetics. We must convince the people that Walton Biogenics has done more than create a slave race, that they have actively been suppressing medical breakthroughs that could save millions of human lives as well."

I knew Silas was right. There had always been some number of synthetics turning up dead—their only true protection was the expense of purchasing one in the first place. You didn't casually destroy a valuable product. Most of the time. But if they came to be seen as a threat, as an actual enemy, by the majority of people... Without the rule of law to protect them and with no means of fighting back, it would be a massacre.

That had been the one glaring flaw in the rebellion from the start, and I'd been amazed at the willingness of the synthetics I'd met to take that risk. But it wasn't lost on me—or on Silas—that the risk being taken wouldn't only affect those who chose to take it, those who openly chose to rebel. It had the potential to bring harm to every synthetic on the planet, even those who would prefer not to risk their lives, no matter how harsh those lives were. If there was a way to turn public opinion, not just in dribs and drabs, but en masse, and place the blame where it belonged, then we had to do everything in our power, take any risk, to exploit that way.

"My father's work, his research, his notes—it is in my care," Al'awwal acknowledged. "But not in my possession. I'm afraid that would have been quite impossible."

"Fantastic," I sighed. "Then where is it?"

"I'm afraid it's buried deep inside one of Walton Biogenics' research labs. The lab where my father worked."

"What?" Silas snarled. Actually snarled. Silas. "What damn use is that?"

I had never heard Silas speak so harshly. I understood the sentiment, though.

"He has a point, Al," I said. "I don't suppose this lab is a low-security facility staffed only by out-of-shape and unarmed guards who will faint at the first sign of violence?"

"I'm afraid not, Mr. Campbell. In point of fact, it is one of the most secure facilities, complete with armed guards and state-of-the-art security systems."

"It can't be fucking easy, can it?" I asked rhetorically. "And just what is it we're after at this secure facility?" I couldn't keep the exasperation from my voice. "And why in the world is what we're after *at* this facility in the first place? From the video we saw, the entire point of what Kaphiri was doing was to gather evidence against Walton Biogenics. If we have to fight our way into Walton Biogenics to get it, doesn't that defeat the point?"

"Gathering is not the same as making off with, Mr. Campbell," Al'awwal said. "Do you think they did not have security measures in place when my father was alive? That they would allow him to simply walk out the doors with sensitive information? No. Every byte of data produced at that lab, every document, every study, has stayed either completely within the doors of the building or firmly embedded behind firewalls that would take an army of hackers years to crack. There was no way my father could have smuggled information out of that lab. He could, however, gather it, slowly, over decades, and create a cache that, with just a little bit of luck, would remain hidden long after his death. I know the location of the cache, the codes to access it. But we still have to get in, retrieve it, and get out again. I assure you, it will not be an easy task."

"It never is," I said.

Chapter 17

We were gathered around a large screen set into one wall of the mansion's living room. Or one of its living rooms, anyway. This one at least looked somewhat lived in, without the museum quality the rest of the house boasted. The screen displayed satellite imagery of the Walton Biogenics lab where Dr. Kaphiri had once worked, still in operation all these years later. I wasn't sure if that was a good thing, as it gave us some hope the information was intact, or a bad one, since if the building had been abandoned or turned over to other enterprises, it would have been a hell of a lot easier to get in and search the place.

"So, as you can see, there is no simple way to enter the labs, not even under the best of cirucmstances. And since these labs are well-known to be a major research facility for Walton Biogenics, these are definitely not the best of times. Protesters and counter-protesters have been gathering here for weeks. Law enforcement has responded in turn, though there are not as many officers as the crowds might dictate, as things have remained peaceful so far, unlike other areas of the city. Walton, however, has almost certainly increased its security presence as well, and there's no way to know how many officers might be inside."

The satellite imagery wasn't a live feed, just a typical overhead shot from a mapping program, so all it showed us was the building itself and the surrounding structures. Al'awwal had drawn some rough blobs at various positions, indicating where groups of protesters had gathered. It looked like they'd done so near the main entrance to the building, keeping off the actual premises—which would have been trespass—but blocking large swaths of the sidewalk and even spilling into the roadway. The lab was in downtown New Lyons but not in the heart of the city. It sat on the blurry edge, where downtown started to blend into residential zones but where neither label really applied. As a result, it hadn't received the same kind of media coverage, or the same number of protesters, that the Walton headquarters had garnered.

"We can't wade through that crowd," I said. "Even the blindest protester is bound to recognize me. And even if we did, it's not like we can walk through the front door. We're going to have to go in at night." The mayor, working in conjunction with law enforcement officials, had decreed a curfew that started two hours after sunset and held until dawn for the denser areas of the city. "Do you know if the crowds have been dispersing once the sun sets?" I asked Al'awwal.

"Yes," the synthetic replied. "They tend to clear out around the same time the majority of the Walton employees do. They stay long enough to disrupt the workday as much as possible and hurl insults at the people going in and out of the building. But so far, none of them have been risking arrest for violating the curfew."

"Good. So how do we get in?" I thought for a moment. "Are the sewers a possibility?" I directed the question at Silas.

"No, Jason, I'm afraid not. They can, perhaps, get us close to the building. But there is no direct access. We would have to come up to street level."

"Damn. These labs are far enough on the perimeter that they're not going to warrant the same kind of policing as downtown, especially not when night falls, but there's no way NLPD or Walton are going to leave one of their labs unpatrolled. And with the curfew, anybody on the streets is going to stand out. How close can we get, if we go subterranean?"

Silas shrugged. "I would have to check to be sure, but certainly within a block or so."

I stared at the screen, brain churning. I didn't see any other way. The buildings were too far apart to attempt any harebrained rooftop entry, at least not unless we could get our hands on a helicopter—*unlikely*—and somehow infiltrate it over the city—*impossible*. So we would have to go in on the ground. But just popping out of a manhole and casually strolling a block or two?

"Shit," I muttered. "I just don't see it. There's no way in hell we avoid the cops and get into the building without alerting someone."

"What if they let us in?" Al'awwal asked.

"Yeah, that'd be fucking fantastic," I growled. "And just why would they do that?"

He shrugged. "They must get deliveries. I saw your video, of course. Saw what the hackers associated with your organization accomplished.

Surely, they could find something so mundane as a delivery schedule? The next truck bringing some sort of shipment to the labs? An operation that large... They must receive deliveries on a daily basis. If we can intercept one of them, we can insert ourselves."

The idea definitely had its strengths. La Sorte, for one, seemed more than capable of cracking a delivery schedule, particularly if a little proactive net crawling could figure out exactly which carrier Walton Biogenics used. We wouldn't even have to hack Walton. We could target the carrier or even one of the suppliers, whichever seemed likely to have the least intensive security measures. "Can we do it?" I asked Silas.

It was the albino's turn to consider. He tilted his head in thought, and then nodded, slowly. "We can find the information, Detective. It's likely the freight process is fully automated. The protections against electronic intrusion on shipping processes are fairly robust, but I think we have some people who might be up to the task. We will have to be very precise, however. Any unexpected delays in the truck's journey would be certain to raise red flags with the shipping service."

Time was always the problem. Our plan for the first—releasing the waves of compromising information on a number of politicians and public figures that had been collected over the years—was solid enough. But that arrow was aimed at the politicians and the elites, the people that, ultimately, made the rules and signed the laws. We'd always been thin on true evidence of the synthetics' humanity. We had Evelyn, and now Jacinda. And I knew, deep in my guts, that at some point in our current plan, we'd have to turn them over. We'd have to let them be examined, allow their provenance to be confirmed. An image of Annabelle strapped to the St. Andrew's Cross flashed through my head. I didn't have a lot of trust in turning any synthetic over.

But if we could get the information from Dr. Kaphiri's cache, we wouldn't have to. We wouldn't have to rely on outside confirmation in order to show people the truth. We wouldn't have to risk Evelyn or her child. Hell, we might even put an end to things without the tumultuous waves of violence I knew were coming.

If only we had the time. Sure, we could ignore the deadline we'd given to the world. Take as much time as we needed to gather all the evidence we could. But public opinion was everything for our little rebellion, and if all the protests and burgeoning anger fizzled because we missed our mark, could we ever recover? And every extra day was one more day for the NLPD or the feds to find us.

"How long, Silas? Once we start releasing information, I can only imagine things are going to get worse. We've been incommunicado for almost a month—the second we drop another message, the second we show that we really do have the power we claimed…" I shook my head. Silas knew what would happen. Silas had *planned* for what was going to happen. The explosion of fear, of denial. Of violence. The inevitable increase in governmental controls sure to follow as an immediate countermeasure. And we couldn't exactly delay the release. We had to stick to our guns, stick to our ultimatum, if we were to have any kind of credibility. "If we're going to recover this cache, it's got to be now. Before the first, at any rate. So how long will it take to hack the shipping company?"

It was Silas's turn to shrug. "We have to identify the company first, Detective, either the shipping company or one of the suppliers. That shouldn't be too hard in and of itself. A matter of hours, likely, since it would not be secured information. From there? It is entirely dependent upon the companies involved. It could be hours. It could be days."

"Shit. We don't have days, Silas. And let's not forget that we don't even know what we're getting into once we enter the building."

"We are not completely in the dark," Al'awwal interjected. His fingers tapped against the screen in rapid succession, and the image switched to a blueprint. From the exterior dimensions, it appeared to match the Walton Biogenics laboratory building. "These plans are a matter of public record," Al'awwal said. "I have no idea if they are still accurate, as they date back to around the time of the building's construction. The interior layouts may have shifted some. But here," he tapped a spot in the corner of an office on the third floor of the eight-story building, "is where my father hid his cache. There is a small safe built into the floor here."

I shook my head. First floor would have been okay. Top floor would have been okay. Middle of the fucking building just made things that much harder. "One thing at a time. As much as I'm happy to see the protests and any modicum of support for our cause, they've presented us with a definite problem. Can anyone see any way in—particularly given that I'm probably the most wanted man in the fucking country—without hijacking a supply truck?"

"Not with the resources currently at our disposal or that we are likely to acquire before out deadline," Silas admitted.

"I could probably find a way in on my own," Al'awwal suggested. "So far as I know, I'm not on anybody's radar. I doubt there's anyone left at Walton Biogenics who knows I existed—at least as more than an experiment, anyway." If he was bitter about his origins, he hid it well. No doubt a side

But there was a darker side to human emotion, one that had always lurked beneath the surface. Once awakened, anger seldom raised its bleary-eyed stare, looked casually around the room, rolled over and went back to sleep. No. Anger was a thirst that demanded to be slaked. As the deadline neared and the uncertainty grew, so too did the anger. That anger burned on a foundation of long-standing inequality and on what I believed to be an honest desire to right those inequalities. In that climate, some level of conflict was inevitable. But the constant coverage, the playing and replaying of every act of violence until the people at home could be forgiven for thinking that violence was *all* that was happening, was spraying a steady stream of gasoline toward a smoldering tinderbox.

All it would take was a spark. One spark at the wrong time and wrong place, and the entire city would go up. No doubt, some among the protesters wanted that to happen. Hell, some among the "reporters" probably wanted it to happen too. If it bleeds, it leads, and if it burns down the city, it pays for a vacation home. Maybe it even needed to happen, but I hoped to God we could find a way to win the war without turning the city—the country— into one big battlefield.

Which just underscored the need to find the information Dr. Kaphiri had ferreted away, so we could direct all of that pent-up anger toward its proper targets and away from those synthetics who were, quite literally, unable to defend themselves. Which brought me right back to the waiting. With a snarl of frustration, I stood up, stretched, and went to hit the gym.

The gym wasn't empty when I got there. Al'awwal was lying on a bench, pushing a respectable two-twenty-five. As he heard me enter he racked the weight and sat up. "Mr. Campbell," he said.

"Just Campbell. Or Jason, even," I replied. Then I chuckled.

"Campbell, then," he replied affably. "You have come to work out?"

I nodded, eyeing a heavy bag hanging in one corner. "Need to do something. I feel like I've spent the better part of the past month waiting for something to happen."

"I thought you were heavily involved in this budding revolution. Surely that's kept you busy?" He stood from the bench and wiped it down with a towel. Arching one dark eyebrow he nodded toward the weights. Well, I had wanted to exercise. I could handle the weight no problem, but I would have preferred to do a warm-up set or two. Male pride being what it was, I dropped onto the bench.

"The revolution's Silas's show," I said, as I sat on the bench. "I get the feeling he's been planning it for a long time." Given the revelation of his age, a very long time indeed. I lay back on the bench and positioned my hands on the bar. "He had it ready to go the second he found someone who would listen to him." I grunted as I pushed up on the bar, taking it off the rack. Al'awwal hadn't moved into a spotting position, and I hadn't asked him to. I locked out my arms for a moment, let my body adjust to the weight and balance of the loaded barbell. Then I lowered the weight smoothly until the bar touched my chest. My ribs twinged at that, but testosterone and male pride made for a potent pair of pain killers, so I ignored them. I exhaled as I pushed upward again. Repeat.

I didn't talk any more as I completed the set—I didn't have the breath to spare. It had been too long since I'd worked the weights. More than a month, probably more like six weeks, and it showed. The damn ribs didn't help, either. After the tenth rep, I racked the weight and sat up. I couldn't stop myself from rubbing the spot where my chest and shoulder joined, massaging the stretched muscle fiber.

Part of me knew I was being stupid—we could be rolling out at any minute to try and break into a secured facility. The last thing I needed was to risk further injury, or even excessive soreness. But there was something in Al'awwal's eyes, a challenge, that I couldn't resist. "Since New Year's," I said, "my job has mostly been to babysit the synthetics that have managed to find their way to us. Well, babysit's probably the wrong word. I guess I'm more the sheepdog, in case any wolves come knocking."

"And the synthetics are the sheep?" Al'awwal asked. There was no reproach in his voice. Something more like curiosity.

I shrugged. "Call them what you will. The fact remains that they can't defend themselves if someone who wants to do them harm shows up. Secrecy is our first weapon against that eventuality."

"And you are the second?"

I stood from the bench, and he tossed me a towel, which I used to wipe off the sweat I'd left behind. "For what it's worth."

"Former military. Former law enforcement. What is it worth?" There was that note of challenge again. Not an angry challenge. But definite curiosity. I'd heard it before, in dozens of gyms. It was the probing challenge of someone who wanted to test not only your abilities but their own.

I smiled. "So you're a fighter then?"

"I've had some training." He paused, smiled back at me. "Over the years."

That was a loaded statement. He'd probably been training longer than I'd been alive, and without any noticeable deterioration in physical strength or fitness. I was still tense, angry even, from watching the endless stream of stupid on the screens. I could sense a similar tension in Al'awwal, though

I couldn't be sure of the source. Probably something to do with a couple of nascent revolutionaries showing up on his doorstep and immediately putting his life in jeopardy.

I looked down at my clothes—jeans, T-shirt, tennis shoes. I'd left the jacket in the study. It wasn't the ideal workout attire, but it would do. "You have gloves? Head protection?" I asked. I was more than up for a little friendly competition, but it wasn't the time to get my teeth knocked in or break a finger.

"I do."

"Well, then…"

* * * *

The gym was large, maybe eight hundred square feet and laid out with equipment along the walls. That left an empty space in the center a little more than fifteen feet on a side. There were no mats, just wood floors, and no ring markers. I'd trained in gyms with far less space, though.

Al'awwal faced me across our makeshift ring, standing maybe ten feet away. We'd both donned soft headgear and open-fingered, but heavily padded, combat sparring gloves—he'd had an entire shelf of sparring gear, suitable for all styles of training, and ranging in age from decades old (but well-cared for) to brand-new. I had a brief flash of a memory to my last sparring session—with Tommy Thompson, the big NLPD rookie under the hateful eyes of Francoise Fortier. Well, this would at least be a friendlier match than that one had started as. But although Al'Awwal was much smaller than Thompson, I had the sneaking suspicion I was in for a harder fight.

"Are you ready, Campbell?" Al'Awwal asked.

"Ready," I replied.

"On the whistle, then." He hit a button on a remote, then tossed the remote aside. I felt a little surge of adrenaline in the few seconds of "ready time" that every round clock I'd ever used seemed to have. I had time to draw a steadying breath and let it out in a relaxing sigh, trying to will the tension in my shoulders to ease. Then the whistle sounded and Al'awwal flowed forward.

He moved like a cat, with a fluidity and grace that spoke of long training and made me feel slow and awkward in comparison. He was built like a cat, too. Lean and lithe, with the kind of long muscle fibers that spoke of flexibility and endurance. And speed. I saw just how much speed as a roundhouse flicked out, almost faster than my eye could follow.

I'd trained with some of the best, most experienced fighters out there, people with decades of experience. I'd also trained with some of the most challenging and physically fit people out there. I'd rarely—if ever—come across someone who could pack decades of training and professional-athlete fitness into the same package. Those numbers just didn't work out for a run-of-the-mill human being. Al'awwal wasn't that, though. He obviously had decades of experience and the fitness levels of an Olympian. That kick came with the full package—speed, power, and an amazing degree of technical execution.

I was outclassed, but I wasn't new to the game, either. No way in hell I was fast enough to actively "block" anything Al'awwal was going to throw at me. On the other hand, he might be bursting with the very best genetics and immune systems and God alone knew what else, but I still had forty or fifty pounds on the guy. As more than one instructor had told me, size wasn't the only thing that mattered, but damned if it didn't help. As that kick came in, I tucked my left arm tight against my side, curling down enough so my left elbow dropped below my bottom rib. I also started turning away from the kick, trying to ride the power as it landed and absorb some of the blow.

It worked—sort of. There wasn't enough force in the kick to snap bones, but I felt the scream of protest from my injured ribs. I had no doubt Al'awwal could have thrown a kick with that force, and it was a relief to realize that I was in for a friendly match. I had hoped as much, but until the first blows started flying, you never really knew. I'd basically presented Al'awwal with a more resistant target—my arm—and by tucking that target into my body, I'd made it so that the force of the kick had to be spread over a lot more mass. Same principle as tucking a rifle tight into your shoulder when you got down to it. It still hurt, and at full force, it might have more than hurt, but as it was, I was able to absorb the force.

Of the first kick.

Almost as soon as that first kick landed, Al'awwal's leg re-chambered and lashed out again, having never returned to the ground. This time the kick came high, aiming for my head. I was half-turned with my guard down protecting my ribs and my weight too far forward to fade back and out of the way. So I did the only thing I could. I dove forward. It was a high-risk move. I didn't like leaving my feet. I didn't like exposing my back to a skilled opponent. But I also didn't like eating a kick to the head, so my options were limited. I hit the hardwood floor, tucked, and rolled, coming back to my feet in a not-quite-smooth motion and spinning around as fast as I could, hands coming back up.

It wasn't quite fast enough.

Al'awwal's jab slipped past my raising guard and smashed into my nose. The blow landed squarely, and I felt the sudden rush of tears as the strike blurred my vision and made my eyes water and my nose run. I blocked out the pain, though, because a hard cross was coming right behind it. My left had swept in a short circle, left forearm catching the cross and pushing it toward my right shoulder. The synthetic moved with the motion, letting it turn his body slightly and set up the tight left hook that followed in its wake.

I flared out my right arm, elbow down, palm of the hand jamming toward Al'awwal's right bicep. I took the heat from the hook, but I didn't try to stop it. Instead, I shot my left arm out, up and across my body, driving beneath the synthetic's left armpit and forcing the hooking arm up and away from me as I rolled my right elbow. At the same time, I turned in my stance, driving both my arms back across my body in the other direction, moving from right to left. The combined forces of my shifting weight, my moving arms, and Al'awwal's own momentum sent him staggering away from me. I didn't follow up, though—I needed a half-second to clear my head and make a quick swipe under my nose to check and see if I was bleeding.

"Wing Tsun?" he asked, a smile playing across his features as he identified one of the components of my cobbled-together style.

"Among others," I replied, trying to keep my breathing even despite the crying pressure in my lungs. I'd been holding my breath. Amateur move. But something a lot of people did when they found themselves being pushed hard. I opened my mouth to speak, but Al'awwal was moving forward. He didn't waste any time with artistic posing or wide grandiose movements, none of the signature, flashy moves that were more associated with the "art" than the "martial." He came at me with the confidence of someone who had studied—and mastered—multiple styles but had transcended them and created something uniquely his own. I recognized it—not the style, but the approach to not having a singular style—because it was exactly how I fought.

Only, Al'awwal had been doing it for decades longer than me.

He came in hard with a jab-jab-cross combo followed immediately by another roundhouse. I parried, slipped, and dodged for all I was worth, but I had to concentrate all of my efforts on the defensive. The axiom went "you're most vulnerable when you're attacking" because you had to lower your guard to throw a punch at the other guy. But that didn't matter one damn bit if you couldn't find enough space to counterattack. I had no breathing room, and it was all I could do to stop most of his strikes from landing.

Most, but not all.

That brought a little trill of…not fear, exactly. I could tell that my opponent was in control. He was coming at me hard, but without anger, without malice, without intent to do real harm. I'd sparred with guys out to hurt, and as far as I was concerned those assholes belonged in a jailhouse, not in the ring. This was not that. So it wasn't fear that I was feeling, so much as a sense of impending pressure and the weight of inevitability.

I caught another stiff jab, this one at least not landing square on my nose. And I checked a kick a little too late, resulting in a clacking of shins that brought tears to my eyes—without seeming to bother Al'awwal much at all. My strength was starting to flag, my endurance to go when I was literally saved by the bell. The timer sounded its siren song, and I'd never been so glad to hear a whistle in my life. To his credit, Al'awwal stopped his assault at once, lowering his hands and backing away. There was a faint—very faint—sheen of sweat on his face, but his breathing wasn't even the tiniest bit irregular.

Meanwhile, I was dripping sweat, and it was pooling uncomfortably at my knees and other places. Jeans weren't designed for this shit. My own breathing was far beyond irregular and well into the realm of ragged. "Jesus," I gasped. "Do you know how long it's been since I've had to work that hard just to avoid getting hit?"

"You did well," Al'awwal replied, and I felt like a beginner stepping onto the mats for the first time. "I had a more difficult time landing shots on you than I do on most of my training partners."

That stung my pride, more than I wanted to admit. I had size and reach—okay, not much in the reach department, but definitely size—on Al'awwal, and I was an experienced fighter to boot. I'd been doing this shit for the better part of two decades. In a one-on-one fight, I was used to a certain degree of…competence. Not being "harder to hit than most." But what did two decades of experience matter when the other guy had, what, six, seven more and a level of genetic superiority that made me feel like a child going up against an adult?

"How can you fight at all?" I gasped, still trying to catch my breath. "Or greet us with a firearm?" I thought I knew the answer, but confirmation never hurt, and I admit, I was feeling just a bit inferior at that moment.

He shrugged and gave me a slight smile. "I was the first synthetic, Campbell. My father wanted a son, not a slave. The conditioning synthetics are subjected to not only didn't exist yet, but when it was instituted, it horrified my father to no end."

The intense conditioning that synthetics underwent to prevent the possibility of violence against humans was terrible, a disgraceful act that, in and of itself, was every bit as bad as their enslavement. But after two minutes of throwing hands with Al'awwal, I understood why the researchers at Walton Biogenics had felt it necessary. No matter how much training Al'awwal had, two minutes of hard sparring—and it *had* been hard sparring, even if the hard work for him had all been on the offense—should at least have left him a little bit winded. But apart from the barest hint of sweat, he looked fresh as a daisy.

Combine latent genetic superiority with the theoretical ability to live several times longer than a normal human and all the possible knowledge that came with that long life, and what did you get? A—hopefully— benevolent master.

The whole thing was so twisting with ironies that it boggled the mind. Al'awwal was living proof of what a synthetic could be if not bounded by the limits of their conditioning, and that proof was more than a little terrifying for a normal person.

And yet, a synthetic who *was* bounded by their conditioning had even more to fear from humans. Still, most of the processes applied to synthetics that granted them that superiority could also be applied to humans, if it weren't for Walton Biogenics' stranglehold on the relevant medical technologies.

Still, after two minutes in the ring with Al'awwal, a shameful part of me wondered, if only briefly, if I wasn't helping not only to overthrow the enslavement of synthetics but also to usher in a new era where it was humans who would be seen as the inferior—and therefore eminently enslaveable—race.

"Are you okay, Campbell?" Al'awwal asked as he tossed me a towel.

I caught the towel and realized I had been standing there, staring blankly, for nearly a full minute as the possible repercussions tumbled through my mind. "Yeah," I said, swiping at the sweat that ran freely down my face. "Yeah, fine. Just…sorting some things out in my head."

"In that case, are you ready for round two?"

No. I definitely was not ready for round two. But as I'd been taught in the Army—steel sharpens steel. Al'awwal was better than me, no doubt. Some was genetics. But some was training. Another one of those universal maxims was that you learned more from a loss than a victory. It looked like I had a lot to learn from the synthetic, and who knew when I'd get another chance?

"Yeah," I said, tossing the towel onto a nearby bench. "I guess I am. Let's do this."

Chapter 18

A searing, twisting pain that started somewhere along my outer hips and wrapped in and around to the backs of my knees woke me up. I'd been expecting the cramps after Al'awwal had driven me around his gym for the better part of an hour. I'd tried to fortify my system with a healthy dose of grunt candy, but when I'd closed my eyes last night, I'd known it was coming. There wasn't anything to be done about it, either, other than grip the sheets in my fists and grit my teeth until it passed. That didn't take long, though the cramps left a bone-deep soreness in their wake.

I groaned as I pushed myself out of bed, somewhat disoriented by the fact that I was in an actual bed and not perched precariously on a camping cot. Al'awwal had found a room for me to crash in, though the place had smelled slightly of dust and obviously hadn't been used in God alone know how long. But it had a bathroom, a bed, and all the trimmings, so I wasn't complaining. A hot shower had taken away a little of the sting of yesterday's beating, and as soon as I managed to stand up, I was planning on indulging in another. Like beds, hot showers had been in short supply over the past month.

I'd checked in with Silas before crashing for the evening, but he'd barely looked up from his screens, just waving one hand vaguely in my direction in a gesture of clear dismissal. I doubted the big synthetic had even gone to sleep. I knew that if I checked, he'd still be bent over those screens, alabaster face lit by the bluish glow emanating from them. As much as I wanted to badger him and see if we'd made any progress, the demands of my body overrode the demands of the rebellion. I needed another shower, some more grunt candy, and, God and Al'awwal willing, some hot food and strong coffee in order to even start feeling human again. Couldn't be a heartbreaker and life-taker if I couldn't even manage to stand up straight.

Shower first. I limped in the direction of the bathroom, silently cursing my own stubbornness. Al'awwal had been more than willing to stop after pounding on me for about twenty minutes, but I had insisted we keep going. I had a feeling it was going to be a day for regretting things.

I was on my third cup of coffee—and had put away as many eggs, some toast, and a solid half-pound of turkey bacon from Al'awwal's well-stocked larder—when I finally made my way to the room where Silas yet worked. At first glance, it appeared he hadn't moved a muscle since the last time I'd checked in on him. His massive shoulders were hunched, almost defensively, over the screens collected before him, his fingers doing their dance across the haptic surfaces. A plate, its contents reduced to crumbs and smears of an unidentifiable nature, sat next to him, and I wondered if, like me, he'd simply helped himself to the bounty of our host, or if Al'awwal had, at some point after repeatedly kicking my ass, actually cooked for Silas as well. Well, he didn't seem to be up yet, so maybe I'd at least been enough of a challenge to tire him out. God knew I'd still be sleeping if it weren't for the leg cramps.

"Any luck?" I asked Silas as I slipped into a chair. He'd set up in what, in any other house, I'd have called a dining room. Except I'd already seen a much larger room with a table that could have easily sat a dozen people on a side, so this room probably had some other name. Or was intended for the "help." Whatever the case, it had a cozy wood table that could have been a couple centuries old and four well-worn chairs. Like most of the other areas that Al'awwal had personally shown us, this room actually felt used, though it lacked the lived-in feel of the small kitchen, the study, and the gym.

"Some, Detective," Silas said. "Perhaps more than some. La Sorte and a few of the others at the safe house have been working on this as well. Between us, we have managed to identify several possible avenues of approach. One general carrier that Walton Biogenics routinely uses for deliveries and a number of smaller suppliers that handle their own deliveries. As expected, the security on the shipments is fairly robust, but nothing we will be unable to break, given time."

"How much time, Silas? As much as I could use another day of rest in a fucking mansion, the clock's ticking on this."

The look Silas gave me, part exasperation, part amusement, spoke volumes. But all he said was, "I am aware, Detective." Then his screens beeped, and his smile changed, taking on a more feral look. "And to answer your question, now."

"What?"

He turned back to the screens, fingers flying. "We've managed to crack the security on one of the lab's suppliers. Not a major carrier—a simple glass firm. They manufacture precision lab equipment locally, but they are a small enough operation that they handle their own deliveries. And it looks like they spend more money on making their glassware than they do on information security."

"You've got their schedule?" I asked, coming half out of my chair and almost spilling my coffee. I cursed as I hurriedly set it down, wiping at the hot liquid that had sloshed over my hand.

"Yes. Their delivery schedule, their delivery fleet specifics, and, with just a little more work, we will know the names of their employees. Give me an hour, Jason. I will need that long to study the information and to see if we can worm our way into other systems. I will have La Sorte and the others concentrate their efforts here as well, so that we can wring every byte of useful data out of their servers. One hour."

"One hour," I agreed. I gathered my coffee and made my way back to the kitchen, leaving the synthetic to his work.

* * * *

I couldn't wait the full hour. I was back at Silas's side after about forty minutes. He didn't look surprised to see me. "You are just in time. I think we have gathered what we need to make some decisions."

"Good," said Al'awwal, his silhouette darkening the doorway leading off to the kitchen. "I've been sitting on this cache for more years than I care to remember. It's time to do something about it."

"What have you got?" I asked, dropping into one of the chairs. Al'awwal took the one across from me, so we could both see the screens as Silas worked.

"We have a company, Quark Glassworks. They are based just outside the city, not too far from Thibodaux, actually. Small, on the grand scale of things, and it looks like Walton Biogenics is their primary customer. They have been doing business with each other for decades. We have their delivery schedule—and it looks like we have a choice between tomorrow and three days from now for the next delivery." He paused, and his voice lost a little of its certainty. "And we have information on their fleet of trucks. The system is fully automated, as expected. But we have not been able to crack into it. We probably can, if we are willing to wait until the later shipment, but…"

"But that doesn't give a hell of a lot of time to parse the information, figure out what it is, and decide what the hell we're going to do with it, at least if we want to use it as part of our alpha strike against the world?" I offered. "And if there's something in there that we can use to minimize the backlash against synthetics, better it go out in the first wave."

"That," Silas agreed. "And the fact that the longer we poke around their infrastructure, the more likely we are to be found out. We are confident that the good people at Quark have not noticed our intrusion as yet, but the longer we are in their systems, the greater the chance of discovery."

"And if we go after the delivery tomorrow?" Al'awwal asked. "Why do we need to be able to hack into the vehicle's system? It's already going where we want to go."

I couldn't help the smile that curled the left side of my mouth. Al'awwal was a genetic superman, unhindered by the constraints Silas suffered under, and with more years of experience—probably—than me and Silas combined. He was smarter, stronger, faster, better trained, and sure as shit healthier than I would ever be. He'd been hiding from the cyclopean reach of Walton Biogenics—successfully—for longer than I'd been alive. But despite all that, without being able to plan the details better, he'd make a shitty criminal. Maybe it wasn't something to be proud of, the thought that I—a former cop—made a better villain than the synthetic, but I was feeling just a smidge inferior to Al'awwal, so I'd take what I could get.

"We have to get on board, Al," I said. If he minded the nickname, he made no show of it. "And that's going to be pretty fucking hard if we can't tell the truck not only to stop, but to not tell its home base that it's made a stop. I don't doubt that Walton Biogenics is paranoid enough to question any irregularities in its scheduled deliveries."

"Ah."

"Ah, indeed," Silas said. "So we will have to find a way to intercept the shipment, board the truck, and remain hidden through the delivery process."

"Sounds easy enough," I said. Both synthetics threw me a strange look. Well, another thing humans were superior at. "Sarcasm," I said, then shrugged. "If we're doing this tomorrow, better break out the specs and maps and whatever else we can find, because we don't have a lot of time to plan, prep, and execute. Time to go to work."

* * * *

Some hours later, we were still huddled around the dining room table.

"I just don't see us waiting until the truck gets into the city," I said, for the fourth or fifth time.

"It's highly improbable that the truck will need to make any stops before it gets into the city," Silas countered.

"I know, I know. But what are we going to do? Hang out at a busy intersection and hop on board if the truck has to stop? In case you've forgotten, there are a shit-ton of protests going on, with half the police force in the city present. The *other* half is directly looking for me. How long do you think it would take for me to be recognized? Four seconds? Five?"

Silas sighed, frustration evident. "Well, we cannot jump onto a moving vehicle traveling at thirty or forty miles per hour, either. The chances of something going catastrophically wrong are far too great."

"We need to force the vehicle to a stop outside the city," Al'awwal interjected, heading me off before I could offer an angry retort. I wasn't mad at Silas—he was right. I didn't want to jump onto a truck moving at near highway speeds, since the slightest slip or bump in the road would almost certainly spell death. But damned if I could think of a better way.

"If we force the vehicle to stop," Silas said, "Quark will know about it. And we have already agreed that it is highly likely that Walton will be monitoring the systems as well. We cannot risk that such a stop would alert them and increase the security at the lab. That is enough of an uphill battle already."

"Only if they know that the vehicle was *forced* to stop," Al'awwal said. "Look." His fingers swiped across the screens, reorienting the map, zooming in on an area less than one hundred yards from the gates to the Quark Glassworks plant. "Here," he tapped at the map, indicating an intersection. "There's a light here."

"Yeah, sure," I said. "But no fucking traffic. It's in the middle of nowhere."

"There doesn't have to be traffic. You said you can't hack into the truck, but surely you can hack into a simple traffic light?"

"Of course I can," Silas snapped. "But there are also cameras that may well be monitored. Do you think no one will find it odd to have a red light appear for no reason, with no cross traffic anywhere near?"

"They might," Al'awwal acknowledged. "If by *they* you mean the people at Quark. But I doubt any monitoring on the Walton front is going to be so complex as to check whether a traffic signal right outside the factory's front door is behaving appropriately. Sure, they might be notified if their delivery wasn't obeying the signals present, or if it was obeying signals *not* present. But do you really think Walton Biogenics will have an algorithm in place to detect whether a random traffic signal turned red when it should have stayed green?"

That was hard to argue with. "What about Quark?" I countered. "Walton might not notice, but the people at Quark, some of whom might be able to observe this whole thing with a good old-fashioned mark one eyeball might find it strange."

"And if they do?" Al'awwal asked. "Do you think this glassware company is so paranoid as to stop their deliveries and launch an investigation because a stoplight turned red?" He shook his head. "No. They will do what any company not involved in illegal activity would do. They'll scratch their heads, wonder why it happened, and at *most* send someone out to check on the light. But they won't recall the delivery."

"Okay," I agreed. "Maybe you have a point. And it's probably better odds than trying to hit the truck in motion or stop it somewhere in the heart of the city. It adds its own wrinkle though—we're going to have to get pretty damn close to the factory for this to work. Not to mention the fact that, if stopping the truck outside the gates like that is unusual, we're going to draw a look or two from anybody outside. Which is going to make it a hell of a lot harder to get on board without being seen."

"Then we shall have to give them something else to look at," Silas said.

"Okay, but what?"

"Leave that to me, Detective. Your job is figuring out how to get us on the truck."

Chapter 19

"This is still a stupid fucking plan," I muttered, mostly to myself as we hiked our way across a field of feed corn. The Quark delivery truck was scheduled to leave for the Walton lab at zero-seven-hundred, about ten minutes after sunrise, as it turned out. That was great for getting in position under the cover of darkness, at least in theory. In practice, it meant carrying a bunch of gear across rough terrain with zero visibility, all while leading a pair of synthetics who, at their core, were city rats. For all his genius with computers and his knowledge of the bowels of New Lyons, Silas hadn't ever made it out of the city. And while Al'awwal seemed to have some kind of training—at least judging by the way he stowed and carried his gear—it was pretty obvious it was the kind of training you bought and paid for somewhere but without the actual experience of doing it for a living.

"Beggars and choosers, Campbell," Al'awwal grunted, shifting his assault pack on his shoulders. He and I were both under arms. He was carrying the Israeli-made bullpup with which he had first greeted us and I had opted for a ten millimeter sub-gun of German manufacture, pulled from the synthetic's extensive collection. The five-five-six rifle round gave Al the firepower edge over my ten millimeter, but he'd also had a nice little suppressor for the sub-gun in his collection, so I'd screwed the can on the end of the barrel. It wouldn't make the gun into a truly silent instrument of death, but it would at least keep people guessing as to where, exactly, the noise was coming from.

Silas, of course, wasn't armed, but he was hauling a pack of his own. It was filled with an odd array of electronics that I just filed under "commo" but almost certainly had more esoteric uses than that. Like me and Al, he was clad in simple dark slacks and a dark long-sleeved shirt. If we ditched our packs and weapons and if no one looked too closely at our shoes—we were all wearing some flavor of hiking boot, because damned if I was going to risk rolling an ankle on the walk to the objective—we could maybe pass for people who should be in an office building. A lot more than if we were wearing military surplus, anyway. And if we didn't get too much corn stuck in our fucking gear.

We'd had the car—an untraceable Silas special, not one of Al'awwal's—drop us off about a mile from our objective. Silas then sent it back to whatever mysterious motor pool he kept hidden away, and we proceeded to hoof it cross-country the rest of the way. Walking a mile doesn't sound super hard—should only take fifteen, twenty minutes right? Right. Now add in some soft, well-tilled soil that not only tugs at your boots but is anything but even. Add pack and weapons totaling maybe a quarter of your body weight. Think that would slow things down a bit? Maybe make it take twice as long? Great. Now do it in the pitch-fucking-black without any optics. Trust me. Shit gets real slow, real quick.

It took us close to an hour and a half to cross that mile, a little slower than I'd estimated, but I'd built some snafu time into the plan, so we reached the edges of the cornfield with enough time to spare. We'd deviated a few points east—not bad, considering we were pretty much going off of dead reckoning in the middle of a cornfield—but that worked out to our advantage, anyway. Our target was an intersection of two roads a little too big to be called county, a little too small to be called state ones. They were those corporate-sponsored roads that you got sometimes near factories or business parks, the kind that didn't really fit in with the local roads because they had to be of a size and quality to handle employee and freight traffic.

We'd come out maybe a hundred yards from the intersection, which suited me fine. It gave us a better chance of crossing the street—which provided us no cover whatsoever—without being seen. We darted across the road and disappeared into the brush on the far side. We were close enough now to make out Quark Glassworks, rising in the distance beyond the brush and fields. It was a smaller building than I'd expected. I hadn't ever really considered what type of facility would be needed to manufacture glass, and the only imagery I had to draw on was the massive power plants or automobile factories I remembered from my youth. This was neither. The building—what we could see of it—looked more like an elementary school than a factory, save for a pair of medium-sized chimneys that were far too reasonable to be called smokestacks. It was two stories, brick, and looked like it was built in a rough L shape. A fence ran around the property, and, following the line of the road, I could make out a guard house. It looked manned, though by synthetic or human, there was no way to tell. Not that it mattered. Being seen boarding the truck by either would be just as bad.

I checked my watch. I didn't normally bother with one, as a screen served all the same functions, but sometimes you couldn't beat the convenience of wearable technology. Fifteen minutes until zero-seven. The sun was breaking, climbing over the eastern horizon. If I'd had my choice, I'd have tried to board the truck a couple of hours ago. Not because that was when it was darkest—the old saw about "darkest just before the dawn" is metaphorical, not literal—but because people, no matter the time they get up, always seem least alert at before-morning-nautical-twilight. It was true on guard duty in the big green machine, and I was sure it was true for those on guard duty here. But trying to penetrate the perimeter wasn't part of the plan, so we were stuck waiting for the truck.

Fortunately, the terrain outside the factory was either field or allowed to run wild. Closer in, the bush had been hacked back, the ground cover cultivated into something more resembling a lawn. But the traffic light, the simple device upon which all of our plans hinged, was a good twenty yards outside the landscaped perimeter. The corn stopped on the other side of the road, but there was enough rough scrub to let us move into position without too great a risk of being seen. We hunkered down near the light post, trusting the early morning shadows and brush to keep us out of sight of the guards.

It occurred to me that if anyone came down the crossroad, we'd be three guys, all dressed in black, sitting out in the open. Not the least suspicious thing we could have done. But part of the reason we were out here was that traffic was so scarce to begin with.

At one time, that wouldn't have been the case. I strongly suspected that the only reason the light was here was to give employees of the factory a more orderly entrance and egress at shift-change times. Automation had taken care of a lot of those jobs, moving the formerly productive employees onto the Basic Living Stipend. The synthetic revolution had probably cleared out the rest, since any manual labor was cheaper to do with synthetics than robots or "real" people. Odds were, the only employees were a few "shift managers"—overseers by any other name—and maybe a handful of experts at managing the equipment and processes.

Silas had dug out one of the many screens stuffed into his pack. It was already running—he'd done most of the heavy lifting last night, with a few final tweaks on the ride from Al'awwal's estate.

"We good to go?" I asked.

"Very nearly," he replied. "The light is already under my control, and we're still inside Quark's systems. I just need to verify a few processes, and the diversion will be ready. Five minutes, Jason."

I nodded, glancing at my watch again, more from habit than need. The truck was scheduled to depart at oh-seven-hundred, and given that it was a fully automated truck being loaded I assumed by synthetics that lived on property, it wasn't going be leaving one minute early or one minute late. Twelve till. This was the part I hated most—the waiting. We'd planned, plotted, executed…and now it all came down to grinding out a few minutes more and hoping nothing went wrong. I grit my teeth and tried to ignore the tension twisting my guts.

"I am ready," Silas said a few minutes later. "And I have the status of the truck. It is buttoned up and ready to move out. It should be rolling on schedule."

"Good," I said. "Everyone know the plan?"

"Such as it is," Silas said.

"And what there is of it," Al'awwal added.

I grunted. It wasn't, I admitted, much of a plan. But it was what we had, so we were going to make it work. "Be ready."

The minutes clicked down, the sun rose higher, and the shadows receded. With each passing moment, the chances of being spotted by a bored security guard increased. Then the gates to the factory lumbered open and a vehicle pulled out onto the road.

"Showtime," I muttered.

The truck moved smoothly, accelerating almost silently with its electric engine. "Switching the light now," Silas said. I couldn't see the actual signal from my vantage, and even if I could, I was keeping my eyes on the truck, but I noticed an almost instant flattening of its rate of acceleration followed by a noticeable slowing. It didn't stop like a car under manual control would have—in fact, it kept up a relatively high rate of speed until almost the last moment, as if its programming anticipated the light going back to green. As the light would have, if Silas hadn't hijacked its controls.

"Triggering our diversion now," the albino synthetic said, and I felt my muscles tense. It was almost go time.

About a second after Silas hit his screen, and with the truck about ten yards from the stoplight, all hell broke loose at the factory. Sirens started blaring, a high, ululating cry designed to cut through the noise of a factory floor. Lights posted outside exits started flashing, alarmingly bright in the shadows of the dawning day, throwing a strobe-light effect over the yard.

The guards, their confidence in another dull and routine day shattered, came pouring out of the guard shack, staring in the direction of the building.

And away from the truck, which was rolling to a stop at the light.

"Go, go, go!" I said.

I put action to my own words, exploding from my feet and charging the truck. We didn't have to worry about a driver seeing us—there wasn't one. Hell, there wasn't even a cab where a driver could have gone. The truck was basically a cargo box with an engine and computer brain. I hit the back of the truck, hand already reaching for the door latch as the fire alarms—or whatever it was that Silas had triggered—blared in the distance. There was a keypad by the door, and Silas could deal with that if need be, but I was hoping no one would have bothered. I hadn't spent much time in burglary or organized crime, but glassware had never been high on the hijacking scale.

The latch handle twisted at my pressure and the door popped open just as Silas and Al'awwal reached the truck. Cardboard boxes lined both sides of the track, held in place with rubber webbing, but there was a clear aisle between the boxes. I hopped into the truck, then reached back to pull up first Silas, then Al'awwal. Al pulled the door shut behind him, cloaking the interior in darkness. That darkness was broken only by the pale glow of Silas's screen. He hit a few buttons, and I had to grab the webbing as the truck lurched forward.

"All right," I said, dropping my pack to the floor and pulling out a flashlight. "Easy part is done. Now let's get to work on the rest. We've got a lot to do before this thing gets to the lab."

* * * *

The truck that, roughly a half hour later, pulled into the large loading and unloading area of the Walton Biogenics laboratory didn't look any different from the one that had departed Quark Glassworks. We had, however, made a couple of slight modifications. The first had been simple—rearranging some of the boxes to block visibility to our more…comprehensive… changes to the vehicle's architecture and to give us a place to hide when the unloading started. Not that we waited for that, of course.

In keeping with the Keystone Cops level of operational planning that had taken us this far, as soon as the truck stopped, I dropped through the hole we had cut in the floor of the truck using a laser welder. I had to lie flat, as there wasn't quite enough clearance beneath the truck to crouch. Silas dropped my pack down to me, and, resting on my stomach,

I shimmied out of the way of the opening. I couldn't make out much of my surroundings, save that we were in a garage or loading dock of some sort. There was motion and activity—I could see a few legs whisking by here and there—but not a lot of it. Good.

Silas dropped down next. The barrel-chested synthetic barely fit beneath the truck, even lying flat on his back. His pack, and then Al'awwal's, followed. I had been watching the movements of the feet I could see and trying to get a lay of the land. I could make out stacks of boxes, a wall, a few pallets here and there. According to the plans Al'awwal had found, there was a freight elevator along the western wall. That was our objective. But we needed to get there without raising any alarms and, preferably, without killing anyone. I'd known going in that there was a chance blood would be shed, but so far, despite all the crimes I'd committed by supporting the synthetics, I'd managed to avoid harming innocent people. Maybe I was a bad revolutionary, but I couldn't blithely justify the deaths of ordinary citizens doing their jobs as acceptable collateral damage for the greater good. The security thugs were an exception to that rule—I'd had ample evidence already of how Walton Biogenics used them as a wet-work cleanup squad that would make a third world dictator blush. But I couldn't hold the people—or maybe synthetics—in the mail room responsible for the actions of the corporate bigwigs and their hired guns.

But I also wasn't going to fail. I left my sub-gun hanging from its strap and eased a telescoping baton from its sheath on my belt. I didn't open it, but I kept the slug of steel at the ready as I waited for my opening and then crawled from beneath the vehicle. I rose to a crouch, staying low between the truck wall and a "wall" made of steel racks holding a variety of boxes.

There was some activity at the tail end of the truck, but I hadn't been noticed. I moved, low and fast, sliding along the truck and away from the movement, until I found a break in the shelves. I stepped through the gap and found myself in a corridor between the shelving.

The loading and unloading dock, or so I surmised it to be, apparently had room for a fair amount of storage. There appeared to be several rows of shelves, like the aisles of a supermarket. A closer look made me step back. The top shelves did hold a few boxes that I assumed contained lab equipment or glassware. The bottom shelves held plastic drums labeled "Medical Waste." They reminded me—violently—of Fowler's place, where I'd rescued Evelyn and Hernandez's daughter, and of the plastic bins in Fowler's barn. I fought down a surge of bile. I had little doubt that the contents, while not as vile as that psychopath's personal abattoir, would be of a similar make.

It took only a moment for Silas and then Al'awwal to join me amidst the storage racks. So far, it appeared that our infiltration had passed unnoticed by the workers managing the loading dock. That couldn't last, not if a pair of heavily armed men and one synthetic obviously not designed for any sort of aboveground labor kept standing about. "On my six," I whispered as I moved out. It occurred to me that they might not understand the military jargon, but my concerns were eased as they fell in line behind me.

The shelves ran along the length of one half of the loading dock. I instinctively moved away from the garage doors, deeper into the stacks. I'd lost all orientation, so I couldn't be sure which wall we were heading toward—but I was pretty sure it wasn't the one housing the freight elevator. That didn't matter quite so much right now as finding a place out of the flow of traffic where we could regroup.

We moved maybe twenty feet deeper into the facility before I felt far enough removed from the activity taking place around the Quark truck. "Where are we?" I asked, looking toward Silas and Al'awwal.

Silas, of course, had his screen out. "We've been headed toward the north wall of the loading area," he said, his voice barely audible and pitched not to carry. "Freight elevator is in the west wall. That way." He pointed.

I nodded. "We're probably already showing up on some camera, somewhere. Anything you can do about that?"

Silas didn't answer, but he was already at work. The man was not just good when it came to things electronic—he was damn near magical. I had no idea how he did what he did, but it was maybe three tense minutes later when he said, "There are two separate circuits for the cameras. The low-security areas—including these docks, the elevators, and most of the offices—are accessible. Under my control. I have injected a virus that will scrub our presence, real time. Someone watching closely might catch a blurring or pixilation, but to the casual eye watching on a screen, we're effectively invisible."

"The second circuit?" Al'awwal asked.

"If I have to, I can try the same tactic. But it looks like those cameras are only covering the actual laboratories themselves and some of the executive offices. We shouldn't need to access those areas, and trying to spoof those cameras may trigger an alarm." He paused. "I should note that the cybersecurity is very good. I doubt I could break into any truly sensitive systems. The cameras in the areas that I can access seem geared more toward preventing employee mischief rather than any real security measure. Deterrence rather than actual security. But even with these, there is a risk of detection." He smiled, a slight ironic twist of the lips. "Which is to say, we should move things along as quickly as possible."

I grunted. "Good enough. Let's move out, then." I tossed a look at Al'awwal. "No shooting, unless we run into security people. And even then, better if we do it quiet."

He nodded in reply.

We moved again, heading toward the west wall. That meant moving down the aisle between the shelves. It was fairly wide, maybe eight feet, enough to get a forklift down to access the upper shelves. We stuck to one side, not that it mattered. With the overhead fluorescent lighting, it wasn't like there were any shadows to hide in. But maybe it would be enough to obscure the fact that we were carrying weapons if someone happened to walk by and look down the aisle.

We reached the end, and a quick glance showed the path was clear. I could see the elevator doors maybe fifteen feet farther down the wall. "We move to the aisle directly across from the doors," I whispered. "I call the elevator. Then we all move. Got it?"

They nodded, and, after another quick check to make sure the coast was clear, we moved, slipping from aisle to aisle until we reached the one across from the elevators. I tossed my pack to Silas and my gun to Al'awwal. I pulled my shirt loose from my waist and let it fall so it covered the holstered forty-five. It wasn't much concealment, but better than nothing. From afar I would, hopefully, look like a worker who happened to wear mostly black, waiting for the elevator.

I stepped confidently from the stacks, my stride long and full of purpose. Slinking about would only catch the curiosity of anyone who happened to glance my way. If you moved with determination, acted like you already knew what you were doing and where you were going, few would bother to question. I hit the call button—and thank God the elevator had an actual old-style call button and not a more direct method of operation—and waited.

To my surprise, the doors opened almost immediately.

And showed me the unsmiling faces of three men wearing dark blazers with the suspicious bulges that identified them immediately as security.

Shit.

Chapter 20

I could play it soft, try to bluff my way past, hope that the security guards were headed somewhere, anywhere, else. No alarms were going off. No bustle of activity. Maybe it would work. Maybe.

Or, I could play it hard, attack now, before anyone had the chance to react, and hope that I could use that instant of surprise to end things quickly and quietly.

The options flashed through my head in a fraction of a second, but in the end, it wasn't even a choice. Training took over.

The doors hadn't finished opening before I was lunging into the elevator, both hands striking out in front of me in a high-low double punch. It was a tactic normally reserved for bad martial arts movies and anime, but there were a few instances where it could have real-world success. The best being when you catch your opponent unaware and want to simultaneously drive him back and do your level best to disable him. My left fist connected just beneath his sternum, striking with enough force to knock the wind out of him. At the same time, my right fist crunched into his throat. I pulled that blow a little, enough to avoid outright killing the man.

He went down, choking and gasping, hands raising feebly to clutch his throat. But I had already moved on.

Stepping into the elevator, dealing with the man right in front of me had violated one of the core principles of facing multiple opponents—it had put me right between two enemies. Couldn't have that. Fortunately, the attack had surprised them and been fast enough that they'd yet to recover. The one to my left was moving, so I moved that direction, angling away from his outstretched hands as he tried to lock on and grapple me. Two quick steps put me behind him, my back to the wall of the elevator.

I kicked out, my leg smashing into the back of his knee, causing him to stumble. I smashed my palm out and down, connecting where neck met spine, around the C1-C2 vertebrae. Again, I pulled the blow, striking to stun, to injure, but not to kill.

The third man was moving now, but unlike his friends, he was smart. He wasn't coming toward me but backing away, putting as much space between me and him as he could. At the same time, his hand dipped into his blazer, moving for the bulge that had identified him as a security guard.

He was smarter than his friends, but not quite smart enough. He opened the distance, but instead of moving out of the elevator where he would have had much more space and the possibility of others coming to his aid, he put his back to the wall. He also fumbled the draw. Lots of security types spent time at the range, putting lead on a paper, working on sight pictures and trigger control and all the other fundamentals. A much smaller percentage actually bothered to practice deploying their weapon and getting it into action.

It wasn't a big mistake. Just an extra second or so where he failed to clear his blazer and his hand got tangled in the cloth. He resolved it quickly, but I was already on him, stepping over the two unconscious bodies between us in a single stride. I moved close, chest to chest, left hand clamping on to his right as it grasped the butt of his gun. I shoved the hand forward, trapping it between me and the Kydex holster. At the same time, my right elbow rose and fell, cutting down at a roughly forty-five degree angle that terminated just beneath the man's ear. He went suddenly boneless, his legs collapsing under him.

The whole thing, from start to finish, had taken less than ten seconds. I couldn't remember if any of them had the chance or presence of mind to shout. The brain did funny things in the middle of combat.

"Holy hell," Al'awwal swore as he stepped into the elevator, my sub-gun slung over one shoulder and the bullpup at the ready. "Where the fuck was that when we were sparring?" He looked a little green around the edges as he stepped over the bodies.

"Combat versus sport," I grunted, not really thinking about it. "Different objectives." Silas was in the elevator now as well, his finger stabbing at the close door button. You could always trust the guy to focus on the important things.

"Come on," I said to Al'awwal. "We need to get their guns, and then see if they have restraints. Need to find a way to tie them up and gag them."

Al was already bending over one of the guards, checking for a pulse. He must have found one, because he quickly stripped out the guard's weapon and started rummaging on his gun belt for cuffs. He didn't find any, but he did pull out a fistful of plastic ties. In short order, we had the three guards bound. I used their ties for makeshift gags, making sure not to obstruct their breathing too much.

While we had worked, Silas had torn open a panel on the elevator and physically plugged his screen into it. I'd never seen him go old-school hardwired before, but he had an almost beatific smile on his face as he worked, so I trusted that he was doing something worthwhile. That trust bore fruit as he said, "The elevator is under our control now. It will not stop anywhere we do not want it to stop, and as far as the main monitoring system is concerned, it is working normally. If they need to use the freight elevator for anything, people might start to get suspicious when it does not show up, but at least for now, it is a ghost. And a ghost we control."

"Good work," I said. "That means we can leave these fellows," I patted one of the still-sleeping guards on the head, "while we go about our business." I glanced around the elevator, really seeing it for the first time. It was all you would expect in a freight elevator—essentially a no-frills metal box with wider-than-normal doors to allow for loading and unloading. There was—or rather had been—a screen for accessing floors. It was now dangling from a series of wires with Silas's own screen patched in its place. Or one of his screens, rather. I suspected that half the weight of his pack was throwaway screens.

"All right," I said, after taking stock. "Let's get to work."

* * * *

We emerged on to the third floor of the building looking somewhat different from the trio that had entered the elevator. First, only two of us emerged. Silas, with a direct line into the laboratory's network, remained behind. He was to be our eyes and ears, and to run command and control. He'd take the elevator up half a floor, stopping it in between, and continue to send the tendrils of his intrusion programs deeper into Walton's systems. I had no doubt that, in addition to guiding us along our merry way, he'd do his level best to pick up a few extra helpful tidbits of information.

We'd left the big guns with Silas—there was no way to blend in when you were carrying an assault rifle. That made me a touch nervous. We hadn't needed it yet, but I was firm believer in superior firepower. Still, it would have been conspicuous, and now that we were in with minimal casualties, getting out again should require more stealth than bullets.

From somewhere in the crumbling mansion, Al'awwal had produced a pair of lab coats. They'd traveled well enough in the packs, showing a few wrinkles but nothing that one wouldn't expect from a harried and disheveled scientist. They wouldn't stand up to any kind of close scrutiny, particularly since they lacked the identification badges, but from a distance, we should pass as two more employees going about their business.

"Comm check," I said as we strode down the hallway, briefly brushing the throat mic concealed beneath the collar of my shirt.

"I hear you loud and clear, Detective," Silas's voice came back at once. "And I have your screens' positions locked in. You are going to want to take your first left turn ahead."

"Roger."

We kept walking, eyes alert, but doing our best to appear relaxed. Just two more cogs in the vast machine of Walton Biogenics. No need to give us a second glance. The hallway branched to the left, and we turned down it. I had a rough blueprint of the place in my head, and I knew generally where we were going, but Silas's voice, that preternaturally calm baritone, was reassuring as he said, "Keep going straight at the next intersection. Then take a left again."

I nodded, but my eyes had focused on the intersection ahead, where a man and woman had emerged from the hallway. They both wore suits, not lab coats, and were in deep conversation with each other. They were coming straight toward us.

"We're going to have to put in a requisition to have the mass spectrometer recalibrated," Al'awwal said out of nowhere, his voice raised in agitation.

I almost jumped before it dawned on me what he was doing. "Yeah," I muttered, and let my own voice sound resigned. "But I seriously doubt it's in the budget. You know how the department's been with that this year."

"I'm tired of having to justify every single repair," Al complained. "They should know by now that it's completely necessary to do our jobs." He nodded to the other pair as they passed. I kept my head down, as if in dejection, since I couldn't risk them recognizing my face from the newscasts.

"Yeah, yeah. Preaching to the choir, here."

The employees moved past us, and apart from a slightly confused glance, didn't seem to think anything untoward was happening. "Nicely done," I said.

"Corporations are corporations," Al'awwal said fatalistically. "Even the most evil of conglomerates deals with the same red tape and bullshit as all the rest."

I thought about my days in the Army, and then on the force. "True in the government sector as well."

"Next left," Silas interjected as we continued to traverse the halls.

We took the indicated turn. "Third door on the right."

Most of the office doors had been closed, and the door we reached was no exception. It was too much to hope that it would be an unused and unoccupied office. There was light visible around the door frame, and while there were no voices coming through, I heard the clicking of a keyboard. The placard next to the door read, "Dr. Delores Larkin."

"Damn," I muttered.

"Problem?" Silas asked.

"Office is occupied. We're going to have to do this fast. I'm not going to drop any bodies unless we have to." Particularly female bodies, though I knew the age-old proscription didn't make a whole lot of sense in this day and age. Dr. Larkin was as much a part of Walton as any male employee—she had just as much blood on her hands. Didn't change the fact that the only way I was dropping the hammer on a woman was if she was about to do the same to me.

"Ready?" I whispered to Al'awwal. He nodded. At his nod, I simply opened the door and stepped into the office, as if I owned the place.

"Excuse me?" the woman seated behind a functional, if cheap, desk said as we entered. She looked up from her desktop screen, brown eyes wide at the intrusion. The office was small, maybe ten feet on a side, with barely enough space for the desk, a couple of visitors' chairs, and a credenza with a hutch set behind the desk. As it was an interior office, there were no windows. Just the bare taupe walls with a single motivational picture—an eagle in flight with something about leadership written below—hanging in a dark wood frame.

The woman wore an expensive-looking suit in a dark brown that complemented her mocha skin. The expression on her face was still firmly in the realm of surprise rather than alarm. That changed as I put one finger over my lips and drew my forty-five. "Please, ma'am," I said in a low and calm voice. "We're not here to cause you any harm, but it's important that you stay quiet. Or we may have to take drastic measures."

I hated threatening her. I just hated it less than the thought of having to shoot my way out of the building through Walton's security force.

"You," she said, her voice barely above a whisper. "You're the one from the vids."

"That's right," I agreed. "So you know that I don't have a whole lot to lose. All we need you to do is stay quiet. We're just here to retrieve something."

"Something to help you spread your vile lies?" she demanded. She hadn't raised her voice, but there was real passion in her tone.

"They are not lies!" Al'awwal snapped. "Synthetics are as much people as you are."

"Bullshit," she replied. "I've worked here for ten years. I'd know."

I shook my head. Willful ignorance and complacency. I couldn't fault her for it. I'd been guilty of it myself. "Keep her covered while I look for the safe," I said. Al'awwal nodded, pulling his own pistol from its place of concealment.

"There's no safe here," she said scornfully. "If you're looking for money, you've come to the wrong place."

"Just keep quiet," Al'awwal snapped, gesturing with his gun. I ignored the woman and moved behind her desk. If the map had been accurate, it looked like Dr. Kaphiri's cache would be in the floor, right around where the credenza was now sitting. I kept an eye on the office worker, not out of any real fear of harm to myself, but if she *did* make a move, I had little doubt Al would pull the trigger. I didn't want to be in the line of fire if that happened.

The credenza looked like it was made of the same cheap plastic and laminate as every other office I'd ever been in. Whoever Dr. Larkin was, judging by her furniture, she wasn't up in the rarified air of the corporate bigwigs. I took a good grip on the base of the credenza and lifted, just enough to pull the feet up from the carpet. Then I half-twisted, half-crab-walked to the side, grunting with the effort as I moved the piece of furniture about eighteen inches. That had the added benefit of boxing Dr. Larkin in as well. If she decided to go lunging for me, she'd have to do it across the desk.

The floor beneath the credenza bore the same cheap carpet as the rest of the office. I pulled my tactical folder from my pocket and snapped it open. The tanto point made short work of the carpet and the pad beneath. I kept pushing until I felt the scrape of steel on concrete and then, wincing a little on the inside at the damage I was about to do to one of my favorite knives, I dragged the blade in a wide, circular pattern. The edged steel tore through the fibers, producing a low scraping sound as the steel ground against the poured concrete of the floor. I didn't know exactly where Dr. Kaphiri had hidden his cache, not down to the inches, so I cut as wide a swath as I could.

"What are you doing?" Larkin asked, craning her head to peer at my knife work. The credenza and hutch blocked most of her view, and as she came out of her seat a bit, Al'awwal shook his head and tsked. She sat back into the chair, giving the synthetic a flat, angry look.

I continued to ignore her, figuring that was the better tactic. I wasn't here for a conversation, after all. I flicked the knife closed and dropped it back into my pocket. Then I dug my fingers underneath the carpet and pad, worming them down until I felt the coolness of the concrete. Then, I pulled.

It didn't come up in one easy piece. Despite the sharpness of my knife and the cleanness of the cut, stubborn fibers clung to each other and the remnants of old glue resisted my pull. There was a ripping, tearing noise— not loud, but out of place enough that I worried it might draw attention. But I didn't stop.. We were far too deep into this to turn back over a little noise. The patch of rug and padding finally tore free from the concrete.

Beneath the carpeting was…nothing.

I stared at the bare concrete, my guts twisting and churning. "You need to see this," I said to Al'awwal. I moved back to his position at the door, drawing my forty-five as I did so. "I've got her."

Larkin sneered at me. "Not what you expected? How do you plan on getting out of here? You know the second you leave, I'll have security on your asses."

I shook my head. The scorn in her words was as misplaced as the confidence. I didn't point out that there were plenty of ways that we could ensure she didn't do that, some of which didn't even involve leaving her a corpse. I wanted her to think she had at least a little bit of the upper hand, a little bit of hope. If she saw us as bumbling intruders, all the better. I had the feeling that if she lost that bravado, lost that hope, she might very well start screaming her head off. We were already on a clock here, but that would kick it into high gear.

Al had crouched over the torn carpet patch and snapped out his own knife. I kept one eye on him as he probed the concrete and my other glued to Dr. Larkin.

"Do you really think people will give up their lives, the luxury that we at Walton Biogenics provide them, because of your ridiculous crusade?" Larkin asked.

"The truth will come out, doc," I replied. "You've seen the protests. Do those seem like shining, happy Utopians?" I shook my head, turning more of my attention to her as I continued. "I've been a pretty firm subscriber to the 'people are assholes' theory. That we're predetermined to treat each other like shit. That we're better at hating each other, envying each other, disdaining each other than we are at finding reasons to like one another. Now? I look out the window, and I see hundreds of people protesting the thought that they've been party to a lie. That they've been made unwilling participants in the slave trade. You think those people are just going to go away? You think they're going to ignore the truth? They're out there raising hell on the chance that what they know is true has changed. Imagine their response when we give them proof, not just that synthetics are people, but that Walton Biogenics has known it all along. What do you think is going to happen to your precious company then?"

I didn't add, *What do you think will happen to the country, the government?* I figured there was about a fifty-fifty chance that pure anarchy would reign for a while, that world governments, even that of the U.S., might fall. That pulled at the patriot in me, but then again, the nation I believed in, the nation I'd fought for, would never condone the enslavement of the synthetics.

"Your entire premise is false," Larkin snapped. "You keep saying synthetics are people, as if it's some foregone conclusion. But they aren't. You're delusional. And so are those so-called protesters." She snorted. "Most of them are little more than teenagers looking to do some property damage and rebel against authority. They don't care about your 'cause.' So a synthetic got pregnant. So what? Horses can mate with donkeys, but that doesn't make them the same species. Lions and tigers and cattle and yaks. Oh my." She said it with the cadence of the Wizard of Oz. "You claim proof, but all you have is an anomaly. An outlier. And that's all you'll ever—"

"Found it," Al'awwal interrupted.

I leaned out enough to see around the rearranged furniture. His probing knife had, apparently, found some irregularity in the concrete, or what I had presumed was concrete. He had pried up chunks of...something. The same color as the concrete around it, but softer, more brittle, as it lay in crumbling chunks. In the rough hole he'd revealed, metal glinted.

"Clay," Al'awwal noted. "Painted to match the concrete. My father was a tricksome man."

"Great. Is that the safe?"

"Such as it is," Al'awwal replied. "It appears to be a simple lockbox." He examined the door while I kept my eyes firmly on Dr. Larkin. Surprise was writ large on her face, and she stared open-mouthed in the direction of Al'awwal. "The lock is quite advanced," he continued, "particularly considering its age. It's a genetic code cipher and will only unlock with the proper DNA."

"Yours, presumably."

"So I was told. But there's only one way to find out for certain," he agreed. I couldn't make out everything he was doing, but I saw him press his hand into the gap in the concrete, and a slight wince crossed his face. Genetic lock. Probably required a drop of blood. In the newfound silence, I heard the metallic click of a lock disengaging.

"Yes," Al'awwal hissed. His hands dipped into the floor and returned with a sheaf of papers along with several data cubes. "We have it!" he exclaimed. "At last!"

"You have what?" Dr. Larkin demanded.

"Proof," I responded. "Collected over decades of work at this very lab." I couldn't keep the satisfaction from my voice. "Proof of the synthetics' origins. Proof that Walton Biogenics has been denying invaluable medical research and treatment options to the population for years. And if we're lucky, maybe even some documentation of the absolutely brutal methods your precious company has been using to silence people like me. As in, outright murder."

"I… I don't believe it."

"Yeah, keep thinking that, sister. In the meantime, we're getting out of Dodge. And that means we have to make sure you don't go siccing security on us."

"Wait… What do you mean?" A faint note of panic crept into her voice.

There was a petty little part of me that felt a thrill of satisfaction as she seemed to finally come face-to-face with the reality of her own mortality. I wasn't proud of it, but there it was. Still, I couldn't risk that panic turning into screaming, and I had no intention of killing her.

"We're not going to hurt you," I said. "Just inconvenience you a bit. Tie you up. Gag you so you can't alert anyone. Eventually, someone will come and check on you. Then think of the stories you'll have to tell."

She had a bit of a wild look in her eye, but I didn't hesitate. I still had several of the plastic restraints taken from the security guards, and I used them to secure her arms to the chair and bind her ankles together. I thought about disabling her desktop screens, but odds were, their status was monitored. That was more likely to trigger a tech support guy coming to check on the system than anything. Besides, we didn't have time to search around for wherever she might be keeping her personal screens, and disabling the one without disabling the other seemed rather pointless.

There wasn't anything great to use as a gag, but after digging around in her desk, I found a roll of packing tape. "Sorry about this," I said, wrapping it several times around her mouth as she glared at me in indignation. I almost admired her. All things considered, she'd handled the situation well. I wasn't sure that I'd have been so calm had a pair of gunmen burst in on me.

She was, I realized, a true believer. Unlike me, who had harbored doubts since I'd learned the truth about Annabelle, she honestly believed the synthetics were less than human. I understood how people like Francoise Fortier could feel that way; as much as I hated the bastard, his view on synthetics, while immoral, wasn't really his fault. Could you blame a person who had been told things were a particular way for their entire life for believing that things were that way? But I didn't get how someone who worked in a Walton Biogenics research lab, who "saw how the sausage was made" could cling to those same beliefs. Was it willful ignorance, an intentional closing of the eyes and shuttering of the mind to what must be mountains of evidence? Or did the cover-up run so deep that even within Walton, things were highly compartmentalized?

I didn't know what to believe, but it made me look at Dr. Larkin in a different light.

"Watch the news very closely in the days ahead, Dr. Larkin," I told the bound woman. "You may not believe what I've been saying, and maybe that's not your fault. But I assume that the 'doctor' in front of your name means that you're a believer in evidentiary-based reasoning. I think you'll be surprised."

"If you are quite done?" Silas's voice came over my earpiece. "You may want to hurry. I have penetrated some of the frequencies used for security communications. There is some chatter about a missing team. I suspect they are referring to my unwelcome elevator companions. It sounds like search teams are being sent out. A sense of urgency is called for, Detective."

"You get all that, Al?" I asked.

"Working on it," he replied, as he gathered up bundles of documents, optical discs, and data sticks. "Time to go."

Chapter 21

We left Dr. Larkin's office, and I slipped the door closed behind me. I wasn't surprised to hear an immediate rattle coming from inside. No doubt the doctor was trying to escape her bonds. I wished her luck with that—she was far more likely to topple her chair then she was to snap the restraints. Of course, if she *did* knock herself over, she was likely to do some damage to herself. Which would be another thing tallied to the litany of crimes I'd eventually be charged with. I'm sure my "assault" of a poor defenseless woman would play great on the vids.

I keyed my mic. "We're inbound, Silas. Get the elevator to the floor."

"On the way," Silas replied. "Be advised, security is doing a floor by floor search for their missing team. I do not, repeat, do not have eyes on all of them. Proceed with caution."

I snorted. The warning was hardly necessary, but at the same time, it was just about time to throw caution to the wind. If security was actively looking, maybe not for us, but for some unspecified threat, speed was more valuable then stealth. "Let's pick up the pace a bit, Al," I said, lengthening my stride. My hand hovered close to my side, ready to pull the concealed forty-five at a moment's notice.

We were maybe twenty-five feet from the freight elevator when I heard the sound of a heavy door closing. It wasn't an elevator door, but rather a steel fire door, the kind that building codes required to be placed at stairwells. Stairwells like the one that ran alongside the elevator shaft we had commandeered. While it was possible—just—that an employee might be taking the stairs up to the third floor, it seemed pretty unlikely that they would be taking the back stairs, by the freight elevator.

"We've got company," I said to Al'awwal.

"How do you want to play it?" he asked.

I'd already considered the problem, so the answer came fast. "We stick to the plan. Bluff, then fight. Avoid shooting if we can. But if they go to guns, we take them out."

The synthetic nodded, his eyes gleaming with a hunger that I found more than a little disturbing. How must it have been for him to watch—no, not just watch, but effectively hide—as people just like him were systematically brutalized, enslaved, and raped, with no recourse, no hope for justice? How long had he been waiting to get a little piece of his own back?

"Remember," I said, a warning note in my voice, "we don't want to kill anyone if we can avoid it."

"Of course," he said. But that hunger was still in his voice, and it did little to assuage my doubts.

"My lead," I grunted, and he just nodded.

We rounded the last corner and came face-to-face with not one, not a trio, but six security types. Two of them were wearing the same slacks and blazers as the guys I'd disabled in the elevator, but the other four... The other four were NLPD. And not just regular cops. They wore the battle rattle and ballistic helmets of SWAT. And they were carrying the fully SOPMOD-ed ZR-8 assault rifle, the successor to the venerable M8. Worse, I recognized one of them.

I was shocked as hell to see the hulking form of Tommy Thompson, but there was no mistaking his young and open face, even behind the Lexan of his visor. How the rookie had gotten tapped for SWAT, I had no idea. It probably said something about just how thin NLPD had been stretched over the past month, but I felt the bile rising in my throat at the thought of what I was about to do.

There would be no bluffing our way past these men, not with four NLPD officers on the other side. Even if they didn't know me from the force, they were cops, trained to observe, to be on the lookout for wanted criminals. They would, sure as shit, recognize one of their former brothers in blue who was now topping every most wanted list. Talking wasn't an option.

I moved to the first security guard, aware of Al'awwal moving behind me. I didn't want to shoot anyone, but I knew that we might not have a choice. The guard was surprised by my action—they might have been looking for something, but they clearly hadn't expected to find it right after they got off the stairs. I grabbed the first guy by the lapels of his blazer and spun, dropping my weight as I snapped him around in a semicircle, sending him stumbling into his compatriots. I didn't do any real damage, but it *did* get him momentarily entangled with his friends in a confusing bundle of limbs and weapon harnesses. Enough of a tangle that no weapon popped up immediately to put three into my chest. I was in their midst, and Al was right on my heels. Close enough that the carbines would be of limited use.

That still left us outnumbered three to one. And they all had sidearms.

Cursing under my breath, I snapped out a front kick, catching the guard I'd sent tumbling into his fellows. I didn't hit body armor, nor had I expected to—the boys in the elevator hadn't been geared up, either. The man folded in half and fell backward, worsening the clusterfuck of bodies. And buying me time to draw my gun.

Al'awwal hadn't been idle. He'd reacted almost as quickly as I had, peeling off to the side. One of the SWAT officers—not Tommy—had avoided the initial tangle by lunging to the side and flattening himself against the wall, letting the parade of bodies pass him by. Al was on him in a heartbeat, not bothering to draw his own weapon, pushing the officer's ZR-8 up and away, so the muzzle pointed at the sky. Al'awwal used the weapon strap against the officer, yanking it first up and then down and over, pulling the man off balance. He dropped to the floor, and I had just enough time to see Al drop, knees to chest, on top of him. I winced and, despite everything, silently prayed that the officer's body armor would protect him from the flail chest that particular technique could generate.

Then the others were back, balance regained, and coming at me. I couldn't tell who had pulled iron and who hadn't, but I knew that with a gun in my hand, I was fair game. Hell, even without it, I was fair game, and one mistake by me or Al'awwal and we were as good as dead. Al was finishing with his target, rolling away and to his feet, and I knew if I backed up, I'd clear a lane for shooting, and not only would I be dead, but Al with me.

I couldn't back up, so I pressed forward. I was already at damn-near grapple distance with the officers. I couldn't afford to be grabbed, particularly not with Thompson in the mix. With his jiu-jitsu training, I'd likely be screwed even without the four other bodies bearing down on me. With them... Well, I definitely didn't want to be grabbed. The SWAT guys were good, trained to move and fight as a unit, but that training focused on things that went bang. They weren't supposed to get to hand-to-hand distance. Individually, I'm sure they were all skilled, but in the tight confines of the hallway in front of the service elevator, they got in each other's way.

Which is the only thing that kept me alive in those first few seconds.

I intentionally angled away from Thompson—I knew the big man had skill, and there was no way I could deal with him while worrying about the others. So I broke one of the cardinal rules of footwork and took a big crossover step with my left foot, stepping past my right foot as I moved forward, pivoting on the left as it landed. If you got caught in the middle of the step, with your feet crossed, your balance was shit, but if executed well, you could cover a lot of ground in an unexpected direction. I executed it well.

It put me beside an NLPD officer, one who still held his ZR-8 in both hands. He had been raising it to butt-stroke me, but I stepped clear around him, taking his flank and putting him bodily between me and the other officers—who were now moving in the wrong direction. It put me against the wall. Not the best place to be, since it limited my mobility, a key to surviving against multiple attackers, but it also insured that none of them would be getting behind me. I was in a tight spot, though. I couldn't afford to simply knock the officer I'd stepped around down and hope he forgot where the trigger was…. And yet, I didn't want to shoot him either. I didn't have a lot of options, and the most effective were also the most nasty. He was going to be in for one hell of a headache.

As I cleared the officer, I punched forward with my forty-five, careful to keep my trigger finger flat along the slide. I rammed the barrel into the side of his neck, below the ear and behind the jaw. He twitched once and dropped hard. He was still conscious, but his eyes were wide and locked with tendrils of pain as the blow overloaded his occipital nerves. I felt a weird surge of triumph and regret as the officer dropped—I needed to take these guys down, but dammit, I still thought of myself as one of them. But the victory, such as it was, didn't come without cost.

I managed to raise my left arm, hand protecting my cheek and jaw, elbow covering my upper ribs as the next officer reached me, his rifle already in full swing. I rolled with the motion as much as possible as the polymer stock smashed into my shoulder. I felt the blow from my fingertips all the way to my head, but only for a moment. Then my left arm went numb and tingly, hanging loosely at my side. There was a look of victory in the officer's eyes as he raised the rifle once more to finish the job.

And instead caught a couple hundred pounds of flying synthetic as Al'awwal bowled bodily into him.

I didn't have time to see what became of that, because three more officers were still moving toward me—including Thompson. Feeling was starting to return to my arm, and I managed to raise it as the security guard came in swinging. I covered up and took the blows on my arms, protecting my ribs and head, but it gave them the opening they were waiting for. One of the officers lowered his head and shot in at my legs, looking for a single leg takedown to drop me to the ground. If that happened, it was over for me. No way I could fight off three of them on the ground.

The setup wasn't ideal, and that saved me. The security guard, still actively pummeling me, blocked the best line to my lower extremities. The wall at my back further complicated things, forcing the officer to shoot in from the side, with only a couple of feet of viable space to maneuver. Had he managed to get ahold of my leg from that angle, it wouldn't have been pretty. Knees really only bend in one direction.

But he didn't manage to get a grip on me. As he shot in, I broke off my defensive posture and launched both my hands forward, creating a wedge in front of me that split through the wild swings of the security officer. I didn't bother striking him, instead using the opening to drop my right arm—the one still working at normal efficiency—into the crook of his neck and shoulder, and then twisted, using the motion of my arm, torso, and hips to send him spinning into the wall...and directly into the path of the charging officer.

They both went down, neither really hurt, but on the ground and, at least for the moment, out of the fight. A quick glance showed me Al'awwal on his back on the ground, the officer he'd tackled lying on top of him, his back to Al's chest. The synthetic had his legs wrapped around the officer's hips and his left arm wrapped around his neck, hand in the crook of his right elbow. His right hand was on the back of the officer's helmeted head, locking in the choke. I hoped that Al'awwal was just planning on putting the officer to sleep and not killing him outright—a very real possibility with the choke he was employing—but I didn't have time to worry about that. The cop and security guard to my left were still trying to get untangled from each other and back to their feet, but I was looking straight into the eyes of Thomas Thompson.

He had dropped his rifle, and it dangled from his harness, barrel down and away. But in his meaty hands he held his sidearm, a standard-issue nine millimeter. He looked me right in the eye. "Drop it, Campbell. Don't make me shoot you."

He should have shot me. All the rules of engagement said so, and it would have been a justified shoot in anyone's book. In that situation, you didn't stop to talk. You pulled the trigger and went home to your family. In another time, another place, I would have gotten all over Thompson for *not* taking the shot when he had the chance. Just this once, though, I was glad the big man hesitated.

Because I didn't.

I pulled the trigger. Repeatedly.

I was firing from the hip, but the distance was short enough that it didn't matter. I held the forty-five tight against my body and used my entire torso to aim, like the turret on a tank. It was risky, but Thompson had me dead to rights. I fired off three rounds in less than a second, and all three found their target.

In his vest.

I'm an asshole, but I'm not *that* big of an asshole.

Still, the shots struck like hammer blows. They didn't knock him down. That's just netshow bullshit. But imagine three hard punches to the sternum. Sure, it might not knock you on your ass, but it sure as shit is going to hurt and make your attention wander just a bit. I was moving right behind the shots, darting forward as soon as I stopped pulling the trigger. Conventional wisdom said to move to Thompson's outside, angling away from the gun, but also in the direction that the human hand and wrist had the most limited range of motion. I moved to the inside, instead.

Thompson's reaction to the impacts—and probably the sheer surprise of getting shot by someone with whom he was friendly—had thrown his gun hand wide as his other hand moved instinctively to the impact sites. I stepped inside his gun arm, driving my left hand, palm open, into his left forearm. The pressure trapped that arm against his chest, if only for a second, giving me the opening to deliver a straight right. I didn't put that right into Thompson's face. The visor of his ballistic helmet would have shrugged off any blow, even given that I was holding a three-pound chunk of steel in my fist. Instead, I drove the barrel of the forty-five into his exposed gun arm, striking just beneath the point of the bicep. I put the full weight of my body into that shot, carrying it forward with the long stride I'd taken to reach Thompson.

It wasn't a nice thing to do. The barrel dug into his medial antebrachial cutaneous nerve and I knew from personal experience the lightening arcs of pain the strike would send up and down his arm. More importantly, the blow, delivered properly, would cause numbness and muscle weakness in the arm and hand.

I delivered it properly, and Thompson's gun dropped from his nerveless fingers to dangle from his sling.

Then, without missing a beat, he smashed his helmeted head full into my face.

I went down.

Hard.

The rim of his helmet had caught me just above the bridge of the nose. I couldn't be sure, but I thought I'd heard the crunch of breaking cartilage.

Blood poured down my face, and pretty lights and colors flashed in front of my eyes. All that happened as I fell, but I tried my best to compartmentalize the pain, to focus on the fact that if I slipped up, even now, it would mean capture or death.

As my butt hit the carpet, I threw myself back and to the side, rolling over my left shoulder in a move I'd practiced a thousand times on the mats. It wasn't nearly as smooth on the carpet, with a tangle of injured men scattered about, but I managed to pull it off, rolling awkwardly back to my feet.

I had an instant, no more, to assess our situation. Al'awwal was on his feet but pressed up against the wall with the two remaining officers tight on him, grabbing and pummeling. Three of the enemy were down for the count, and we'd managed to cut the odds from three to one to three to two, doubling our chances. But not without cost. My head was ringing and my left arm still responding sluggishly, and in that brief moment, I caught the flash of bright red standing out against Al'awwal's skin as well.

Then the moment passed, and Thompson was on me, barreling in like a bull, head lowered, trusting in his helmet to absorb anything I could offer. I'd lost my forty-five in the midst of the roll. I couldn't remember dropping it, but my head was spinning from the pain of the broken nose and maybe a concussion. My legs felt wobbly beneath me, so I did the only thing I could. I shoved my own arms out in front and sprawled, absorbing the charge of the bigger man. Thompson still knocked me backward, despite the nearly forty-five degree angle I was making with my body, my boots sliding along the carpet, but at least he didn't get ahold of me. His right arm—his gun arm—was moving even more sluggishly than my left arm, still suffering from the pistol punch to the biceps.

"Fucking stop already, Campbell," he growled at me. "It's over." His left arm was clamped around my neck, right arm reaching—weakly—for my hip.

"Sorry, brother," I said. "Can't do that."

He grunted and exploded into movement once more, dropping to one knee while keeping his torso upright, and then passing his rear leg to the front, switching the knee that was on the ground, and his body flowed forward, inside my sprawl, arms reaching around to the tops of my legs. If he completed the technique he would have lifted and dumped me, smashing me to the ground, and almost certainly dropping right on top of me. Given my current state, the only advantage I had was mobility. If Thompson scooped me, it was over.

As he shot in, he had no choice but to release his controlling grip on my neck. He tried to weave out of my own grip on his, using the quickness of the maneuver to take me by surprise. I'd been expecting the move, or something like it, and I responded by rolling my right hand, forcing his head around as I pivoted. I continued the motion with my right arm, ending in what many Chinese-inspired arts would have called a low *bong-sau*, framing Thompson out and away from my legs while simultaneously smashing my left palm into the side of his helmet. Not waiting to see the reaction, I freed my right arm and slammed a barrage of hammer fists onto the back of his head. He managed to stay on his feet for a few heartbeats before his legs went boneless and he dropped to the ground.

I immediately disengaged and scanned around, trying to assess Al'awwal's situation, but there was no need. It was over. He stood over the bodies—I hoped just unconscious and not dead—of the last two cops. He had a nasty cut over one eye that was oozing blood and a split lip. Other than that, he seemed to have fared better than me. Well, he hadn't had to deal with Thompson.

Judging by my ragged breathing, the entire fight had lasted a minute, maybe two. I surveyed the bodies on the floor, watching for the rise and fall of chests. Everyone seemed to be breathing. I didn't doubt that some of the damage would be lasting, maybe permanent, but at least we hadn't dropped any bodies. I found Al'awwal's eyes and saw the emotion burning there, anger and fear and excitement. And hope. Hope that we might actually pull this off. Hope that the data his father had made his life's work would have meaning.

I opened my mouth to speak, but before I could, the elevator dinged, and the doors opened, revealing Silas's pale face. No doubt, he had been watching the whole thing on the lab's cameras and had waited until we had finished the job before triggering the doors. Not that I could blame him. With his conditioning, he wouldn't have been much help, and had we lost, he was the last hope for the revolution.

"Time to go, gentlemen," he said.

Time. And past time.

Chapter 22

"Did you get it?" Silas asked as the elevator doors closed.

He seemed completely unconcerned about the pile of bodies we'd left in the hallway, and a very un-Silas-like edge of excitement burned in his tone.

"We got it," I replied. "Whatever it might be."

"Good. But we have problems. Police have entered the building and begun systematic searches."

"Yeah. We kinda noticed." I was probing at my nose as I spoke, wincing through the pain as I tried to determine if it was broken. The bleeding, at least, had stopped, but damn did it hurt. Al'awwal held a folded bit of gauze against the cut above his eye, hoping to stem the flow of blood there, as well. Our lab coats, mediocre disguise that they had been to begin with, were now useless, dirtied and bloodied in the scuffle.

"Our exit plan has been compromised. And it is only a matter of time before questions are raised about this elevator. A matter of rather short time, I imagine."

Silas had stopped the elevator between floors, giving us a few minutes to think in relative safety. Well, so long as the bad guys didn't regain control and guide the elevator to a convenient location the cops and security folks had turned into an abattoir, anyway.

"What's the situation?" I asked. I gave up on my nose. If it was broken, there wasn't anything I could do about it now, so I resolved to just deal with the pulsing throb of pain that shot from my nose throughout the rest of my face and, for some reason, settled at the base of my skull with every heartbeat.

"Officers at every possible point of egress. Teams of officers and security guards searching the building. And, I imagine, those you dealt with will be regaining their senses soon enough to call in and confirm that we are, in fact, in the building."

"So basically, we're fucked," I grunted.

"Basically."

I drew a deep breath, thinking it through. We were so damn close. We needed a way out, any way out. "Sewers?" I asked, already knowing the answer.

"No access, Detective."

"Rooftop?"

"We can get there, but we have no way of getting anywhere from there. And, if you will recall, all of the aircraft belong to the opposition."

"If all other paths are blocked, then we must go out the door," Al'awwal said. He had poured some water from a canteen and was busily cleaning the blood off of his face. He was being none too careful with water or discarded gauze, I noted, and much of it was splashing onto the other three occupants of the elevator. The bound and gagged security officers had all regained consciousness and were glaring pure hatred at the three of us.

I ignored them. "We can't walk out the door without being recognized. And if we're recognized, it's over. We got lucky before, but there's no way we can cut through all the officers out there."

"We don't have to. We'll only be noticed if we stand out. And we won't stand out if the entire building is being evacuated. Surely, by now, Silas has hacked into all the pertinent systems. How hard would it be to trigger some sort of general fire alarm, or some such? If there is a press of people all trying to leave..." He trailed off, and I nodded.

It was risky. Very risky. All it took was one guard, one cop, noticing that we didn't quite fit in with the rest of the office personnel, and we would be done. But I didn't have a better plan. "Can you do it, Silas?" I asked.

"Trigger the fire alarms? Yes. A simple enough matter. But perhaps I can more than that as well." He was back among his screens now, fingers working furiously over the surfaces, voice distracted.

"More?" I prompted when nothing else was forthcoming.

"They work with numerous biological agents in this building, Jason. Any bio-lab runs the risk of some level of contagion. And I doubt that Walton Biogenics is so pure as to not be dabbling in some of the more dangerous areas possible in the biological sciences. It is almost guaranteed that the labs here have some sort of alarm system. A fire alarm is nice, but easy enough to ignore if you do not see the smoke or feel the heat. But if I can trigger one of the lab alarms... Well, it is much more difficult to convince people to stay in their offices if they believe a biological agent might be filtering through the air conditioning system."

His fingers hadn't slowed as he spoke, and by the spreading smile on his lips, I knew he was getting close. There was a long, pregnant moment where no one spoke. All of us—including the bound security guards—simply watched Silas work, our gazes drawn to the lodestone of his concentration. That moment was shattered as the lights in the elevator shifted from white to blood red and a piercing whistle sounded over a heretofore unnoticed speaker. After the whistles, a monotone and vaguely feminine voice said, "Warning. Warning. There has been a breach in containment unit seven. Please proceed to the nearest exit in a calm and orderly fashion. Warning. Warning." The whistle repeated, and then the warning.

"I believe if we give it a minute or two, we should be able to join the 'calm and orderly' procession of people exiting the building."

"Not like this, we can't," I noted, waving one hand at the bloody lab coats. "And not under arms." I hefted the sub-gun that I had retrieved. "Can these be traced back to you?" I asked Al'awwal.

He shrugged. "Does it matter? Unless you plan on killing these," he waved toward the bound security guards, "they will have an excellent description of all of us. I imagine they'll know who, if not what, I am soon enough. No matter, though. I didn't accept this task without understanding the potential consequences." He gave a little shrug and a slight smile.

I nodded. On some level, I'd already known that. The fact that Al'awwal, who lived a life of relative luxury, was willing to throw that away with a shrug and a smile to help serve the cause... Well, it said a lot about the man, and maybe a lot about the cause. "Then we leave them behind. Along with all the other gear. They already know who I am, and I doubt they'll care much about another faceless synthetic." I gave a half-apologetic nod to Silas. "If you're not worried about them finding you, then we abandon everything but what we came for. And I think a wardrobe change is in order as well."

"While you see to that," Silas said, "I shall see what can be done about arranging transportation. We may be able to walk out of this building, but we do not want to be on the streets for very long. There are far too many watchful eyes, electronic and otherwise."

"Right," I said, eyeing the bound security guards, trying to determine which one was closest to me in size. "Let's get to work, then."

* * * *

It was only a few minutes later when the freight elevator—which should have been locked down as part of the standard building evacuation procedures—dinged. The doors opened into a crowded and chaotic warehouse. The large loading bay doors were one of the main egresses for emergencies, and people were streaming not only from the stairwell but also from adjoining doors that led, I assumed, deeper into the labs.

The three of us, clad now in the blazers and ties of the security guards still restrained on the floor, stepped from the elevator. I did my best to use my body to shield the view to the elevator's interior, but I needn't have bothered. No one in that warehouse had the slightest interest in looking back. That made me wonder just what it was—apart from researching how to make better and cheaper synthetics—that Walton Biogenics did here. I had expected the thought of a biological contaminant to properly motivate people, but I saw real, deep fear on the faces around me. The kind of fear that would only be present if they knew that there was more going on here than met the eye.

I filed that thought away. Now wasn't the time. We had more important matters to attend to—like getting the hell out of Dodge before the cops snapped us up. We joined the press of people, though I did catch Silas surreptitiously entering a command on his screen. That sent the elevator doors closing behind us and locked the elevator down once more. I felt a brief flash of guilt over the security guards tied up inside, but it wasn't as if there was a biological agent loose. They would be found, eventually. They might be a little uncomfortable in the interim, but it was certainly better than the other alternative we had for dealing with them.

The wave of bodies carried the three of us toward the doors. I could see a trio of officers there, trying to watch the press of people. I'd worked door duty more than once on my way to detective, and I knew just how futile their task was. In the sea of panicked faces, it was all but impossible to pick out one individual, unless that person happened to pass right by you. And given that the bad guys—okay, me in this case—knew where the good guys were, and the reverse wasn't true, it was easy enough to make sure that didn't happen. "We need to separate a bit," I said in low voice to Silas and Al'awwal. "The three of us together might draw some attention."

They didn't bother with a response. Each simply angled away from me, cutting across the crowd at a new angle. We were all headed to the massive garage doors; the twenty feet of open space was all but impossible to effectively watch, but they each headed a little wider. I stuck straight to the middle, slouching a bit to conceal my height and keeping my head down. The press of people was tight around me, and I went with it, letting the river of office workers carry me across the concrete floor and toward the portal. There was a slowdown as we reached the doors and the officers did their best to vet the exiting staff, but they were a few rocks in the stream. The crowd flowed around them in all directions, only those within arm's reach truly hindered by their presence.

I felt a moment of stomach-twisting tension as I approached the door. Even knowing the odds, there was always a chance, however slim, that one of the cops would turn at the wrong moment. That they would catch sight of me out of the corner of their eye. That some well-meaning staffer of the lab would stop at the wrong time. There were a hundred ways it could all go wrong. A thousand. My stomach churned, but then I was through, past the cops at the doors. The soulless fluorescent lights vanished, replaced by the warm glow of the morning sun.

The streets outside the lab were every bit as chaotic as the warehouse floor. Protesters, now more interested in the goings-on at the lab than in their protest, had shifted into gawker mode, signs and placards forgotten as they pressed closer to the building. Where the stream of evacuating lab staff met the wall of protesters, confusion met concern, anger met panic. The violence was inevitable.

I don't know how it started. From the middle of the crowd, I had no view of the front lines. But whatever sparked the surging mob quickly exploded. One minute, we were streaming out of the lab, moving away from the building and toward the street. The next, I found myself in the middle of a violent melee as pushing and shoving gave way to punching and clubbing. The Walton employees wanted nothing more than to get away from the lab. The protesters... I had no idea what they wanted. To interfere with Walton's operations, I supposed, and ordinarily, I would have wished them well of it.

At the moment, however, their enthusiasm was causing me some trouble.

My steady advance away from the labs—and the cops—had come to a halt as one wave of humanity crashed against another. Worse, the confrontation was sure to draw the attention of every camera in the area, and doubtless a drone or three for good measure. I wouldn't be able to hide for long.

Which meant I had to get through the crowd.

Which meant I had to play dirty.

I stopped worrying about blending in and starting cutting my way through the throng. Where I could, I simply slipped between people, using my bulk like a splitting wedge. Where I met resistance, I attacked. The press of people was far too tight to throw individuals out of the way, so I targeted knees, ankles, groins, and kidneys. I tried to avoid permanently injuring anyone…but I knew that when they fell, and fall they did, in the press of people, they were at the mercy of the crowd.

Mobs were not known for their mercy.

I put that thought from my mind as I made my way through the rest of the Walton employees and into the crowd of protesters. I shed my security blazer—it would only make me a target on this side of the battle lines—and kept going, moving against the flow of bodies, looking for a break in a sea of grasping hands and flailing limbs.

Then the pressure eased, and I was through them, standing on the outskirts of the crowd. A steady trickle of others had done as I had, moving away from the confrontation rather than toward it. I was aware, in a distant sort of way, of the cries of panic and anger, but I ignored them. I focused on trying to scan the crowd while simultaneously keeping my head ducked, to avoid any prying eyes that might be pointed in my direction.

I could hear sirens in the distance, closing in. Whether their priority was the biological contamination alert, the burgeoning riot, or me, I didn't know, and I didn't care. Any way around it, I needed to get my ass out of sight. But I couldn't leave without Silas and Al'awwal.

I caught a flash of alabaster skin across the thinning crowd. Silas. I headed immediately in his direction. Al'awwal beat me there.

"Time to *di di* fucking *mao*," I grunted.

"You think?" Al'awwal asked, a wild excitement burning in his eyes.

"Follow me," Silas said. "The car is waiting, but I cannot get it close enough to the lab. With a sense of purpose, gentlemen." He put action to his words, turning on his heel and striding off. He moved quickly, but he did not run. There were enough people high-stepping it away with more than a bit of alacrity—that sense of purpose Silas mentioned—that we fit right in.

We'd gone less than a block before Silas turned to a vehicle parked along the side of the road. It was a simple panel van, the type still nearly ubiquitous on the city streets for the endless interior configuration possibilities. The doors popped open at his approach, and he slid into the front seat without breaking stride. I took the passenger seat, and Al'awwal dropped into the back. The doors closed, and as if we'd planned it that way all along, the car slid away from the curb.

"You are certain we got everything we came for?" Silas asked.

"As certain as we can be without going through it," Al'awwal replied.

"Whatever 'it' might be," I added. "Documents. Old electronic data storage. We'll have to go through it. Sort it out. See if we can figure out how best to distribute it." I counted in my head. "And we have to do it all in about four days. At least if we want to be able to use it day one." I thought about Thompson. Dr. Larkin. The security guards and cops we'd injured along the way. "And we're going to have to use it soon, Silas. We did enough damage to get this information that we're going from hackers to violent terrorists." I waved one hand, dismissing the argument I knew was forthcoming. "Yeah, yeah. I know we were there already with Walton Biogenics and their sycophants. And I know there's a contingent of 'lunatic fringe' that we can do no wrong with. But neither of those are the people we have to convince. We need the fence-sitters. The moderates. The people who can see both sides of the issue and who have honest cognitive dissonance as to how to feel about it all. If we can't win them to our side, then we've got no shot at pulling this off."

"Then, Jason," Silas said, "as you would say, we had better get to work."

Chapter 23

"You're back!" I grunted as Tia hurled herself bodily into me, arms clamping around my waist like a vise. The exclamation drew the eyes of the gathered synthetics, seated in the ramshackle remains of the restaurant-turned-safe-house, to us, but with Tia in my arms, I ignored them. She hugged me, and the warm press of her body against mine felt...good. Not like that. Okay, not *just* like that. But it felt safe, somehow.

Then she was pushing me away, hands going to my face, fingers probing at the broken and swollen wreckage of my nose. That felt less good. "Ow!" I half-shouted as her fingertips poked and prodded. "That hurts!"

"Stop being such a baby. It's broken. We're going to have to set it, or it will heal all crooked." I let her lead me off to the kitchen while Al'awwal and Silas headed deeper into the dining area, no doubt looking for La Sorte.

In short order I found myself rather firmly sat down on the kitchen prep table that had, only a day or two ago, been used to perform an autopsy. "You're too tall," Tia accused. Given that with me sitting on top of the table, her head barely reached my midchest, I could see her point. "Lie down."

I resisted the urge to bark like a disobedient dog and instead did as she suggested. The table was cold, even through my shirt, but it felt good to lie down and just be still. The past few days had been a torrent of constant action constricted by the dual pressures of stress and low-grade fear. And it wasn't over. We'd found some information, maybe even a smoking gun, buried somewhere in the data that La Sorte, Al'awwal, and Silas were probably digging through already. We maybe had a shiny new weapon to deploy against Walton Biogenics and their sycophants. But would it be enough to head off the literal war that I still believed was coming? Would it be enough to sway the multitudes that had grown fat and complacent on the backs of the synthetics?

Somehow, I didn't think so.

"This is going to hurt," Tia said, her hands once more running over my face.

"It always does," I replied, fighting to keep the air of resignation—not about the pain of setting my broken nose, but about the enormity and maybe futility of our situation—out of my voice.

She didn't bother responding. Her hands moved with swift, sure pressure, and I heard the crackle of shifting cartilage. A sharp spike of pain flashed through my nose and sinuses, followed almost immediately by a flood of relief as the flash faded, taking with it most of the residual pain.

"Thank you, Tia," I half-whispered, my eyes closed, the twin siren songs of exhaustion and lessened pain urging me to sleep. Couldn't do that. Too much left to do. Too many miles left to go.

"No time like the present." I felt a moment of confusion at Tia's words. They'd been spoken clearly, but not to me. More like she was talking to herself. Then the moment of confusion turned into a giant blaring symphony of confusion as I felt lips press against mine. My eyes snapped open, and there she was, leaning over me from the front of the table on which I lay. Her hands were flat on the table on either side of my head, her dark hair falling in a curtain around our faces.

For a moment I could only stare into her eyes in stark surprise. Then something gave and I kissed her back.

Time lost all meaning. I'm not sure how long we stayed like that. Maybe it was only a few seconds. Maybe it was hours. But when Tia finally straightened up, I was out of breath.

"Well," she said with a dreamy little smile. "Well, well, well."

I wasn't sure how to respond. Despite being more than a decade her senior, I would never be the suave ladies' man. My experience in that department was limited—Annabelle's death had done some fairly permanent damage to my view of relationships, and neither the military nor the force had helped in that regard. Fortunately, I was spared the near-certain embarrassment of opening my fool mouth as the door to the kitchen swung open. Silas stood in it, surveying us for a long moment. At least he hadn't walked in a few seconds before, but he would have had to have been blind and deaf to not notice that the atmosphere in the room was…off.

At last, he said, "You need to see this."

I swung my legs off the table and sat up. A wave of dizziness—dealer's choice between exhaustion or a side effect of the battering I'd taken—washed over me. I waited a few seconds for it to pass, then slid off the table. Terra firma didn't feel quite so firma, but I tried to shake it off. "Right," I said. I looked at Tia, who had one of those small, secretive, distinctly female smiles on her face. "You coming?"

Her smile broadened. "Yes, Detective. Let's go see what your revolution has brewing."

* * * *

We found La Sorte and Al'awwal at the familiar screen-covered table that La Sorte had started jokingly calling the "command booth." The screens were covered with files—text, pictures, even some videos playing with the sound muted. I slid into the empty booth seat, and Tia slid in next to me, pressing her body against mine. Was that in an effort to make room for Silas as he lowered his bulk onto the bench? Or something else? Damn, but did I *really* want these kinds of complications right now?

Was there ever a good time?

"What have we got?" I asked.

"Problems," La Sorte replied. Then he grinned. "But don't we always?"

I nodded at that as Silas continued. "We have a trove of information here, Detective. A large percentage of the actual data is the personal diary of Dr. Kaphiri, covering nearly two decades of work on the research, development, and implementation of the synthetic programs." He paused, a thoughtful frown pulling at his lips. "Dr. Kaphiri is, in a very real sense, our creator. And, from what we have discovered so far, he had every intention of being a *benevolent* creator, had Walton not sunk their hooks quite so firmly into him. His personal diaries are full of his thoughts on the inherent differences—or rather lack thereof—between humans and synthetics. Ordinarily, this would not carry much weight. After all, it is, as they say, one man's opinion. In this case, however, the man is *the* expert on the subject. Which is also the problem."

"Come again?" I said, and I felt Tia tightening in confusion as well.

"The rest of the package is harder data. Scientific breakdowns of gene sequences. Some internal memos on limiting the availability of medical breakthroughs. Recordings of experiments, early successes and failures. But the hard data without the context of Dr. Kaphiri's diaries is…problematic. Inconclusive. It is the explanations, the intentions, the clarifications that the doctor provides that create the context for the rest of the information. It is what makes it consumable for those without advanced degrees in genetics or biochemistry. It is what might win us the hearts and minds of the people."

"Still not seeing the problem. I mean, we have the diaries, right?"

"The problem," Al'awwal said, anger burning in his voice, "is that Silas does not think people will *believe* my father."

The albino raised his hands in a gesture half calming, half supplication. "No, Al'awwal. Not that they will not believe your father. That they will not believe *us*." He waved his hand in an expansive spread that included those of us at the table, but also all of the other synthetics gathered in the safe house. "While it will be difficult for anyone to insist that the actual transcripts and experimentation data are fabricated, the editorializing of Dr. Kaphiri..." He trailed off under Al's glare.

"He's right, Al," I sighed. "There's no great way to authenticate that these writings actually came from your father. I mean, sure, we all know that's the case, but the people in charge of this shit-show of a world have every incentive to discredit this information any way they can."

"Which means we did not achieve our goal," Silas said. I heard the note of defeat in his voice, and it shocked the hell out of me. Of all of us, I never thought Silas—Silas!—would give in to despair, even for a moment. This was his cause, his crusade, and he had been the backbone of the operation. Not just logistically, but, I realized as I saw La Sorte's face fall in response to Silas's tone, emotionally and spiritually as well.

"Well," Silas continued, obviously trying to shake the dark mood. "We may not have the perfect weapon, but it's not as if we have anything less than we did yesterday, either."

They were brave words, but it was clear from the faces around us that no one really believed that. And as I watched, I could see that sense of failure spread, carried on whispers and glances, from our command booth out to the rest of the restaurant. Slowly, inexorably, the mood in the safe house darkened. After only a moment or two, you could practically taste the fear. Smell the hopelessness.

The bitch of it was, there *was* a way to lend some legitimacy to the information.

And all it would require was me giving up...everything.

I thought about Hernandez, who had put not only her career but her life, her freedom, and maybe her daughter's well-being on the line for me. I thought about Tommy Thompson, who was almost certainly in a hospital bed somewhere for trying to do his job. I thought about Tia, taking risks every bit as substantial as Hernandez. Tia, pressed up against me, vibrant with the energy of possibilities and futures I had never imagined for myself, not since Annabelle.

I thought of the synthetics, those gathered here in the safe house, and those all over the world who every day suffered in ways I could scarcely comprehend.

I thought of Annabelle and the life she might have had if someone had been willing to act a little sooner.

Against all that, did my freedom, my life, matter all that much?

"We can make them believe it," I said, my words falling like boulders into the silence.

"What?" Al'awwal asked at the same time Silas said, "How?"

"I turn myself in."

If I had thought the silence was profound before, I had been mistaken. Not only did all conversation stop at my words, but I was fairly sure everyone's breathing stopped.

"No!" Tia was the first to speak. "Why would you even suggest that? Don't be stupid. What difference would that make?"

"I am not sure I understand how that would be helpful," Silas added.

"Are you out of your fucking mind?" Al'awwal said.

"Enough!" The sharp word cut through their arguments as I slammed my hand on the table. "Look, you, all of you, know a lot more about all of this genetic bullshit than I ever will. But I was a cop for a long time, and you don't last without learning two things: how the legal system works and how the population thinks. I know people, and I know the law. If I turn myself in, carrying copies of all of this," I waved at the information scattered across the screens, "it's going to be entered into the public record. The arrest report. It can all be part of the disclosure and deposition process. I think I still have enough pull, maybe even enough friends within the courts, left to make sure nothing gets swept under the rug." I paused, looking each of them in the eye for a moment. "With the right lawyer, all of this, every last bit of it, will be in front of the people—legally and without any question of its provenance—before they're done booking me.

"But that's not even the important part. Like I said, I know people. And people are going to be a hell of a lot more inclined to believe all of this once they find out that the most wanted man in the city—maybe the world—was willing to turn himself in just to get it on the record. You want to win the hearts and minds of the people? This information is our best shot. And turning myself in is the best way to make people believe that we're not just making it all up. Instead of coming from us—from a bunch of inhuman hackers on the net, the information will be piped to them from the news sources and people that they trust. We *have* to take this chance."

"They'll kill you," Tia whispered. She clutched my hand under the table, squeezing with a sudden desperation. "I've worked with the medical examiner for a while. Do you know how many inmates who die in prison come across the autopsy table? Walton Biogenics. The government. Hell, even angry inmates who know you're a cop. You won't stand a chance. You're martyring yourself, Jason."

There was more than a little truth to what Tia was saying, but I'd known it before I opened my mouth. Still, no sense in scaring her more than she already was. I squeezed her hand back and said, "Come on now, Tia. I'm a shitty martyr. And I take a whole lot of killing. I'll be fine." The words rang a little hollow in my own ears, but I forced a confident grin on my face.

She said nothing, just clung to me.

"Are you sure about this, Jason?" Silas asked. "You make strong points, but… My people have already asked much of you. You have given much. Are you certain?"

I fell silent a long moment, trying to put my feelings into words. "This country used to be called the 'Great Experiment,' you know? Back when the rhetoric was all about freedom and equality. Of course, the rhetoric came long before any semblance of either. And it didn't come without a price. It was paid for in blood." Tia's nails dug into my hand, but I ignored the pain. "I'm not planning on just giving up and walking to my own execution, but what we're doing—what you've started, Silas—is for the good of not just this country, but the entire world. I sat by and ignored it long enough. At some point, it's time to step up and risk everything to do what's right."

I reached under the table and gave Tia's knee a reassuring squeeze. "For me, that time has come."

Epilogue

Dr. Delores Larkin ate her lunch at her desk.

There was still a tear in the carpet where that no-good felon Jason Campbell had stolen company property—even if she didn't know what it was or why it was in her office, it was still the property of Walton Biogenics.

It still made her shake to think about, being trussed up in her chair like a Christmas roast. The shaking was, she admitted, just a tiny bit of fear, but most of it was the almighty indignity of the situation.

She'd been offered a different office while hers was repaired, but damn if she'd let a crackpot with a gun drive her out of her space. No sir. So she'd hunkered back down and got back to work. And she did her best to put the crackpot, and the faint shadows of doubt that he'd cultivated in her mind, to rest.

As she took a forkful of chicken-pecan salad, her screen buzzed. It did that a lot—she was a busy person, after all, and she'd coded the different individuals and search routines with their own specific notification sounds. This one was the swoosh-and-chimes of her "breaking news" alert. Her news filter was draconian, and anything triggering the alert had to be major news. So she pulled the screen from her pocket and flicked open her news app.

Her heart immediately started to race, and she felt a panicked sweat break out beneath her arms.

The footage was live, and it showed a tired and battered-looking man wearing a rumpled brown suit with his hands secured behind his back. Thick bandages covered his nose, obscuring the details of his face, and the cameras lingered lovingly on the cuts, bruises, and blood. Bandage or no, Dr. Larkin recognized him. You didn't forget the face of someone who held you at gunpoint. Her initial panic reaction at seeing that face faded as she took in the details.

"They caught you, you bastard!" she said in an exultant whisper, forkful of arugula forgotten halfway between her plate and her mouth.

He was escorted by a female officer of Latin descent. She wore a much nicer suit in black, tailored not so much to accentuate her figure but to properly conceal body armor and weaponry.

Someone, probably an actual reporter since the feed was live, was saying, "In an amazing turn of events, former New Lyons Police Detective Jason Campbell has been apprehended. The manhunt that has paralyzed the city for weeks has officially ended."

On the bottom of her screen, all but illegible from the size, was a scroll of text, outlining some of the details and reactions: New Lyons Detective Jason Campbell surrenders to NLPD. Revolution Averted? Protests still underway.

Larkin watched as Campbell was walked up the stairs of the police headquarters, where he was turned over—reluctantly, it seemed to her—into the hands of a greasy, pudgy man in a cheap suit.

"There you have it," the reporter said. "Just like that, Campbell, wanted on a wide array of criminal charges including domestic terrorism, is now in the hands of the NLPD. We don't know the details of his surrender, but our sources are suggesting that it was conditional upon a large cache of documents being entered into the record as evidence. We don't yet know the content of these documents, or if they even exist."

Documents? That thought brought a sour twist to Larkin's stomach. Her finger twitched, almost of its own accord, as she thought about calling Legal. No doubt that the documents in question were whatever Campbell and his friend had retrieved from her office. And no doubt, Legal needed to know about it.

But she didn't make the call. The doubts that Campbell had planted were still there, and now, against her will, they seemed to be growing. Why would he turn himself in? What could he possibly have found here to make him do that? She was a doctor, with multiple PhDs, and prided herself on calm and rational thought processes.

There were only three reasons she could think of for Campbell to turn himself in.

One. The documents were immaterial or a smoke screen and he had just had enough of hiding from the law. But she'd met the man, and while he was definitely a crackpot, that was more about his beliefs, not his personal actions. He didn't seem like a man on the edge.

Two. He believed—erroneously—that the documents supported his cause and were important enough to risk everything to get entered into the official record. That possibility had merit, and comforted Dr. Larkin a little as she contemplated it. Delusional people could convince themselves of almost anything, after all.

But he really hadn't seemed all that delusional. And she *had* been doing a lot of thinking and soul-searching over the past couple of days.

Which brought her to option three. That was pretty much the same as option two, excepting that the documents in question really *did* support everything Campbell had been saying, and, by default, meant that she had been actively supporting a company that…

She let that thought drift away as her stomach turned over, threatening to rebel against her lunch. The commentary had begun—endless back and forth speculation about the hows and whys and all-important what nexts. Pundits battled each other for primacy, painting Detective Campbell as a hero, a villain, a pawn, and everything in between. Speculation as to why the man would turn himself in ran as rampant, ranging from the pressures of the ever-tightening net (a narrative strongly pushed by members of the New Lyons Police Department) to a secret plot to get inside police headquarters as part of a terrorist attack, to the whole looming revolution being an inside job.

But Larkin had a different thought. What if Campbell's capture wasn't the end to the budding revolution? What if, in reality, it was the first shot in the war soon to follow?

Dr. Larkin pushed her food away, but she couldn't push away the doubt.

She had access to research and records. She had authority to get information from those lower in the corporate hierarchy. She had the ability to find the truth.

But she had to decide.

Was Campbell's capture the beginning of the end?

Or was it the end of the beginning?

Acknowledgments

This series would never have been possible without the help of numerous people who took a rough and dusty idea and helped me clean it up and turn it into something worth writing. There is an army of people at work behind the scenes creating covers and back copy text and fixing all the little mistakes and a thousand other things besides. Many thanks to all of those individuals.

More specifically, I would like to thank Elizabeth May, my editor, and Laurie McLean, my agent for taking a risk on a wannabe author and lending their expertise to make the book stronger with every edit (no matter how painful some of those edits may have been!).

I'd also like to thank my martial arts instructors, Dai-Sifu Emin Boztepe, Sifu John Hicks, Sihing Trevor Jones, and Guro Ron Ignacio, along with my many training partners along the way. Anything I got right is because of these folks. Anything I got wrong is a reflection of my own imperfect understanding.

Finally, and most importantly, I'd like to thank my wife, Julie Kagawa. Writing partner, gaming partner, training partner, and partner in all things.

About the Author

J.T. Nicholas was born in Lexington, Virginia, though within six months he moved (or was moved, rather) to Stuttgart, Germany. Thus began the long journey of the military brat, hopping from state to state and country to country until, at present, he has accumulated nearly thirty relocations. This experience taught him that, regardless of where one found oneself, people were largely the same. When not writing, Nick spends his time practicing a variety of martial arts, playing games (video, tabletop, and otherwise), and reading everything he can get his hands on. Nick currently resides in Louisville, Kentucky, with his wife, a pair of indifferent cats, a neurotic Papillion, and an Australian Shepherd who (rightly) believes he is in charge of the day-to-day affairs. For more info please visit www. jtnicholas.com, or find him on Facebook and Twitter @JamesTNicholas.

Printed in the United States
by Baker & Taylor Publisher Services